AN LEABI
HO

ELIZABETH BOWEN AND THE DISSOLUTION OF THE NOVEL

Also by Andrew Bennett

KEATS, NARRATIVE AND AUDIENCE

READERS AND READING (*editor*)

READING READING (*editor*)

Also by Nicholas Royle

AFTERWORDS (*editor*)

TELEPATHY AND LITERATURE

Elizabeth Bowen and the Dissolution of the Novel

Still Lives

Andrew Bennett
University of Bristol, England

and

Nicholas Royle
University of Stirling, Scotland

Foreword by
Ann Wordsworth

St. Martin's Press

First published in Great Britain 1995 by
MACMILLAN PRESS LTD
Houndmills, Basingstoke, Hampshire RG21 2XS
and London
Companies and representatives
throughout the world

A catalogue record for this book is available
from the British Library.

ISBN 0–333–60760–0

10 9 8 7 6 5 4 3 2 1
04 03 02 01 00 99 98 97 96 95

Printed and bound in Great Britain by
Antony Rowe Ltd
Chippenham, Wiltshire

First published in the United States of America 1995 by
Scholarly and Reference Division,
ST. MARTIN'S PRESS, INC.,
175 Fifth Avenue,
New York, N.Y. 10010

ISBN 0–312–12048–6

Library of Congress Cataloging-in-Publication Data
Bennett, Andrew, 1960–
Elizabeth Bowen and the dissolution of the novel : still lives /
Andrew Bennett and Nicholas Royle ; foreword by Ann Wordsworth.
p. cm.
Includes index.
ISBN 0–312–12048–6
1. Bowen, Elizabeth, 1899–1973—Criticism and interpretation.
I. Royle, Nicholas, 1957– . II. Title.
PR6003. 06757Z515 1995
823' .912—dc20 93–39875
CIP

Contents

Foreword

Foreword

Ann Wordsworth

> Nowadays painting occasionally makes us realize that what it wants to create, its 'production', can no longer be works of art, but corresponds rather to something for which there is not yet a name. The same applies to literature. That towards which we are advancing is not perhaps what the future will in fact disclose. Yet that towards which we advance is vacant and full of a future we must refrain from freezing in the traditions of past structures.[1]

This intimation and warning is Blanchot's, from his essay 'The Book to Come', and its sound is not easily heard by academic ears. The traditions of past structures are familiar and apotropaic and they hold both critic and reader in a benign literary history which assimilates the new to its own patterns: Elizabeth Bowen 'is what happened after Bloomsbury ... the link that connects Virginia Woolf with Iris Murdoch and Muriel Spark'. But the nameless space which Bennett and Royle's study invokes is unmapped and we, whether resentfully or with relief, find ourselves denied the positioning of the canon and the accommodation of character and plot to the suavities of paraphrase. These are such stable critical practices that to write without their architecture requires a different address, a mobility which must take the reader out of the known context and into a space which is more truly that of the novels themselves. The words of the sub-title *Still Lives* enact this movement by an indeterminate pressure of adjective and adverb, noun and verb, which breaks down the resistance of the phrase as a single defining term. Under this pressure Bowen's vocabulary is sheered from the mimetic function and its supposed relation to her sensibility and freed to make transitions that surpass the activities of plot. 'Writing is eventful.'

Bowen's novels and the corresponding chapters of this book are generated around the energy of words and phrases – going, abeyances, dream wood, sheer kink.... The world of experience is no longer separable from a linguistic drift; nothing pins activity to any constitutive authority. The Cogito and the House of Fiction alike are transgressed. Mirages of selfhood, the re-enactments of the dead on the unwitting bodies of the living, the tensions of heat and stillness and erotic expectation are all loosened from their explanatory contexts and given a figurative energy, unreified and unconstrained. Bowen's language, only seemingly representational, becomes the generator of what moves through the novels, across and beyond the traditional space of literature.

The course and process of this language are not easy to trace and it is through theoretical work that Bennett and Royle find a mode adequate to the eventful writing of the novels. Their readings are performative, not critically prejudged, not tautological like paraphrase. Theory, therefore, is not used, as is so often the case, like a talisman to give power and a safe passage to a critical work through the authority of cited names – Derrida, Freud, Nicolas Abraham, Maria Torok. ...

(A talisman, nevertheless, for this foreword: to cite Derrida's 'single definition of deconstruction, one as brief, elliptical and economical as a password': *'plus d'une langue* – both more than a language and no more of a language'.[2] This too is intimation and warning to artist, critic and reader alike.)

This volume, so old-fashioned in its apparent scope – a single-author study of a 'minor' figure whose work is most often read as a charming but dated embodiment of traditional literary and social values – follows instead processes of dissolution, 'of loosening, fading away, breaking up, unsolving'. The precarious beauty and comedy of the novels is dispersed through a writing of life/death which the critical work in its turn mobilizes through the uncanny exchanges of language. *Elizabeth Bowen and the Dissolution of the Novel* sets a precedent for more readings and rereadings of other novelists enfolded in traditional criticism whose future has not yet been opened.

Notes

1. Maurice Blanchot, *The Siren's Song* (Brighton: Harvester Press, 1982) p. 248.
2. Jacques Derrida, *Mémoires for Paul de Man* (New York: Columbia University Press, 1986) p. 15.

Acknowledgements

When Jane Gallop learnt of this project she exclaimed incredulously: 'You're co-writing a book? How can you co-write a book?' Still uncertain as to how we might want to answer such a question, we would like to acknowledge the appropriateness of that incredulity and our thanks for the perverse pleasure which we derived from it. To give an account of how this book was written would, we suspect, necessitate the writing of another. Suffice to say that there are many people without whom this study would not have been possible, even though they may have made no identifiable, and certainly no culpable contribution to it. In the first place we must register our indebtedness to the example of Michael Gasson, most passionate and exacting of Bowen readers. In a more immediately practical sense, we would like to thank Robert Cooper at the University of Tampere in Finland, for driving us into the extraordinary environs of Bowen's work (we were asked to teach *To the North*), and to thank our students for all their enthusiasm and interest. In particular we should like to thank Pia Hovi, Asko Kauppinen, Joel Kuortti, Leena Lehto, Maarit Piipponen, Riitta Santala, Tiina Sarisalmi and Arto Schroderus. We would also like to take this opportunity to express our gratitude to Ralf Norrman, for all his generosity and support as Professor of English at the University of Tampere. More generally, we are very grateful to the University for its assistance in enabling us to set up the *Bowen Newsletter*, now based at the University of Stirling, Scotland, and the University of Bristol, England. Thanks, too, to everyone who has given their critical support and encouragement in the broader and expanding area of Bowen studies, especially Bill Readings, Sarah Wood and Ann Wyatt-Brown. For detailed and invaluable comments and suggestions regarding various parts of the manuscript we are very grateful to Valerie Allen, Derek Attridge, John Bayley, Rachel Bowlby, Maud Ellmann, Jacqueline Hall, Ann Wordsworth and Robert Young. Finally, this book could never have happened without the love, patience and support of Ann Bennett, Anna-Maria Hämäläinen-Bennett, Minnamarja Rasi, Kathleen Royle and Maxwell Royle.

The authors and publishers would like to thank the following for permission to use copyright-material:

Jonathan Cape Ltd, on behalf of the estate of Elizabeth Bowen, for the extracts from the following novels by Elizabeth Bowen: *The Death of the Heart, The Heat of the Day, A World of Love, The Little Girls* and *Eva Trout;*

Curtis Brown Ltd, London, on behalf of the estate of Elizabeth Bowen, for the extracts from the following novels by Elizabeth Bowen: *The Hotel, The Last September, Friends and Relations, To the North* and *The House in Paris;*

Alfred A. Knopf Inc., for the extracts from the following novels by Elizabeth Bowen: *The Last September,* copyright 1929, 1952 by Elizabeth Bowen; *To the North,* copyright 1933, renewed 1961 by Elizabeth Bowen; *The House in Paris,* copyright 1935, renewed 1963 by Elizabeth Bowen; *The Death of the Heart,* copyright 1938, renewed 1966 by Elizabeth Bowen; *The Heat of the Day,* copyright 1948 Elizabeth Bowen; *A World of Love,* copyright 1954, © 1955 by Elizabeth Bowen; *The Little Girls,* copyright © 1963 by Elizabeth Bowen; *Eva Trout or Changing Scenes,* copyright © 1968 by Elizabeth Bowen. All the above extracts are reprinted by kind permission of Alfred A. Knopf Inc.

Finally, the authors would like to thank the Institute for Languages and Intercultural Studies at the University of Aalborg, the Department of English Studies at the University of Stirling, and the Department of English at the University of Bristol for assistance in covering the cost of the permission fees.

ANDREW BENNETT
Tampere, Cambridge, Aalborg

NICHOLAS ROYLE
Tampere, Widworthy, Stirling

List of Abbreviations

DH	*The Death of the Heart* (1938)
ET	*Eva Trout* (1968)
FR	*Friends and Relations* (1931)
H	*The Hotel* (1927)
HD	*The Heat of the Day* (1948)
HP	*The House in Paris* (1935)
LG	*The Little Girls* (1963)
LS	*The Last September* (1929)
TN	*To the North* (1932)
WL	*A World of Love* (1955)

CS	*The Collected Stories of Elizabeth Bowen* (1980)
MT	*The Mulberry Tree* (1986)
TR	*A Time in Rome* (1959)

All page numbers refer to the Penguin editions, except *The Mulberry Tree* which is published by Virago.

Introduction

Introduction

> 'Isn't she pretty at all?'
> 'I'm afraid not.'
> 'Spotty?'
> 'I'm afraid she is, rather.'
> 'Oh dear, poor little thing.'
> 'It's horrible,' said Julian, lighting her cigarette for her, 'to be talking like this about a child. But she rattles me terribly. I can never just look at her; I always feel as though I were catching her eye.' (*TN* 37–8)

This passage of dialogue from *To the North* is not only an amusing evocation of Julian Tower and his interlocutor Cecilia Summers and of the relationship between himself and his fourteen-year-old niece, the orphaned Pauline. Working with the stereotype of the 'spotty' adolescent, this passage also concerns a reversal of conventional roles: adults are frightened of children, rather than vice versa; more particularly, it is the adult male rather than the young female who seems given to being hysterical. A number of other questions arise: how can or should one talk about children? What does it mean to 'just look'? What is going on in this 'catching' of the eye?

Our book proposes new and different ways of thinking about the twentieth-century novel. It does this, above all, by providing the first theoretically informed reading of the complete novels of the Anglo-Irish writer Elizabeth Bowen (1899–1973). All of Bowen's novels are still in print and she continues to enjoy a large readership among the general reading public on both sides of the Atlantic and elsewhere. But she is only now beginning to be recognized by current academic criticism and by radical theorists alike. In particular she is emerging as a significant figure within several key areas of contemporary study and interest: twentieth-century women's writing, Anglo-Irish and minority literatures, writers of the thirties and forties, postcolonialism, and postmodernism. Oriented and impelled by close readings of Bowen's work, *Elizabeth Bowen and the Dissolution of the Novel* maps the transformations of the twentieth-century novel in general.

This century has seen fundamental changes in the form and

conception of the novel. Obvious examples would include the long-recognized experimentalism of modernists such as James Joyce or Virginia Woolf, or the more recently acknowledged postmodern practice of writers such as Paul Auster or Jeanette Winterson. The originality of the present study, however, consists in the adoption of a rather different perspective.

> Regarding Cecilia more kindly, as one regards an oyster soon to be opened, or an engaging new novel certain to entertain, [Lady Waters] hesitated between other lines of approach, while Cecilia, smiling and not unconscious, looked down at her pretty hands. (*TN* 88)

Attempting to bring out the strangeness of such suspense – the anticipation and hesitation, the veiled cannibalism and the enigmatic notion of reading people – we focus on the novels of Elizabeth Bowen precisely *because of* their apparent conventionality and stability: they supposedly represent a tradition of the realist novel untouched by the vagaries of modernist or postmodernist experimentalism. Our book thus theorizes the dissolution of the twentieth-century novel through careful, if perhaps unexpected, readings of a novelist whose work has been taken (however tacitly) to embody the very bulwark of the conventional and 'proper', of traditional realism and conservative 'society'. Bowen's novels are also especially appropriate to the theoretical and political project of this present work since they are (unlike the work of, say, Woolf and Joyce, or Auster and Winterson) written and published across a broad historical period, from 1927 to 1968: spanning the central five decades of the century, the novels embrace the concerns of both modernism and postmodernism as well as engaging with the historical specificity of two world wars, the changing role of women and the nuclear age. Finally, our book is itself, we believe, a new kind of literary critical writing. Like the novels of Elizabeth Bowen, it would seem to accommodate itself to highly traditional notions of literary criticism (a focus on 'life', close reading, the affective power of literary texts, etc.) but at the same time it represents powerful, theoretically-informed sites of cultural and ideological disruption.

In order to give some sense of the welter of traditionalism out of which our analyses erupt, we might begin by considering one of the most basic accoutrements of novel-publishing in the twentieth century: blurb. Blurbs can be highly revealing. The blurbs on the backs of the Penguin editions of Bowen's books are explicitly and consistently author-centred, oriented towards the author's personal experience, imagination and feelings. These blurbs at once assume and promote readings of the novels as reflections or representations of Bowen's 'own experience' (*HD*). The novels variously give us 'Miss Bowen's [*sic*] most brilliant qualities' (*HP*), 'her genius' (*H*), her 'originality of mind and boldness of sensibility' (*WL*), her 'insight' (*TN*), her capacity for being 'daring' and 'passionate' (*FR*), her 'intense sensibility' (*ET*). Inevitably perhaps, these blurbs declare Bowen a 'major' writer. While we would not wish to detract from the importance and accuracy of such judgements as they pertain to the writing, we would nevertheless suggest that the effect of such praise is also damning. It is damning, first, on account of the forms of subordination it guarantees regarding the relations between a text and its author: consistently to present the meaning and power of novels in terms of the 'experience' and 'sensibility' of their author is to strangle such novels, so to speak, at birth. The 'life' of the novel is blotted out by the focus on the 'life' of the author.

But there is a more specific form of damning praise in what the blurbs tell us about the canonical status and classification of Bowen's work. In a statement which can be found on the back cover of both *The Death of the Heart* and *The Collected Stories of Elizabeth Bowen*, Bowen's biographer Victoria Glendinning tells us: Bowen 'is a major writer. ... She is what happened after Bloomsbury ... the link that connects Virginia Woolf with Iris Murdoch and Muriel Spark'. *Elizabeth Bowen and the Dissolution of the Novel* breaks not only with the subordinating effects of such an evaluation of Bowen but also with the very assumptions of what 'major' entails, of the literary and cultural significance of 'Bloomsbury', and of a literary history governed by metaphors of continuity and complementarity (linkage and connection). Countering and parodying descriptions such as Glendinning's, we would suggest a few alternative blurbs of our own: 'Bowen's novels are like Jane Austen on drugs'; 'Virginia Woolf is a major writer. ... She is the link that connects George Eliot with Elizabeth Bowen'; 'Bowen's work constitutes the Other of James Joyce'; 'Together with Beckett's, Bowen's are the greatest comic novels written in English this century'; 'Bowen's novels are what happened after modernism. They embody nothing more and nothing less than the dissolution of the twentieth-century novel.'

* * *

The novels of Elizabeth Bowen are open to fundamental rereadings, to readings which at once transform the status and importance of Bowen's work and effect a deconstruction of everything that is seemingly most conventional and reassuring about the very notion of the novel.[1] The distortions of conventional Bowen criticism concern above all the modes of categorization that have been imposed on her novels. The historical scene of this could be sketched as follows. In a classic strategy of canon-formation, Bowen is first identified as a novelist of manners or sensibility. This category is at the same time subsumed within the larger category of 'realism'. Judged according to the conventional protocols of such fiction, her novels are then misread – and valued as important, but minor. In this way, Bowen's work is slotted into genealogies and lineages comprising such writers as Jane Austen, George Eliot, Henry James, Virginia Woolf, E. M. Forster, Rosamond Lehmann, Ivy Compton-Burnett, Muriel Spark and Iris Murdoch. Within these traditions Bowen's work is assessed by certain (inappropriate) criteria, and (therefore) found to be of secondary significance. A certain tautology ensues: if you read Elizabeth Bowen as a minor Virginia Woolf, then that is precisely what you will find – a minor Virginia Woolf. Indeed, it is often those critics who acknowledge the evocative power, the haunting singularity of Bowen's work, and would elevate it to university syllabuses and course-book status, who insist most strongly on such misleading comparisons and thus serve to bolster and perpetuate distorted readings of her work.[2]

Bowen's work, then, is often judged according to certain protocols of 'realist' fiction. Realist novels are conventionally thought to entail representations of 'people', for example, who are open to characterological analysis just as 'real' people are said to be. And in a double gesture, such 'people' are thought to reflect 'real' life, while simultaneously being distinguished from it by their self-evident bookishness or fictionality. Critics' commonly expressed reservations about Bowen's inability or refusal to distinguish the real from the fictional, together with the opposite claim that her writing is not realistic enough, means that her work is marginalized within the realist tradition. Our study seeks to question such assumptions. Again, to take an example from the early novel *To the North*, there is Emmeline listening (or appearing to listen) to Cecilia:

> Emmeline started. She had sat staring so fixedly at Cecilia that Cecilia had disappeared; instead, she had seen spinning sen-

> tences, little cogs interlocked, each clicking each other round. She sat blinking at this machinery of agitation. (*TN* 98)

Being stops and starts. Stared at, people disappear. People uncannily *become* words and sentences, a machinery of agitation, caught, spellbound. We argue that the notion of character (that is, people, real or fictional) is fundamentally transformed in Bowen's writing: her novels derange the very grounds of 'character', what it is to 'be' a person, to 'have' an identity, to be real or fictional. We explore not only the persistently strange but crucial significance of the notion of 'still life' itself, but also the force and pervasiveness of a number of other concepts and motifs characteristic of the form and operation of the twentieth-century novel, though largely unrecognized till now. Rather than talk about character, we talk for example about people 'being thought'. Rather than talk about plot, we talk about notions of 'going'. A ceaseless 'machinery of agitation', reading in turn has to do with forms of trance or of what Bowen calls 'dream wood'. The 'realism' of the novel in the twentieth century is dissolved, along with other preconceptions according to which critics and readers have responded to the apparent conventions of this genre.

* * *

Following the dislocations of modernism and postmodernism, what does the twentieth-century novel have to tell us about what used to be referred to, in such apparently unequivocal terms, as life? What would it mean to speak of the novel as still life? What happens if we put aside assertions about 'the death of the novel' and consider instead the multiple resonances of 'dissolution' – of loosening, fading away, breaking up, unsolving? In what ways might the very reading of a novel stage its dissolution?

Still Lives: these words of the sub-title constitute a focal point and a dispersion. Our study attempts to spell out the multiplicity and heterogeneity of senses to which the title phrase gives rise. There is, to begin with, the fundamental paradox whereby 'still life' conveys death – as the French term, *nature morte*, more explicitly suggests. To speak of still lives in the context of the twentieth-century novel is to invoke questions both of representation (supposedly realistic depictions of life) and of death (life stilled). Complicit with the derangement of 'character' in the novels of Elizabeth Bowen is an unsettling of distinctions between life and death. Bowen's writing is pervaded by the forces of dissolution and mourning. In fascinating and highly singular ways, her novels examine the disquieting truth that in the midst of life we are in death. On the one hand they investigate the idea that (to adopt Antonia's words in *A World of Love*) we are generally 'far too quick to assume that people are dead' (*WL* 37). On the other hand, they consistently suggest that we are also far too quick to assume that people are alive. Perhaps more candidly and more lucidly than any other novels written in English in the twentieth century, Bowen's trace the profound but shifting ways in which the living are affected by the dead. These novels provide an extraordinarily rich and challenging account of how lives *are* still, of how lives are programmed – socially, emotionally, erotically – by the dead. 'Living', in this context, bears what Proust called 'the burden of obligations contracted in a former life' – even though such obligations may themselves remain unconscious or unknowable.[3] The notion of a former life, however, has less to do with Proustian or Wordsworthian pre-existence than with the life of another, now dead. Haunted or inhabited by the dead, Bowen people live the burdens contracted by other people in their former lives. But lives in Bowen's novels are not linked to the unknown in any consolingly religious sense: despite the attempts of conventional criticism to read consolation into Bowen plots, these novels diverge from everything in or after modernism that might be identified with a 'culture of redemption'.[4] Bowen's texts present us – often comically – with issues of life and death in provocatively secular terms. Again, this puts these novels at the, still in many ways unexamined, centre of the crisis of modern European literature. The ghostliness of 'still lives' is evident throughout the later nineteenth- and the twentieth-century European novel. This ghostliness has to do not only with the past (remembering or trying to do justice to the significance of those who have died) but also with the future: it has to do with what is left of us when we leave, what remains of us, what is still to be.

The present study will inevitably suggest analogies and correspondences relevant to a reading or rereading of other late nineteenth- as well as twentieth-century novelists, including Eliot, Hardy, James, Lawrence, Forster, Joyce and Woolf. It takes Bowen's work as a kind of test case for an exploration of how the phrase 'still lives' draws together the various and strange interweavings of life and death in writing. Part of this variety and strangeness emerges from the consistency with which her novels emphasize stillness. When Louie Lewis sees Harrison sitting at an outdoor concert in Regent's Park, at the start of *The Heat of the Day,* we are told: 'This man's excessive stillness gave the effect not of abandon but of cryptic behaviour' (*HD* 9). As this brief quotation may suggest, what is 'still' in Bowen's writing is bound up with the paradoxical, with what is at once excessive and cryptic. As Bowen observes in her Foreword to *Afterthought* in 1961: 'writing is eventful; one might say it is in itself eventfulness'.[5] She goes on to say that this applies to 'reading' too. The eventfulness of reading is inscribed in the semantic and temporal intricacies of the words 'still lives': 'still', for example, is not only 'silent' and 'motionless' but also 'yet', 'up till now'; likewise 'lives' works as both noun and verb. What is the strange 'eventfulness' of writing? And what is the relation between writing (or reading) and stillness? The elaborations of such questions are, we argue, central not only to an appreciation of the extraordinary novels of Elizabeth Bowen but also to the fate of the novel in the twentieth century.

In 1925, in a diary entry regarding *To the Lighthouse,* Virginia Woolf writes: 'I have an idea that I will invent a new name for my books to supplant "novel". A new —— by Virginia Woolf. But what? Elegy?'[6] Woolf's suggestion of the term 'elegy' instead of 'novel' helpfully directs attention to the particularity and importance of death and mourning in twentieth-century writing. From *The Hotel* (1927) to *Eva Trout* (1968), Bowen's writing is concerned with dissolution – with dispersion, melting, break-up and death.[7] Living, in the work of Bowen, is dissolving. Even a solution – as for instance, emotionally, between the estranged couple Fred and Lilia Danby in *A World of Love* – is described as being 'not so much a solution as a dissolution' (*WL* 104). Ranging between the tragic and the comic, between the poignant and the scrupulously prosaic, Bowen's novels present dissolutions at the level of personal identity, patriarchy, social conventions and language itself – up to and including the language of fiction and criticism. More radically than Woolf's, we want to suggest, Bowen's novels figure a dissolution of the novel as such: Bowen's novels *are* still lives.

* * *

A short outline of the eight chapters which follow may be helpful. Chronologically arranged, each chapter focuses on one or two of Bowen's ten novels. Chapter 1, 'Abeyances', is concerned with

Bowen's first two novels, *The Hotel* (1927) and *The Last September* (1929), and with how they present a new and culturally disruptive poetics of personality. These novels suggest that people, like people in novels, are constituted by thoughts, their own and others': people in Bowen are *being thought*. The chapter examines one particularly pervasive mode of being thought, namely what Bowen calls 'interior quietness', a kind of abeyance or stilling of thought, a catatonic stilling of mind and body *in thought*.

Chapter 2, 'Shivered', focuses on a reading of *Friends and Relations* (1931) and *To the North* (1932). Extrapolating the importance of Walter Pater for an understanding of modernist notions of 'the moment', it explores senses of movement, departure and arrival, in Bowen's work in terms of what we refer to as *going*. The force of going is intimately bound up with pathos and death. In *To the North* especially, we are presented with a dynamic shattering of time and space, reading and identity. In its very title intimating an unsettling translation of Woolf's *To the Lighthouse, To the North* dissolves the conceptual space of the modernist novel.

In Chapter 3, 'Fanatic Immobility', we discuss *The House in Paris* (1935) in terms of the cryptic. Leopold Grant-Moody is what we term a 'traumaturgy', both a work and a theory of wounds. Leopold – his words, figures of speech, actions, body-positions, immobilities – is a product of his father's suicidal self-wounding. But the wounding of Leopold is also his knowledge – what Leopold knows and doesn't know, what he knows because he doesn't know, what he is not allowed to know, what he cannot know. Developing our notion of people *being thought*, we examine the idea, in *The House in Paris*, of people *being known*: Leopold *is* to the extent that he is known, but the novel puts shockingly into abeyance the very possibility of knowing Leopold.

Chapter 4, 'Dream Wood', offers a reading of *The Death of the Heart* (1938) chiefly by way of its figurations of the animal, the heart, furniture and the notion of dream wood itself. We attempt to elucidate the proposition that – whether as characters or as readers – we are all living in a kind of dream wood. Dream wood becomes a kind of metaphor for the twentieth-century novel and for the experience of its readers. Dream wood is, among other things, the condition whereby it is never possible to be ourselves and the condition whereby every pretension to authority or completeness is – laughably, dreamily, erotically – undone.

Chapter 5, 'Sheer Kink', presents a reading of *The Heat of the Day* (1948) which focuses in part on the notions of identity and the erotic but which also investigates the radical forms of 'kink' which Bowen's novel produces in relation to drama, fiction and storytelling. This exploration engages with a Shakespearean intertext, *Hamlet*, and concludes with a theory of characterization in the twentieth-century novel as decapitation.

Chapter 6, 'Obelisk', considers a number of questions concerning the very institution of the novel: What is the relationship between the novelistic and the epistolary? In particular, what is a love letter? And in what ways might it be said that a letter can determine the identity of its addressee? The chapter focuses on a reading of Bowen's fascinating short novel *A World of Love* (1955) in order to engage with other questions considered to be central to an understanding of the novel in its post-Nietzschean, post-Freudian secular mode. What becomes of the curious figure of the omniscient (God-like) narrator in the twentieth-century novel? In what ways are novels concerned with a notion of remembering the future? Focusing on the strange monument which is a central feature of the grounds in which the novel is set, we ask: What is an obelisk?

Chapter 7, 'Trance', offers a reading of *The Little Girls* (1963) focusing on the trance – entrancements, transitions, entrances – of reading. Often described as a transitional novel and, in particular, a novel which critics regard as 'dated', *The Little Girls* itself theorizes the postmodern culture of the transitory. In an exemplary postmodern fashion, then, it presents an intensive and extraordinary 'still life' study of the transitions of time and, in the figure of the revenant, of the uncanny effects of human transience.

Our final chapter, 'Convulsions', concerns Bowen's last completed novel, *Eva Trout* (1968). Convulsions of body and mind litter Bowen's texts and furnish the basis for a theory of novel-reading as convulsion-work. In *Eva Trout*, we suggest, mouth-events – stuttering, sneezing, laughing, yawning and speaking itself – are all figured as moments when the body is caught up in and by its own otherness, when the body lives its own inanimation in the cinematic moment of convulsive animation, when the body is haunted by *its own body* as other. People are dissolved into the inanimate, convulsive immobilities of their own still lives.

1

Abeyances

> That when there is thought there has to be something 'that thinks' is simply a formulation of our grammatical custom that adds a doer to every deed.[1]

Elizabeth Bowen's first novel, *The Hotel* (1927), concerns the fragile intimacies and destructive occlusions and denials of relationships formed and disfigured in an hotel on the Italian Riviera. Talking and thinking structure a narrative which appears to position itself within a tradition of elegant novels of upper-middle-class and aristocratic manners, and to owe much, in particular, to the Italian sections of E. M. Forster's *A Room with a View.* Among the guests at the hotel is Sydney Warren, a young woman ('a probable twenty-two' [11]) who has come to Italy partly in an attempt to evade an impending nervous breakdown, the reasons for which remain undefined. Sydney is described as over-intelligent and neurotic. She becomes friendly with Mrs Kerr, the first of Bowen's dangerously manipulative older women who figure so prominently in the early novels and who feed off the complex, inarticulate and unspeakable psychic torments of younger women – Mrs Kerr is a prototype of Lady Naylor in *The Last September*, Lady Waters in *To the North*, and Madame Fisher in *The House in Paris*. Sydney is fixated, at least half in love, with Mrs Kerr, and in ways that she can neither express nor comprehend, is quietly shattered when Mrs Kerr's son Ronald arrives at the hotel and Mrs Kerr's time and attention are redirected. Shortly before the arrival of Ronald comes an insecure, sexually and emotionally inexperienced, nervous and socially awkward vicar, James Milton. Following her rejection by Mrs Kerr, Sydney becomes engaged to Milton. After realizing that the engagement has been a result of having lived as if in a dream, a kind of still life, Sydney breaks it off and, soon after, both Milton and Ronald leave the hotel.

Such a summary of the novel can only hint at the intimate and intricate pressures of language on thought and relationships, and at the resistant pressures of stillness on the haunting mobility of people, the abeyances which intrude on the fluid and unstable mobility of lives. In the first part of this chapter we shall attempt to elaborate the complex disturbances of thought which figure people, people being thought, in *The Hotel*, and the ways in which people being thought begin in abeyance.

* * *

The Hotel opens in abeyance. The novel opens with an interior quietness, a stopping of body and mind in the stilling thought of the stopping of thought. Out of the novel, out of its first sentence, comes a minor character, Miss Fitzgerald. As *The Hotel* opens, so the hotel opens and a person comes out, only to stop in abeyance, stilled by the shock of this opening:

> Miss Fitzgerald hurried out of the Hotel into the road. Here she stood still, looking purposelessly up and down in the blinding sunshine and picking at the fingers of her gloves. She was frightened by an interior quietness and by the thought that she had for once in her life stopped thinking and might never begin again. (5)

Within the first three sentences of her first novel, Bowen presents a dissolution of writing in a dissolution of thought. Traces of this opening stasis will haunt Bowen's writing for the next forty-five years, as the possibility of still minds and bodies, a stilling or dissolution of the novel. In this thought, the mobilities and fluidities of writing are traversed by the catatonic impossibility of one particular thought – the thought that thought has stopped.

In the third sentence of her first novel, then, Bowen threatens to short-circuit, to explode reading and writing by presenting what we propose to refer to as catatonia, the stopping of thought, an interior quietness, as the condition towards which both reading and the actions of her characters move and out of which they are generated. Bowen's novels are always already finished, stilled, from and by the opening of her first novel. Bowen's novels *are* still lives. Any reading which can occur beyond this opening is a supplementary reading of the impossible mobilities contained within, but not by, the thought of catatonia. Bowen's ten novels will be haunted by this opening, by the paradox of a catatonic thought-stoppage, and by the paradox that the novels are already finished, stilled by such a thought. Reading catatonia: this chapter will seek to inhabit and to sojourn, unmoving, within the terms set out by the opening to *The Hotel*, reading catatonia, reading catatonically, immovably, still in abeyance.

* * *

Such abeyances as the interior quietness which opens *The Hotel* are what we would like to call 'being thought'. In *The Hotel*, as in her second novel, *The Last September*, Bowen figures people in terms of the possibility of thoughts, people being thought. Characterization comprises figurations of thoughts:[2] people in novels are constructed by language, by thoughts, by reading. Hence the dissolution of the novel, insofar as Bowen's texts dramatize the sense that people are only ever in novels, that is, *being thought*. The dissolution of the novel involves, in the first place, a dissolution of the boundaries between so-called people in real life and characters in fiction. The impossible thought that thought has stopped, a kind of *aporia* or abeyance of thought, an impossible bending back of thought onto itself, figural thought, is both that moment when thought becomes impossible and therefore people being thought radically fictional, and the moment of the mind's simulacrum of death, still life. Such impossible and non-temporal moments traverse the mobilities of people through all of Bowen's novels, they are perpetually in transit across all of these still lives.

Bowen's novels can be read, indeed, as attempts to escape the fictionalizing immobility of the opening to *The Hotel*. Our reading of *The Hotel* will highlight the necessity and impossibility of such attempts. For while the fictionality of people in Bowen is figured by absences of mind, forgetfulness, 'abstraction', states of catatonia, the stilling of thought, it is also and equally true that there are no 'people' without them. We shall then attempt to map such abeyances onto a reading of *The Last September* by elaborating a theory of being thought in terms of the question of the boundaries of the self.

What we would like to term 'catatonia' – designating above all the thought that thought has stopped – does not imply simply an *absence* of thought. Instead it suggests a kind of thought short-circuit, a stilling or aporia of the mind.[3] States of catatonia are related to *catalepsy* and *cataplexy*, both of which are crucial to an understanding of Bowen's still lives. *Catalepsy* (from the Greek κατάληψις, 'a seizing upon') is a kind of seizure or trance in which consciousness is temporarily suspended. But catalepsy also has a technical meaning, in stoic philosophy, of comprehension or apprehension. This remarkable cohabitation of two apparently contradictory or antithetical meanings in the word 'catalepsy' suggests that the *suspension* of consciousness produces, at the same time, a sudden *apprehension. Cataplexy,* on the other hand, is most commonly understood as a hypnotic state in animals 'shamming death', the instinctive dramatization of death by animals in certain life-threatening situations. But the condition of cataplexy is also related to extreme emotion or emotional shock. Often described as a kind of defence mechanism of the mind, cataplexy is 'usually precipitated by an uncontrollable fit of laughter or an event that produces overwhelming anxiety or anger'.[4] Finally, cataplexy is associated, etymologically, with amazement. Καταπλήσσειν signifies 'to strike down with terror'.

Catatonia, catalepsy, cataplexy, then, are all crucial to our notion of still lives.[5] Not only can these conditions be read as paradigmatic states of mental and physiological immobility, they are also exemplary instances of the fictional representation of death – still lives. As is particularly clear in the case of cataplexy, such 'states of mind' mime death. Whether as states of trance, absent-mindedness, or forgetting, etc., catatonia radically disturbs – or in a strictly unthinkable way *dissolves* – the opposition between life and death in thought. Moreover, catatonia in general (and cataplexy in particular) disrupts the distinction between fiction and the real by presenting the body not only as a fiction of death, but also – even before that – a fictional body. The body becomes a puppet or a doll, a simulacrum of the body, immobile until moved by another. The notion that catatonia is the condition of people in Bowen, the condition towards and through which people move, suggests that 'real life' is itself hauntingly fictional, still.

* * *

The hotel is the locus of a loss of movement. Hotel lives are lives stilled for the moment. The narrative of *The Hotel* is structured by precisely such a stasis: when Roland Kerr and James Milton leave the hotel, *The Hotel* ends. Indeed, the novel can be redescribed as a dramatization of such a stillness: *The Hotel* is a novel which centres around and never moves beyond the character of Sydney and her still lives. Sydney is a young woman uncertain of her future, uncertain of where to go, what to do beyond the hotel, and she is immobilized by the influence of her friend, the older and curiously menacing Mrs Kerr. All of this climaxes when Sydney gets engaged to the catatonically unimaginative clergyman James Milton. This engagement is subsequently broken off by Sydney after an episode of potentially life-threatening danger on a mountainside. Her moment of danger is both cataleptic in its access of apprehension to an otherwise somnambulistic existence, and cataplectic in its traumatizing effect of shock.

Immobility proliferates. Throughout the novel, stillness in mind and in body haunts the movements of writing and the linear mobilities of narrative. Almost all the people in the hotel are subject to periods of absence or immobility: Miss Pym experiences a 'short blank pause of astonishment' (5); Mrs Pinkerton is 'frozen into an attitude of reflection' (27); Mrs Lee-Mittison sits 'in a state of happy suspension, a pause as distinct from life as a trance' (36); the picnic party is 'stupefied' with social embarrassment (42); Miss Fitzgerald admits to doing 'extraordinary things sometimes ... without thinking ... when I'm thinking hard' (66); James Milton has a moment of 'arrested consciousness' (83), and later he comes 'to a brink' after which 'Time carried on again after he could not say how long a cessation of being' (150); Mrs Kerr 'perceptibly retreat[s] from consciousness' behind the 'mask of her face' (96). Sydney, in particular, has 'a capacity for being still' (59): 'sitting quite still, [she] remained blank for a moment' (61). Sydney is compared to the hotel lift which is regularly immobilized by unexplained mechanical failures: both can be 'distracted, mechanical and at a standstill' (121). She suffers from a 'strange anaesthesia' (141), and her face has 'a strained kind of stillness as though it might at any moment break up into tears' (151).[6] And there are moments when language itself is curiously immobile, rigidified by a curiously inactive syntax whose inversions bespeak a catatonic reading, a fixation on the undecidable reference of, for example, 'still': '"Shall we walk somewhere?" With an expression of being still, though with even greater indifference, at anybody's disposal, she nodded backward indefinitely in the direction of the hills' (123). Here, the still of Sydney's body, her being still, and its indifference to walking and to other people, becomes a temporal still after the interruption of the indifferent clause. The duplicity of 'still' is, itself, still in suspense. The syntax gives an impression of being still, though perhaps not indefinitely, in abeyance.

In *The Hotel*, then, catatonia, interior quietness, is crucially that of its central character, Sydney. There is an intense concentration on Sydney's thoughts throughout: not only do we have access to her thoughts, but the nature and quality of those thoughts are themselves the subject of extensive discussion. In particular, Sydney is repeatedly referred to as more intelligent than other people, for whom her thoughts tend to be a mystery: Veronica, for example, 'thought Sydney queer, rather interesting, and wondered what she could possibly be thinking so hard about all the time' (31). It is a cleverness which is described – by Mrs Kerr – in terms of being a *barrier* to understanding.[7] Our understanding of the interior quietness figured in *The Hotel* will be mediated by Sydney, then, and we will seek to suggest that Sydney's 'thoughts' can be shown to have crucial ramifications in terms of thinking about subjectivity and the boundaries of the self.

* * *

The Hotel repeatedly highlights the interior mobilities of thought, at the same time as it disrupts the boundaries between such interiority and action, events, other selves. But this is not a work of disruption which moves simply from the inside to the outside, for the hallucinatory interiority of thought is itself traversed by a disruptive fictionality. Sydney 'map[s] out for herself a deep-down life in which emotions ceased their clashing together and friends appeared only as painted along the edge of one's quietness'(57). 'Interiority' functions both as an escape from the 'outside', the 'world', and, at the same time, as the construction of other people as fictional. Mapping it out so that she can move towards the unmoving cessation of movement, traverse the topography of her still soul, Sydney is continually tracing these fictions of stillness in history, in the emotions and lives of others. Friends, others, in this psycho-cartography, are supplementary, fictional. Strangely and disquietingly, other people both mark and live on the boundaries between an interior quietness and the outside, between psycho-cartography and the real. The mobilities of people, 'painted along the edge of one's quietness', are figured as fictional embellishments, supplements, parerga to the immobile interiority of 'thought'.

Edges or curbs, borders, the marginal embellishments of the parergon or figure, a painting along the edge and an 'impenetrable façade with no ingress' (118): in short, fiction. It is, precisely, the inescapable sense not only that others are painted along the edge of one's life, that others frame one with a fictional parergon, but that what they frame is the impenetrable pictorial representation of one's life – it is this unavoidable sense of one's own fictionality which holds one in abeyance, stops one short, curbs one on the curb. Mrs Kerr asks Sydney where she wants to walk:

> The facility with which it would be possible for her to cover larger distances and her present complete inability to move from the curbstone presented themselves simultaneously. She could not command the few words, the few movements which should take her away from Mrs Kerr. ... She could see her life very plainly, but there seemed no way into it; the whole thing might have been painted on canvas with a clever enough but not convincing appearance of reality. (118)

Immobility, a catatonic physical inability to move, is explicitly connected with fictionality, a catatonic inability to distinguish our lives, still lives, from fiction. Sydney's 'anaesthesia' involves an inability to penetrate her own life, an inability to disentangle it from a curiously improbable fiction. This stilled fictionality conditions Sydney's existence. But this stilling is not confined to her own life. As with other young women in Bowen's early novels, Sydney repeatedly views the lives of others in terms of pictures, statues, tableaux. But to move these pictures, to make these visual representations of people *moving* pictures, movies, only functions to produce a fictional movement or 'emotion'. As Sydney looks down from a hill above the hotel, she sees Veronica and Victor, two hotel guests, in the embrace of their first kiss: 'To her, looking down unawares, the couple gesticulating soundlessly below her in the sunshine appeared as in some perfect piece of cinema-acting, emotion represented without emotion' (42). Emotion represented without emotion is both an emotionless representation, and, more curiously, a representation of emotion in the absence of itself. The latter formulation would suggest a radical fictionalization of emotion as such: that emotion can be represented as without emotion figures the possibility of emotion only ever being an empty representation, a simulacrum with no referent. As we attempt to show elsewhere in this study, representation without object or origin, however, is no longer thinkable under the regime of representation.

The fictionalization of emotion in the cinematic kiss between Veronica and Victor is also a fictionalization or a stilling of motion: 'their stillness for some moments was profound' (42). And this fictionalization of emotion, through the endangering proximity of the kiss and the redeeming distance of the gaze, leads to Sydney's questions as to the possibility of her own emotions: 'She wondered whether at such a moment she would be cut off from herself, as by her other emotions' (42). The complex duplicities of Sydney's cutting herself off from herself by her own emotions presents an aporia of fiction (in fiction, of fiction and out of fiction) similar to the thought that thought has stopped. Not only does the syntax obscure the relations between 'her other emotions' and 'cut off from herself', but this cerebral moment is itself an instance of Sydney's emotional withdrawal from the 'real', a radical fictionalization of the uncanny interiority of emotion.

* * *

If the thought of others' emotions makes Sydney doubt the reality of other people, the thoughts of others, on the other hand, work to fictionalize Sydney herself. Sydney has a particularly acute sensitivity to the thoughts of others, to the extent that the consciousness of others can come as an electric shock: 'From out of the black shadow that hid the rest of [Mrs Kerr], her scrutiny like a live wire was incessantly tugging at Sydney's consciousness' (12). Similarly, there is a crucial moment in Sydney's life when she is figured as the implex of other people's crossing perceptions, a kind of geometrical projection of the lines of other people's thoughts. The moment is an exemplary instance of how it is that the thought of others stills the lives of Bowen's characters:

> Sydney took no notice of what was being said; she did not seem as though she had heard. She stood between Tessa and Mrs Kerr as inanimate and objective as a young girl in a story told by a man, incapable of a thought or a feeling that was not attributed to her, with no personality of her own outside their three projections upon her: Milton's fiancée, Tessa's young cousin, Mrs Kerr's protégée, lately her friend. (156)

The passage suggests that it is the stilling of thought by others which constructs people as both immobile and fictional: Sydney is constructed as fictional by the immobilizing thought of other people. Catatonia in Bowen is not only an affair of the individual (here, Sydney), it is also, and differently, the result of being catatonically constructed by the thoughts of others.

Rather than thinking themselves, then, people in Bowen are, as we have suggested, *being thought*. And, being thought by others, people in Bowen are stilled, caught up within the cognitive parameters of other people. In Bowen, there is no possibility of escape from the catatonia of others' conceptions and constructions, no escape from the interior quietness which is being thought. To this extent, the conventional notion that Bowen's world is a world peopled with people, a world of manners, of relationships, is undeniable. Even interior quietness is caught up within these networks of relationships: in Bowen there is nothing outside the textured webs of other people's constructions, constructions which are themselves only the traces of other constructions. In Bowen, there is nothing outside the text of the other.

In Sydney, being thought (the construction of consciousness by the consciousness of others) amounts to what Ronald recognizes as a strange kind of anaesthesia (141). And if anaesthesia figures Sydney it is also, more generally, the governing figure of characterization in *The Hotel*. At times, Sydney's anaesthesia amounts to the possibility of non-existence, as when, through the thought that her friend Mrs Kerr is not aware of her, Sydney comes to a kind of extinction: 'The possibility of not being kept in mind seemed to Sydney at that moment a kind of extinction' (14).[8] To this extent Sydney may be compared to other characters in Bowen, such as Cecilia in *To the North*, who begins to dissolve once she is alone, or the eerie conception of Leopold in thought in *The House in Paris*.[9]

In *The Hotel*, it is not only Sydney who is constructed by others' thoughts: one of the most forceful paragraphs in the novel is a speech by another hotel guest describing the way in which she suffers from a dissolution, a disappearance of the self when she is alone. This unnamed guest tries to explain why people go to hotels: as winter comes with its long evenings, she says, living alone she 'begins to feel hardly human, sitting evening after evening in an empty room' (53). Becoming non-human, she begins to dissolve: 'It's not, of course, that I'm nervous, but I really begin to feel – if you'll understand my saying anything so extraordinary – as if I didn't exist. If somebody does come to the door or the telephone rings, I'm almost surprised to find I'm still there' (53–4). The locations and dislocations of this report of disappearance are telling: there is a subtle pressure on the surprise of the quasi-posthumous 'still' which suggests a profound stillness in being alone, a catatonic immobility. And this perception of an existence founded on the perception of oneself by others explains, to some extent, the vicious double-bind of social life: the necessity and impossibility of other people to substantiate one's own existence.[10] In order to live real lives, still lives, people in Bowen must be constructed by others' fictionalizing perceptions: identities are founded on the fictions of others. If we wonder at Bowen's fascination, her obsession, with manners and decorum, with the violently elegant and artificial constructs of social living, then we should remember that these still lives, lives stilled within the claustrophobic, catatonic web of human 'relations', are grounded in the impossibility of there being any other kind of 'life'. In Bowen, there is no other ground upon which we can substantiate our being, construct our still lives, than the fiction of other people, of other people's thoughts, people and thoughts that are, in turn, fictions. Bowen people can only be thought.[11]

* * *

In two crucial passages Sydney meditates on the nature of the hotel and hotel lives, on history, fiction and immobility. Just as, in *The House in Paris*, Karen will desire the violent change of revolution, so Sydney fantasizes with Milton about an invasion of the present by the past, and the astonishing pausations which give us pause at the beginning of *The Hotel*, become, in Chapter 5, those of history itself:

> 'Wouldn't it be nice', she said, suddenly smiling, 'if the Saracens were to appear on the skyline, land, and ravage the Hotel? They all take for granted – down there – that there aren't any more Saracens, but for all we know they may only be in abeyance. The whole Past, for a matter of fact, may be one enormous abeyance.' (35)

In abeyance? Even before providing us with the conventional sense of an abeyance as a 'state of suspense', the *OED* lays down the law. The dictionary is brutal, uncompromising, almost barbaric with the definitions it holds in abeyance, waiting like an insane series of gaping holes to open up texts: '**1.** *Law.* Expectation or contemplation of law'. Just waiting, in the abyssal anarchic pause of history before the law. 'Abeyance', the *OED* further informs us, is from the medieval Latin *batare*, to gape, stand open. This opening, this gaping hole which is history before history – history without history – this rent of time, this abeyant time of history, would designate the very temporality, the still time of *The Hotel*. To the extent that the past is an abeyance, it presents an aporia, a gaping blockage to thought, to the present, to mobility. Just as Miss Fitzgerald's catatonia opens *The Hotel* with the fear that she may never escape her abeyance of thought, the notion of the abeyance of history would suggest the impossibility of history's ever properly beginning.

Dissolution of the time of the novel in the ghostliness of the present: such would also be the force of Sydney's visit to a graveyard after her initial refusal of Milton's marriage proposal and after the shock of finding Mrs Kerr rejecting her (86). Accustomed to thinking of death as merely a 'spontaneous fine gesture' (87) at the end of life, Sydney now finds that Mrs Kerr's rejection is itself inscribed by and within death: death is 'the last and most humiliating of those deprivations she had begun to experience' (87). Looking at the graves, Sydney is 'oppressed by the thought' that death is the 'end of the future', a future towards which she has always been able to escape:

> Looking up to watch a bird fly slowly across the sky, she realized that living as she had lived she had been investing the future with more and more of herself. The present, always slipping away, was ghostly, every moment spent itself in apprehension of the next, and these apprehensions, these faded expectancies cumbered her memory, crowded out her achievements and promised to make the past barren enough should she have to turn back to it. (87)

The present is traversed by its own ghostliness, displaced to a future which will, at some point, necessarily be displaced back to a doubly phantasmatic past. Sydney's present is erased by its own dispersal in time, its temporal dissolution. Rather than being haunted by the past – as, for example, Antonia and Lilia are haunted by the dead Guy in *A World of Love*, or as Clare is haunted by her past in *The Little Girls* – Sydney's displacement of presence to the future makes the present itself ghostly, phantasmatic, hallucinatory. Within this present of ghostliness and dissolution, it becomes difficult, even in the eyes of the dull Reverend Milton, to envisage Sydney as any kind of unity or 'whole': 'Will these evenings, mornings, lights, memories, shadows, half-apprehensions, glimpses, ever fall away or run together and be merged in the whole of her?' Milton asks himself (146).[12]

Such would be the phantasmagoria of the self and of the present, the phantasmagoria of what we can refer to as hotel lives, lives fictionalized and immobile:

> She said [to Milton], 'I have often thought it would be interesting if the front of any house, but of an hotel especially, could be swung open on a hinge like the front of a doll's house. Imagine the hundreds of rooms with their walls lit up and the real-looking staircase and all the people surprised doing appropriate things in appropriate attitudes as though they had been put there to represent something and had never moved in their lives.' (68–9)

A gaping thought, thought in abeyance, as the doll's house of the hotel and of our lives stands open to reveal its fictional stillness, its phantasmagoric stilling. By the end of the novel, the hotel has indeed become a doll's house: 'The Hotel from up here was as small as a doll's house' (175).[13] Not only are lives stilled, immovably, catatonically, but this immobility is itself a fiction: these dolls or characters (in the hotel, in *The Hotel*, and in the world) are, perhaps, simulacra of 'real' people. But these simulacra, this logic of the simulacrum, would suggest that real people are themselves, in turn, simulacra without originals, facsimiles without true origins. 'Real' life is stilled here, presented as a fictional representation of itself. This fictional fantasy of the fantasy of the fictional radically disturbs any possibility of an opposition between the real and the fictional. *The Hotel* is itself an hotel, a doll's house, which is opened up to reveal characters immovably fixed in the positions described in these pages. But what *The Hotel* makes clear is that this fictional world is not simply a world inside the 'real' world. Rather, the 'real' world is inside *The Hotel*, just as it is inside, rather than outside, the hotel of fiction.[14] Cordelia, Sydney's young friend, prefers people in books who 'only exist when they matter' (81): for her, people in hotels are 'hardly *alive*' (81). In conventional terms, hotels are places where people pause, sojourn and seem to lead fictional lives –

fantasy-escapes from the everyday. But hotels in Bowen are also worlds. Hotel lives are still lives, real lives.

Sydney continues her meditation on the still lives of the doll's-house hotel: 'If one could see them like that ... one could see them so clearly as living under the compulsion of their furniture'(69). It is one of the strange, hallucinatory, gaping thoughts which Bowen's novels present, to suggest that these unmoving movables compel our lives, that our lives are driven and restrained by them, moved forward by them and made to stay. As Sydney goes on to explain, to live under the compulsion of our furniture is to inhabit a space and logic in which notions of cause and effect are themselves put into abeyance: Sydney wonders whether it is not the case that the sabbath and furniture are created 'just to discharge the obligations' which they themselves have made. She explains this idea to Milton, the vicar:

> 'Well, just think of this', she continued. 'Though it may have been an Idea in the first place that made churches be built, it was the churches already existing, with rows of pews for people to sit in and a pulpit and things all ready that had to be filled, that made you into a parson.' (69)

Milton's disturbance at such a suggestion makes Sydney immediately qualify it as ludic, an 'amusing' idea, only presented 'for the fun of the thing' (69). Nevertheless, it constitutes a crucial expression of the logic of still lives, lives immobilized by a necessary engagement with fictionality, a logical parasitism or hotelism. By overturning cause and effect, Sydney has suggested a different kind of explanation for catatonia and still lives. In this short-circuit of reason, of causality, the text suggests ways in which we might begin to think the impossible thought of catatonia. This reversal and displacement of conventional notions of cause and effect presents us with an *aporia*, a generative abeyance of logic, an interior quietness of reason. In this reversal, cause is effect and effect is cause. If this is characteristic of certain forms of (postmodern) thinking, it would seem that one way of thinking catatonia is to think the impossible, the impassable but irresistible structure of logical reversal. What is being thought here is the catatonia of being thought. And this thought suggests that, being thought, Bowen people are traversed by the immobilities of reason, a certain experience of the impossible, the interior quietness of thought.

* * *

Turning to Bowen's second novel, *The Last September* (1929), we find that it too can be defined through its abeyances: characters, once again, are prone to mental and physical stilling. Immobility – ultimately, of course, the immobility of death – is the condition towards which they move. Like people in *The Hotel*, people in *The Last September* are subject to stillness, interior quietness. Francie has mental 'absences' from her husband, 'long queer relapses into silence', such that she earns 'the right to ask curious things, as from a death-bed' (19), and her life is characterized by 'blanks and rifts' (22). During one insomniac, uneventful night in Danielstown, 'darkness clamped round' people's 'waking brains' with an 'insane pressure' (107–8). On another occasion, a gunman's face seems 'numbed into immobility' (125). In this novel, Gerald, in particular, is 'half hypnotized, consciously barren' (95), like 'a waterfall stand[ing] still' (184). Gerald stands 'with the vigour, grief and indifference of a tree that cannot help growing' (189). Lois Farquar stands 'still in alarm' at the sight of Mr and Mrs Montmorency (70); she is described as having 'her consciousness in a clamp' (77); she is 'vacant' (154); she feels 'quite at a standstill' (168); she stands 'not quite thinking' (186) – and then 'her mind halted' (190).

While *The Hotel* presents the doll's house hotel-world as a paradigm of still – immobile, fictional – lives, *The Last September* presents an Irish country house, a house still occupied by the Anglo-Irish, surrounded by the violence of the 'Troubles' and finally destroyed by fire, as another and different locus and simulacrum of still lives. *The Last September* centres on Lois, a nineteen-year-old woman who lives with her aunt and uncle, Lady Naylor and Sir Richard, after the death of her mother Laura. The novel concerns September 1920 in Danielstown, an Anglo-Irish country house and its demesne, and the visits by Hugo and Francie Montmorency, old friends of the Naylors. Mr Montmorency, once in love with Laura, recognizes in Lois traces of her dead mother. In Part II of the novel, Marda Norton, another friend of the Naylors, arrives from England. Lois, her brother Laurence, and Hugo are all, in their different ways, fascinated and enthralled by Marda, but at the end of Part II she returns to England to marry. Most dramatic, and pivotal to the final, third part of the novel, is Lois's engagement to a young British soldier Gerald Lesworth, and his death in an ambush by the IRA. In this love story, however, even before the physical 'actuality' of Gerald's death, love itself is interdicted by Lois's aunt Lady

Naylor. By discreet psychological and social manipulation, Lady Naylor manages to foreclose emotion between the young lovers by enclosing it within the constrictive, immobilizing structures of society, of still lives. The novel ends, after the dispersal of guests from Danielstown, with the burning of the house by Irish paramilitary forces.

* * *

As in *The Hotel*, people in *The Last September* are traversed by the immobilities of thoughts. People in these novels are being thought: thoughts, constantly dissolving in abeyance, construct still lives. In *The Last September*, the peculiarly physical figuration of thought or the stopping of thought, is even more pronounced than in *The Hotel*. Francie, the invalid wife of Hugo, has a mind, for example, which 'lay back in the silence' when 'her thoughts ached' (17), and later, 'her mind clenched tight, like a fist' (105). Slightly differently, Lois suffers from a 'panic of thoughts' (172) at an emotional crisis, and then, when the crisis breaks, she is constricted by the trees in the plantation where she and Gerald are talking, and where 'thought and movement were difficult' (190). The curious pressure of the physical on thoughts cannot only be construed as a dissolution of a Cartesian representation of consciousness – it also maps thought onto bodies or inanimate objects, and makes thought somatic or inanimate. Thus thoughts can be like lights (105), or minnows can be like thoughts: 'Minnows, disturbed like thoughts, darted shadowy over the clear yellow stare of the stones' (174). Similarly, a man – here a paramilitary soldier – can be, in profile, 'powerful as a thought' (34).

This intense pressure which the novel brings to bear on the physicality of thought, and which forces thought to be physical, suggests, in the first place, the importance of what we have called *being thought* – that is, the way in which people are constructed, physically actualized, in thought. The dissolution of the novel would involve, among other things, an intense and unremitting pressure on such an intersection of thought and the physical. And this pressure cannot be recuperated as 'merely' a disruption of classical dualism. The physicality of thought is also, more importantly, a rigorous disfiguration and dissolution of the very possibility of characterization. If people are figured in Bowen's early novels as being thought, the figuration of thought works in at least two ways. Firstly, it concerns the impossible space of novelistic representations of people – the impossible figuration or embodiment of people in books, characterization as the illusion of the physical actualization, the hypostasis, of being thought. Secondly, it does not stop short at the putative boundaries of 'books', but bends back within the non-novelistic. In her powerful elegiac essay on childhood reading, 'Out of a Book' (1946), Bowen reminds us that 'the characters in the books gave prototypes under which, for evermore, to assemble all living people' (*MT* 51). People are not compared to characters, but *assembled* by them. If being thought designates the logic and operation of characterization in the novel, *The Last September* is far from a hermetic metafiction, a self-enclosed and self-reflexive labour of fictionality. *The Last September*, like all of Bowen's novels, suggests the power of thought to figure people, which is to say that if characters in novels are being thought, then these characters are people: people being thought, 'figure[s] out of a book' (*MT* 53).

The dissolution of the boundaries between thought and the physical in *The Last September*, is also, finally, a dissolution of the boundaries of the self. *The Last September* presents the boundaries of the self above all in terms of a politics of private space and private property, a politics which is figured by the infringements of the borders of the Naylor's demesne by paramilitary soldiers. Such infringements occur at least three times before the final invasion and burning of Danielstown at the end of the novel. Each time, however, the notion of boundaries is itself questioned by the very status of Danielstown as an Anglo-Irish domestic enclave in Ireland. And this problematic of boundaries is further exacerbated by the (invited) intrusions of British soldiers into this enclave. The complex, even strictly undecidable question of nationality – Irish, English, Anglo-Irish, 'British' – figures the grounds upon which an undeclared war is being fought out. And the impossible and paradoxical loyalties involved in this war are inseparable, we suggest, from the question of the politics of the self.

The first occasion on which Danielstown is penetrated, its borders disrupted or dissolved, occurs when Lois is walking alone near the edge of the demesne. The scene crystallizes the questions of self, thought, nationality, politics, haunting, which pervade *The Last September*. Lois starts to walk down a shrubbery path and begins to be disquieted by the touch of plants and haunted, it seems, by a name:

> A shrubbery path was solid with darkness, she pressed down it. Laurels breathed coldly and close: on her bare arms the tips of leaves were timid and dank, like tongues of dead animals. Her fear of the shrubberies tugged at its chain, fear behind reason, fear before her birth; fear like the earliest germ of her life that had stirred in Laura. (33)

From the opening of the novel, Lois has been presented in terms of her dead mother, 'the ever-living Laura' (80); Hugo, Laura's ex-lover, doesn't recognize Lois when they meet, but his wife thinks that 'she's the image of Laura' (8). Lois is recognized, known, because she is the image of her mother, a simulacrum or phantom of the dead, a fiction, 'like a novel' (88). As she walks in the shrubbery, Lois's fear seems to be a fear of the name of the mother: the 'laurel', plant of poets, the signifier of linguistic profusion, is also the path down which Lois walks in the name of her mother Laura.[15] The laurel path, then, is Laura, a path which is enclosed by animistic, phantasmagorically breathing laurels. Walking down the path of Laura, Lois is haunted by the encrypted name of her mother as by the fear of an originless presence. 'Laura' signifies not only a path, but also a crypt, or a series of crypts, an 'aggregation of detached cells' (*OED*). If Laura haunts both Lois and *The Last September* more generally, she does so, not least, by figuring people as collections of detached cells, solitary crypts of the self, being thought, the boundaries of which are constantly invaded by others' minds and movements. Invaded, not least, by the thought of the dead. As we shall suggest in various ways in the present study, for Bowen, people are figured, characterized, given identity, precisely by the thought of the dead – their thoughts about dead people, and dead people's thoughts about them.

Lois 'thinks of herself as forcing a pass' through the laurels:

> High up a bird shrieked and stumbled down through dark, tearing the leaves. Silence healed, but kept a scar of horror. The shuttered-in drawing-room, the family sealed in lamplight, secure and bright like flowers in a paperweight – were desirable, worth much of this to regain. Fear curled back from the carpet-border. … Now, on the path: grey patches worse than the dark: they slipped up her dress knee-high. The laurels deserted her groping arm. She had come to the holly, where two paths crossed. (33)

Fear, shrieks, horror, tear into carpets, drawing rooms, the discourse and paraphernalia of Anglo-Irish life. The sealing, the security of shutters, the exclusion of tears in the fabric which Anglo-Irish social life had appeared to offer, are all subject to ineluctable invasions, hauntings, tears of the mind, encrypted horror. The paperweight security of family life is an illusion or fiction of life, still life.

Just as it is 'grey' light which eerily threatens to envelop Lois, so it is light which gives her the uncanny sense of a presence before she hears the steps of a man:

> First, she did not hear footsteps coming, and as she began to notice the displaced darkness thought what she dreaded was coming, was there within her – she was indeed clairvoyant, exposed to horror and going to see a ghost. (33)

In Lois's clairvoyance, the boundaries of the self are turned inside out, so that what threatens, fear, the violent intrusion of the alien across the borders of the self, are understood to be within. What is outside, the ghost, fear, horror, is inside the borders of the self. In clairvoyance, Lois is exposed to the horror of a dissolution of the boundaries of the self. But, above all, such dissolution in *The Last September* relates to the question of political and national boundaries. The dissolution of the boundaries of the self is mapped onto the problematic construction of political boundaries in the Ireland of 1920. What Lois is sensing here is an Irish paramilitary soldier, walking 'powerful as a thought' through the demesne (34): 'In gratitude for its fleshiness, she felt prompted to make some contact: not to be known seemed like a doom: extinction' (34). To be known, however, might be to risk another kind of doom, physical extinction, death. The man who intrudes on the demesne is an armed soldier intent on the destruction of Anglo-Irish demesne boundaries, intent on the destruction of the very binding of Anglo with Irish. The soldier's intrusion is a function of this war, a war over the identity of a nation: he is a soldier fighting in order to establish both 'Home Rule', the elimination of a foreign political body from the government of the country, and in particular, a rebalancing of power away from the political and economic dominance of a small occupying minority – the Anglo-Irish (and predominantly Protestant) landowners. This double gesture of exclusion – the exclusion of the intrusion from outside and the exclusion of the intrusion from within – is founded, as Lois recognizes, on the question of national identity:

> It must be because of Ireland he was in such a hurry; down from the mountains, making a short cut through their demesne. Here was something else that she could not share. She could not conceive of her country emotionally: it was a way of living, an abstract of several landscapes, or an oblique frayed island, moored at the north but with an air of being detached and washed out west from the British coast. (34)

Lois is haunted, then, by intrusions from beyond – and already within – the boundaries of her self, a self which functions in terms of phantasmatic political and national identity. The instabilities and mobilities of both constructions of identity make her vulnerable to such incursions. The Anglo-Irish constitute a nation at once within itself and beside itself, paranational. Both sides of the silent hyphen in 'Anglo-Irish' are irremediably fissured, split within themselves: such fissuring would be the very condition of Lois's identity.

The scene is echoed somewhat later when Marda Norton and Hugo Montmorency are talking. Hugo amuses Marda not least in that 'his negativeness was startling' (80). As they talk, Marda suddenly interpolates with the two questions which are constantly and silently hanging over all conversations in Danielstown – 'How far do you think this war is going to go?' and the supplementary but equally crucial question for the Anglo-Irish themselves: 'Will there ever be anything we can all do except not notice?' (82). 'Don't ask *me*', Hugo replies, but then tries to give an answer:

> 'A few more hundred deaths, I suppose, on our side – which is no side – rather scared, rather isolated, not expressing anything except tenacity to something that isn't there – that never was there. And deprived of heroism by this wet kind of smother of commiseration. What's the matter with this country is the matter with the lot of us individually – our sense of personality is a sense of outrage and we'll never get outside of it.'
>
> But the hold of the country *was* that, she considered, it could be thought of in terms of oneself, so interpreted. Or seemed so – 'Like Shakespeare', she added more vaguely, 'or isn't it'. (82)

A sense of outrage is a sense of passing beyond bounds and for personality to be constituted by an outrage suggests the paradox of a personality which is beyond its own bounds: personality is an outrage of itself. The bounds of personality can never be transcended or exceeded because 'personality' here is always already outside itself. Marda's vague and confusing comments on Hugo's statement seem to be an attempt to reduce it to the commonplace notion that national identity involves a sense of oneself as a part of a larger whole, just as, for Marda, Shakespeare is at once himself and more than himself. But this analogue is a reductive misconstrual of Hugo's statement. Identity, both personal and political, is necessarily outside itself. Being thought, then, would be the political construction of the subject as irreducibly exterior to itself.

* * *

Questions of national identity are most clearly focused in *The Last September* on the notion of being English. Paradoxically, it is precisely on account of their self-identity that the English are presented as non-human. The comments of Lady Naylor suggest that the identity of the English is sub-human: she declares that she wouldn't want to live in England because 'I wouldn't live among people who weren't human' (27), and that 'Really altogether, I think all English people very difficult to trace' (58), suggesting not only that their genealogical origins tend to be confused and obscure, but that English people are, themselves, somehow untraceable, leaving no trace, and to this extent non-existent.[16] Lady Naylor's comments can be taken to highlight the absurdities of a certain arrogant construction of national character. More dramatically, they epitomize Gerald. At the climax of his affair with Lois, Gerald is specifically described as 'outside himself with passion' (190). For Gerald, Lois's English lover, questions of personal and national identity simply do not exist: he is certain, as a British soldier in Ireland, that 'right *is* right' (92). But if Gerald is sealed within the certainty of his own national and personal identity, his certainty of self, his self-identity amounts to a curious impersonality. Gerald appears both to lack a 'personality' and to lack a 'person', to be literally non-human:

> He did not conceive of love as a nervous interchange but as something absolute, out of the scope of thought, beyond himself,

> matter for a confident outward rather than anxious inward looking. He had sought and was satisfied with a few – he thought final – repositories for his emotions: his mother, country, dog, school, a friend or two, now – crowningly – Lois. Of these he asked only that they should be quiet and positive, not impinged upon, not breaking boundaries from their generous allotment. His life was a succession of practical adjustments, into which the factor of personality did not enter at all. (41)

Gerald is a negative person, a non-person, partly, it seems, because of this rigid construction of boundaries. Paradoxically, this rigidity of borders and the denial of their transgression, both for him and for other people, rather than constructing a person, excludes it. Gerald is a non-person, he is and always has been, in some sense, dead: 'he was *not*, at all' (52). The extent of Gerald's impersonality might be gauged in Lois's inability to describe him in letters to her friend Viola: 'And there arose, recurrently, the difficulty of describing Gerald' (51). Gerald cannot be figured, he can only be seen, in fact, dead. Gerald can only be evoked, called from the dead: Gerald can only be described or perceived as if, or if, he is dead:

> As she stood looking at Gerald by the privet hedge, he emerged from the mist of familiarity, clear to her mental eye. She saw him as though for the first time, with a quick response to his beauty; she saw him as though he were dead, as though she had lost him, with the pang of an evocation. (52)

Lois can only picture Gerald, describe him, but also can only see him, as if he is dead. She can only call him or recall him from the dead, he can only be evoked. And seeing him now, for the first time, Lois wants to 'run indoors' and write a description of him to Viola. Gerald is non-human, a non-person, precisely because he cannot be described. The description, figuration, representation of people in thought is what constitutes a person in Bowen. People are only people to the extent that they can be thought, evoked, (re-)called from the dead. For Gerald to be a coherent, stable, finally self-identical subject, is to be non-human, dead. People in Bowen are only alive to the extent that they are traversed by death, only 'real' to the extent that they are traversed by figuration, by fiction. What Bowen calls 'the boundaries of the self' (100) must be constantly subject to invasion and incursion in order for a subject to be thought: the boundaries of the self must be in abeyance, riven by constant invasion, intrusion, transgression, by the fictional, the phantasmagoric, the spectral, the remembered – traversed by death and by the other of thought or other thought. The world – both within and beyond every national and political boundary – is peopled in abeyance, being thought.

2
Shivered

> No, there is no such thing as being alone together. Daylight moves round the walls; night rings the changes of its intensity; everything is on its way to somewhere else – there is the presence of movement, that third presence, however still, however unheeding in their trance two may try to stay. Unceasingly something is at its work.
>
> (*HD* 195)

'Still Lives' is, among other things, an oxymoron. It strangely mixes stillness and movement. In the first place it concerns what is without life or motion ('still') but is, nevertheless, animate or moving (that which 'lives'). But there is a further strangeness and mobility within the word 'still' itself. For 'still' never settles into one determination or another, whether as adjective, adverb, noun or verb. It never settles, for example, into being 'motionless' any more than it settles into 'yet', 'even so', 'nevertheless'. 'Still' is never still; it keeps going. What does it mean to say that 'still' is not still, that 'still' keeps going, that sense keeps going?

This chapter will focus on a reading of *To the North* (1932), but will also take a brief detour by way of *Friends and Relations* (1931). To the extent that a story or plot may be attributed to *To the North* it could be said to concern two women, Cecilia and Emmeline, who live together in a house in Oudenarde Road, St John's Wood, London. These two women are bound to one another by absence and by mourning, by the death of Cecilia's husband and Emmeline's brother, Henry. Against a satirical background of upper- and upper-middle-class English society in London (during the week) and in their country cottages, second homes or elsewhere (at weekends), *To the North* could be said to sketch the process whereby Cecilia decides to marry a perfectly eligible but dull man called Julian Tower and, in greater detail, to delineate the development and consequences of Emmeline's fatal affair with a two-timing 'bounder' called Mark Linkwater. Overwhelmed by the disintegration of her affair, Emmeline is to kill herself and Mark in a car-crash, leaving

Cecilia and Julian back in St John's Wood, waiting. It might seem appropriate to describe *To the North* as a tragedy.[1] In particular, the novel presents an individual, Emmeline, with whom we are encouraged to strongly sympathize or identify. Emmeline could be said to suffer tragically – not only from the brutality and infidelity of her lover, Mark Linkwater, but also, in subtler ways, from the insouciant infidelity of Cecilia. She lives with Cecilia in the 'unspoken good faith' of 'a quiet marriage' (148); but Cecilia, unable to attend to Emmeline's unspoken pain over Linkwater, blindly carries on preparing for marriage with Julian Tower and for the envisaged and inevitable '[falling] to bits' (207) of the women's shared home in Oudenarde Road. Finally, as befit the protocols of tragedy, Emmeline may be assumed to die, and this death coincides, quite precisely, with the end of the text. This death seems terrible, unjust, unnecessary, but at the same time unavoidable and, in some strange and painful respect perhaps, appropriate.

The account of *To the North* offered in the preceding paragraph is at once reasonably straightforward and thoroughly impossible. It presupposes a reading of the novel as a literary and fictional tragic narrative, predicated on the basis of the most classical literary critical concepts, namely the constitutive role of plot, of a linear narrative progression or unfolding, and the determining force of character. In particular it presupposes a central character or central characters whose being and identity is guaranteed by assumed notions of what a person or human individual is, of what stands as a legitimate and acceptable fictional representation of persons or individuals, of what is meant by psychological and characterological realism, etc. *To the North* leaves none of these concepts or presuppositions intact. Rather, it sets in motion a quite systematic, if extremely strange, displacement and re-elaboration of them. To say this is not to deny the tragic force of *To the North*. Quite to the contrary: the novel is intensely moving – it is riven with tragic force and pathos. But this pathos, this power to move should be articulated or apprehended within the context of the conceptual displacement and re-elaboration which the novel sets in motion.

Our argument, in other words, is that the tragic power of this novel is inseparable from an acknowledgement of its displacements of concepts of person and individuality and from a dissolution of the linearity and teleological structure of narrative. A focal term for this analysis will be 'going'. *To the North* calls up and inscribes a movement, a sense of departure or *going* irreducible to notions of psychological realism, narrative unity and coherence, or the plot-based centrality of a self-identical character. *To the North* calls for the logic of a departure or going *within* pathos, in other words for a notion of pathos that is grounded neither in the certitude of self-identity nor even within the traditional conceptual space of 'departure' or 'going'. While such a theorization of pathos may ultimately resist being thought, its promise or its threat signals a notion of tragedy not only as that which leaves its audience without identity, whether individual or communal, but also, more radically perhaps, as that which conditions the very possibility of experience.[2]

Everything is moving, everything is going. *To the North* is in motion from its title onwards. As in the opening sentence, with its to and fro syntax and prepositions, its twisting inversion of the title ('from the north'), its animism breathing life into the wind: 'Towards the end of April a breath from the north blew cold down Milan platforms to meet the returning traveller'(5). Cecilia is going to the north, engulfed in a movement which is at once described and enacted by the text, a going which sets the text's opening *in media res* and traverses its ending, undoing all closure. Even through the catatonic sustenance of affliction everything is going, departing: 'Getting up steam, the express clanked out through the bleached and echoing Milan suburbs that with washing strung over the streets sustained like an affliction the sunless afternoon glare'(5). Even when the train stops the movement goes on: 'At Chiasso they stopped dead, it appeared forever. Rain fell darkly against the walls of the sheds; Cecilia began to feel she was in a cattle truck shunted into a siding' (5). Even in the stillness of still lives, even beyond the movements of falling rain, and the effects of darkness and light, of shunting and 'siding', even beyond the movements of appearance ('it appeared') and feeling ('Cecilia began to feel'). Alongside and beyond all of these there is movement, a sense of *going* as that which exceeds every representation or figuration of movement. As the opening page of *To the North* suggests, 'going' is linked to death: 'As the wait prolonged itself and a kind of dull tension became apparent, [Cecilia] sent one wild comprehensive glance round her fellow travellers, as though less happy than cattle, conscious, they were all going to execution' (5). This 'going' also, it becomes evident, is closely allied to madness, in particular to what the text characterizes as the 'wandering' of insanity – as in the mobility of Emmeline's eyes in which Cecilia believes she sees 'a wandering icy gentleness like insanity's, gentleness without an object' (228).

In certain respects, then, *To the North* conveys that there is no stillness, there are no still lives. As in our epigraph from *The Heat of the Day*, there is no life, no experience, whether in solitude or with another, without the unceasing work of a movement which remains inassimilably other, a movement which can only be *figured* through a 'third presence' but which necessarily and ceaselessly eludes that figuration, that stilling. The movement and the force of this 'going' marks all perception, all experience, even when it is a matter of the classical topos of *topos* or place itself, the stillness or fixity of a house, of furniture or ornaments, of a painting or a moment. As in the description of Cecilia's looking about the drawing-room at Oudenarde Road, on her return from Italy:

> Clear as a still-life in the limpid afternoon light, the ornaments smiled at each other and might be supposed after midnight to dance and tinkle: candlesticks dropping with lustres, tapering coloured candles, fans tilted aslant, shell tea-caddies, painted patch-boxes, couples of china cats spotted with flowers, ramping dark ivory Chinese dogs, one widowed shepherdess with only the clock to smile at, a tall rosy clock from Dresden (a heart on its pendulum, silent under a shade), a small gold clock, ticking. (20)

In this analogy with the (fictional) stillness of a still life, there is the movement of anthropomorphism and phantasmagoric metamorphosis ('smiled', 'dance', 'tinkle'), of present participles ('dropping', 'tapering', 'ramping'), of a syntax which precisely conveys non-arrest, mobility and heterogeneous or discontinuous accumulation.[3] There is, above all, the movement of time, 'ticking'; but this movement cannot be assimilated to the sensible or intelligible, to a commonsense perception of time as a continuous, homogeneous, linear unfolding or narrative. How many clocks are there? How many of them are 'silent' and how many 'ticking'? And what *is* a clock? The accumulative, estranging repetition of 'clock' – together with the syntactical isolation of 'ticking' at the end of this still-life sentence – evokes a kind of hollowness and disquiet. The description intimates the sense of a disturbance of temporality which is not reducible to an opposition of 'silent' or 'ticking', a mobile or immobile clock. Such a disturbance, we would suggest, does not conform to any horology, or even to a simple failure or negation of the horological. Rather, this disturbance, this movement, is *at the same time* death; it is a movement of otherness within the present; it is, among other things, the movement of widowing, marking the silence or death of the heart.

This movement is unpresentable. It marks the very condition of perception and experience as well as the impossibility of any perception or experience – whether of time or place or self or other – ever coinciding with itself. To recapitulate our epigraph from *The Heat of the Day*: the 'presence' of the unceasing movement of otherness can never in fact be present-to-experience, for in this way it would cease to be 'on its way' and 'unceasing'; this 'third presence' can only ever be a figuration of what unceasingly remains unpresentable. This movement, this going overruns every stillness, every possible still life, including every experience of love, all romantic rapport or pathos, every emotion or 'moving of the feelings' (*Chambers*). It inscribes itself even as the condition of possibility of the desire for still life *par excellence*, in other words the desire for death. It is this desire which seems to be embodied by Emmeline, to embody her. Among the trees at St Cloud, during her weekend with Mark in Paris, for example, she

> longed to stand still always. She longed suddenly to be fixed, to enjoy an apparent stillness, to watch even an hour complete round one object its little changes of light, to see out the little and greater cycles of day and season in one place, beloved, familiar, to watch shadows move round one garden, to know the same trees in spring and autumn and in their winter forms. (144)

Again, the movements of this description, its very syntax, underscore the necessary fictionality of any 'stillness'; they pose stillness or fixity as always merely 'apparent', as necessarily phantasmagoric. Beyond these, the description traces the movement of the impossible – the restless longing or desire for a stillness or fixity which cannot *not* be restless, moving as it does among moving shadows, to and fro between the impossible simultaneity of 'an hour' and entire seasons.

The impossibility of this desire is also the impossibility of a stillness in language (whether speech, writing or other), of a stilling of that eerie mobile, language. It is the impossibility of an immobilization of the orders of syntax or sense. Here, in particular, it is the impossibility of freezing or fixing, thus defining or theorizing, a desire which can only be conceived on the basis of its own obliteration, in other words a desire for the stillness of death. There can be no doubt that *To the North* is pervasively concerned with such a desire. It haunts or drives Emmeline with such intensity that, in seeking to emphasize the displacements of notions of character operated by this novel, we might describe her as an auto-thanato-mobile.[4] We can say that Emmeline's is precisely an aspiration towards the condition of still life, but it is necessary to note that this aspiration, this drive, is itself driven: the very representation of this drive is itself worked over by the effects of *going*. There can be no such drive which is not always in advance *written over* by the inescapable fictionality of its representation. In these respects it should be stressed that *To the North* does not stop, that there is no accession to 'still lives' – either in Emmeline or in Markie or in reading. Above all it will be necessary to think: there is no Emmeline, no character or self, pre-existing the eerie dynamics of going, the radiance of what is shivered.

* * *

Death as going or as departure is not presentable or representable: going is the impossible or unthinkable figure of otherness within the present. *To the North*, like *Friends and Relations* and other Bowen novels, is concerned with the radical implications and effects of a conception of the present from which senses of arrival and departure cannot be detached. There is no present which is not uncannily fissured by a Bowenesque temporality of arrivals and departures. In other words, there is no present which is not already, in advance, contaminated by senses of going, of arrival or departure; and by the same token, there is no going, no arrival or departure, which is not itself in turn contaminated. Going, arriving or departing, is never self-identical: going belongs to no present.

The arboreal still life of 'the same trees in spring and autumn and in their winter forms' (*TN* 144) is a fiction overrun, dissolved by the logic of going. There are no 'same trees': 'the same trees' do not exist. Going, in Bowen, bears the force of the thinking of Heraclitus: 'One cannot step twice into the same river, nor can one grasp any mortal substance in a stable condition, but it scatters and again gathers; it forms and dissolves, and approaches and departs.'[5] This statement might be paradoxically described as articulating the uncanny point of departure for Western philosophy. To restrict ourselves to a very recent and narrow context, we may recall that – together with the corresponding proposal that 'All things are in flux, nothing remains' – it also underlies Walter Pater's Conclusion to *The Renaissance* (1868), the short essay which in turn offers an important point of departure for thinking about modernist conceptions of temporality.[6] That Pater's rhapsodic affirmation of the fleeting power and beauty of the moment leaves its mark on the writings of James Joyce and Virginia Woolf – among others – is clear enough.[7] But Pater's text perhaps too easily lends itself to a reification of 'moments', however eloquent and subtle that reification might be. Its essential concern is with the discrimination and experience of 'moments as they pass, and simply for those moments' sake'.[8] To the extent that it tends towards such reification, Pater's Conclusion works away from its own radical exposition of the present moment as 'gone while we try to apprehend it', as being that 'of which it may ever be more truly said that it has ceased to be than that it is': it represents a 'weak' or recuperative reading of Heraclitus. Provocatively dissolute in relation to a Modernist or any other conventionally 'historical' context, Bowen's work is concerned with formations and dissolutions, approaches and departures, *within* the very presence of the present, *within* the self-identity of the same.

* * *

This preoccupation in truth overruns, overflows, all of Bowen's writings, constantly dislocating and disorganizing any attempt to impose upon them any teleological reading, any reading aimed at some fixity of meaning, any reading that might seek to affirm the unity and self-identity of a reader. By way of a passing digression, a minor departure, we could take note of this preoccupation in the novel published a year earlier than *To the North*, namely *Friends and Relations*. In some ways perhaps her most intransigent and least accessible novel, *Friends and Relations* is, nevertheless, exemplary of Bowen's still lives in its relentless and disturbing focus on a notion of the present as always, in advance of itself, inscribed by its disappearance or departure. *Friends and Relations* elaborates a 'ghostly present' (116), a conception of experience as being 'like a too long wait on the platform of some familiar station from which, virtually, one has already departed' (7), a conception of individuals in terms of 'ghostly coming and going' (131) and 'no-presence' (33, 91). *Friends and Relations* impels us towards a thinking of the self, of perception and experience, in terms of what has *already departed*. Thus Janet's coming to maturity – 'as though someone touching her on the shoulder had told her to come away from a party that had hardly begun' (20). Still living, Janet is described as haunting her husband Rodney: 'Before death she had ghosts all over the house; she was preceded and followed' (56). In more than one sense, she is not alone: the text is adrift with this movement of departure. There is Lewis who 'felt he had already departed ... like a ghost' (65). There is the room in the house on Royal Avenue in London: 'Sun streamed in generously; from chairs and cushions colour must already be making a ghostly departure' (23). There is the library at Batts which both contains Janet and Edward and at the same time is 'empty of Janet and Edward, as though both had turned and gone out by different doors, or had never come in' (91). Edward's 'ghostly coming and going' involves a consistent sense of him as 'someone to whom [Janet] had already said goodbye' (131).

Friends and Relations ends uncertainly, evoking a final but undecidable 'alarm of departure': in Cheltenham 'The tourist season was not yet over: a horn in the street, some alarm of departure brought two American visitors hurriedly down the steps of the hotel where Edward had stayed before the wedding' (159). The undecidability of 'departure' as it is figured in *Friends and Relations* – even as that text supposedly (but perhaps never, and never not) leaves or departs from us – clearly corresponds with that of the eerie 'arrival' with which *The Death of the Heart* concludes, or the bizarre and deadly scene in 'the temple of departure' marking the close of *Eva Trout*.[9] Departure, the logic of *going*, in *Friends and Relations* and elsewhere, necessarily entails 'death', but the presence of death can only ever be conceived in terms of a haunting 'no-presence', a no-presence which is nevertheless not simply negative.

This haunting of 'departure' is perhaps most graphically demonstrated in the strange movements of, and within, the sense of that word as it appears in *The Last September*. The third and final section of *The Last September* is entitled 'The Departure of Gerald'. These pages of the text eventually come to cite their title, specifically referring to 'Gerald's departure' (*LS* 193), in other words to the painful breaking-up of Gerald's relationship with Lois, his departure from the house called Danielstown and from the family occupying it. But there is a *last* sense of 'departure' – a sense inextricable from the 'last' of the novel's title – and this concerns the revelation of Gerald's death: 'death' thus comes to remark or replay 'departure' in the title

'The Departure of Gerald', revealing a deathliness and otherness from which no notion of departure can ever truly depart.

Elizabeth Bowen's explorations of going, leaving, departing (or arriving) dislocate the very identity of the self, the very conception of society, love, all friends and relations. There is a work of going and it sets the self apart from itself; it is in this context that the social and political significance of Bowen's writing might begin to be traced. One blazing hot day, after Emmeline has had lunch with Markie and has agreed to his accompanying her on a weekend trip to Paris, she returns to the office in Woburn Place, ominously ruffled by the sense that 'We mustn't lunch out again' (117). She is distracted, appalled:

> Her roll-top in its solemn surround of silence was a monument to the pretence of industry: in vain her stenographer's pointed tapping, in vain the clock: place and time, shivered to radiant atoms, were in disorder. There was no afternoon; the sun, forgetting decline, irresponsibly spun like a coin at the height of noonday. (118)

To shiver is not only, as in the mild convulsion of a body, 'to quiver', but also – and more importantly in the present context – 'to shatter' (*Chambers*), to fragment.[10] What is fragmented or shivered is not only Emmeline's experience or state of mind: it is a shattering or shivering that can be seen to characterize any and every Bowenesque afternoon, or, more precisely, that haunts and thus conditions all 'place and time' in Bowen. In this shivering to radiant atoms is figured a cataclysmic apprehension of the ghostly work of going.

Anthropomorphism makes this shattering afternoonlessness at once more eerie and more generalized: it is the sun that forgets. The vertiginous motion of the sun spins through the wild suspension of the parenthetical phrase, with its interminable present participle ('forgetting decline'), and through the undecidably active or passive, active and passive, 'spun' itself. Here, in this vertigo, the question of responsibility uncannily traces its shadow: 'the sun, forgetting decline, irresponsibly spun like a coin at the height of noonday'. But what is irresponsible here would be the very movement of chance (like the spinning of a coin): the value of both responsibility and irresponsibility are hereby minted in the vertiginous movement of chance itself. It spins through Bowen's blinding syntax: the absence of a comma after 'coin' leaves the phrase 'at the height of noonday' in suspense, undecidably referring to both coin and sun. This, then, would be the chance of going, chance *as* going. An image of chance: unseeable, at the height of noonday, the shadow of a tiny spinning coin in the blinding immensity of the sun.[11] The question of responsibility can be identified with the impossibility of judging or of deciding, suspended as it is here in the spinning forces of the sun as other, the shivering of heliocentrism in a hetero-anthropomorphico-numismatics, the constitutively dislocating necessity of chance. This shivering – not a momentary aberration but rather the chance and possibility of every experience – is what we have been attempting to describe as the work of going.

Going is also the unthinkable space of laughter, ecstasy, soaring rapture, including perhaps what accompanies the seeming hyperbole and surrealism of that shivered afternoon in Woburn Place: 'There was no afternoon; the sun, forgetting decline, irresponsibly spun like a coin at the height of noonday. Emmeline, as though threatened with levitation, gripped the edge of her roll-top' (118). Such, then, would be the shifting grounds or 'changing scenes' of the comedy of *To the North* and other Bowen texts. Going affirms itself only as a movement of otherness, in the grip of laughter, in the promise or threat of what can never be appropriated or mastered. As may become clearer in the course of this study, going affirms the responsibility of conceiving the self and social relations in terms of a movement of *othering*, a movement which poses – in short – the dissolution of the self and of all social relations within the context of the constitutive force of fiction, theatre, literarity, phantasmagoria.

* * *

It would certainly be possible to demonstrate this constitutive force in terms of the ways in which Bowen represents her own life and writing: life is inseparable from its sense of being out of, or in, a book; nominally real people in real life are always 'semi-fictitious'; nominally imaginary people, i.e., characters in Bowen's novels, are on the other hand 'more convincing, more authoritative as humans'.[12] Like Hazlitt in his account of Shakespeare, then, we would wish to indicate the strict impossibility of conceiving 'Elizabeth Bowen' except in terms of a kind of multiple identity, already given over to fiction and difference: in other words, shivered.[13] Adopting a phrase from *To the North*, we would argue that Bowen, like Shakespeare, 'affirm[s] the obvious' (60) – the obvious here being that Bowen, like Shakespeare, is a crowd. Bowen is a multiple being in whom 'characters pre-exist' (*MT* 37); 'Elizabeth Bowen' designates a singularity indissociable from the multiplicitous reality of fictional identities, inextricable from the work of going. In this respect 'Elizabeth Bowen', we might say, has always already *gone away*.[14]

But a conception of the singularity of the individual as fissured, as always in excess of itself, as worked over by the protean dissolutions of going, as given over in advance to multiplicity, to theatre, to fiction and phantasmagoria – such a conception is also, and far more powerfully, furnished by the novels themselves. *Friends and Relations*, for example, in its consistent evocations of the ghostly departure lounge of all perception and experience, focuses on the inevitability of disembodied forms of thought, of thoughts which detach themselves from the self and range with 'delirious boldness' (*FR* 95). It focuses on a notion of the self as inevitably cohabiting with doubles and others, as being (for instance, in the case of Edward) inhabited by some other 'giant and foreign self' (149) or as having (for instance, in the case of Mrs Studdart) a double, 'a confidante, an intimate always present, who did not exist' (157). The very oxymoronism of a 'foreign self' or of a non-existent 'intimate' signals the necessary logic of multiplicity; for by whom could such a 'self' or 'intimate' ultimately be recognized except by a fictive or phantasmagoric conglomeration, a self already subject to a dynamically proliferating logic of foreignness and fictionality?

Nothing in *Friends and Relations* is more memorable, unsettling, distracting than the passage concerning 'everlasting departures' (147) in the thoughts of Lewis. Lewis is leaning against the mantelpiece, having a drink. He fantasizes Janet and Edward departing by ship, eloping together: the mind experiencing this fantasy will later be figured as nothing other than 'the theatre of this large nonoccurrence' (151). The passage is also, and more generally, *about* passage, and about the passage of itself. It is a kind of departure in the text, of the text, a departure in the form of a disjunctive and strange meditation on departure itself: 'Watching a ship draw out you are aboard a moment, seeing with those eyes: eyes that you can no longer perceive. You see the shore recessive, withdrawing itself from you; the familiar town; the docks with yourself standing' (147). Departure here comprises a moment, the 'identity of a moment' which we are told 'has taken everything', a moment in which we are prompted to think not simply about the paradoxical sense in which the one who remains *becomes* those who depart (a structure, it may be noted, already implying self-proliferation) but also about the necessary recognition of this identification as fictive. This is identity in fiction, as fiction. It is the ecstatic treachery of a 'last exchange', a moment sited in irreducible otherness, 'inconceivable', *gone.*

What appears to be Lewis's meditation on departure – this strange passage on the passage of thought, the self, all friends and relations – shifts to the past tense, remarks itself by recalling the departure, remarks itself by departing from itself, keeps going:

> – So you looked back with those aboard, for a moment only. So they depart; traitors to you, with you, in the senses. The ship, those eyes, are for you ashore now inconceivable, gone. Under the very high crane a winch creaks, clocks strike from the dwarfed spires behind. The church hides the hill, terrace blocks out terrace. The crowd that you are breaks up. (147)

Let us leave *Friends and Relations*, then, on this strange note of departure, with the weird pathos of what is referred to in the same passage as a 'tear' for the unknown, a tear for what is 'always to be unknown' (147). Let us leave it in midsentence, at this short but extraordinary clause, 'The crowd that you are breaks up'. Nothing up to this point has suggested that the 'you', which occurs repeatedly throughout the passage, should be understood as anything but second person singular: 'you' as, above all no doubt, Lewis talking to or picturing himself. (Thus the conclusion of the passage in question is marked by a new paragraph beginning: 'Lewis put down his empty glass on the mantelpiece, resolving to see Laurel' [147–8].) The novel at this point, however, dramatizes the very strangeness and undecidability of 'you' – a 'you' which does not stop short of the reader and thus of the dissolution of reading, the dissolution of the novel.[15] How many are we? Of course, the clause can be read straightforwardly as referring to 'you' in the second person plural as a crowd; but the other reading also remains. The preceding and contrary indications of the 'you' as singular, together with the Bowenesque torsion of syntax, leaves *Friends and Relations* leaving us with the alarm of a truly uncanny departure, that is to say with a fragmenting figure of the self as nothing but a crowd.

* * *

'Nothing but' is, however, in danger of sounding merely negative, whereas our concern is rather with the alterity of multiplicity, with fragmentation or shivering, as affirmation. Bowen's novels dramatize a thinking of the self in terms of a shivered multiplicity, fiction and otherness, and there is no doubt that such a drama resonates with a sense of the seductive powers of madness and death. But this logic is also to be affirmed, constituting as it does the literary and ethical adventure of a politics that would accompany the dissolution of the identity and authority of the self. We will draw this chapter to a conclusion, then, by returning to our reading of *To the North* in terms of the affirmation of going and the forms of responsibility that it seems to us to imply.

The negotiations of madness and death in *To the North* are scarcely restricted to Emmeline. Rather, they go with a more general (though historically specific) insistence on personal identity as inhabited by multiplicity, fiction and otherness. Multiplicity is suggested, for example, in the case of Cecilia: 'herself makes a crowd' (193), recounts Emmeline. Similarly, there is the sense of a crowd for Linkwater when he talks to Emmeline: 'Nursing one foot, tipping brandy about in his glass, Markie began to talk very quickly, as though she had been a whole roomful' (72). This can be, in Emmeline's word, 'frightening' (193): *To the North* clearly suggests that such forms of otherness dislocate and dissolve any conception of self as unitary and self-identical. The novel situates such otherness within a particular context. *To the North* happens in the 1920s. The work of going, within which the novel is set adrift, is itself signposted in explicitly historical terms. *To the North* is shadowy with death. Such is doubtless the climate of all Bowen's still lives; they belong to the twentieth-century history of death; their shadowshow is pervasively that of war, whether the First World War or (in the case of *The Last September*) of the Troubles in Ireland or (in the case of *A World of Love*) of two world wars combined. One could say that Henry's death from pneumonia, reported near the outset (12), figures the novel's largely silent, absent 'source' of events – among other things, the culling of young men in the so-called Great War. An ironic source, to be sure: the extent to which, for example, Emmeline's drive towards death is an effect of her failure or inability to accept the death of her brother must remain hauntingly without resolution. We can nevertheless clarify the strangeness and generality of such irresolution. For, as we will show in greater detail in our readings of *The House in Paris* and *A World of Love*, the structure of this deathly logic is precisely *cryptic*: death operates as a force of otherness directing and determining events, characters and experiences in the text. In *To the North* this structure is not confined to the shadows cast by the death of Henry, rather it engulfs the text.

This deathly logic, indissociable from that of going, affects everyone and everything, and constitutes the very historical context of the novel. The sense of a drive towards death is not only Emmeline's, for example, but clearly also Markie's. He is as aware as she is that, as he says, 'we *are* riding for a fall' (184), and he is perhaps even more aware of an accumulating inevitability, of what is 'bound to occur' (202). This sense of the ominous, of shadowy inevitability or (as we shall describe it in our reading of *The House in Paris*) 'dread', is inseparable from the movement of *To the North* and of its historical context. It is signalled by the image of travellers 'all going to execution', on the opening page of the text. It marks the general delineation of Emmeline as 'step-child of her uneasy century' (63). It is eerily inscribed in the blot-like summer during which most of the novel takes place: 'Across the mind's surface – on which a world's apprehension, strain at home and in Europe, were gravely written – the sense of a spoilt summer, so much prettiness wasted, darkly spread like spilt ink' (177). We would argue that the uneasiness of the twentieth century here – at least from the point of view of 'the West' – involves the shadowy effects of the First World War, together with a powerfully secular recognition of the concomitant logic of 'still lives', of life as always already traced by death and of the dead living on. Such death and living on, such *still living*, is most crucially figured in *To the North* by Henry who, though dead and absent from its events, is nevertheless 'generally present' (99). The uneasiness of the century concerns, above all, a decentring of the Western self, its unresting diffusion in a network of death, fiction, multiplicity and otherness.

This is evoked, most intensively, in 'going'. Everyone is going – everyone is in motion. '"All ages are restless. ... But *this* age", Lady Waters went on, "is far more tha n restless: it is decentralized. From week to week, there is no knowing where anyone is"' (170). This somewhat whimsical formulation has its corroboration in the relentlessly locomotive dimensions of the text. As Bowen remarks on someone else's remark, in 'Pictures and Conversations': 'Bowen characters are almost perpetually in transit' (*MT* 286).[16] In transit, then, by foot, by boat, by plane but, most of all in *To the North*, by car.

The locomotive dimensions of Bowen's 1932 text, especially in the context of driving, can be elucidated by brief consideration of an essay by Aldous Huxley, published the preceding year in the collection *Music at Night and Other Essays*. In this essay, entitled 'Wanted, a New Pleasure', Huxley explores the realization that 'as far as pleasures [are] concerned, we are no better off than the Romans or the Egyptians' (249–50).[17] Huxley notes that 'We live in the age of inventions; but the professional discoverers have been unable to think of any wholly new way of pleasurably stimulating our senses or evoking agreeable emotional reactions' (252–3). After speculating on the possible 'invention of a new drug' (254), Huxley suggests that the nearest thing to it, and 'the one genuinely modern pleasure' (255), is speed – in other words, moving at high velocity, in particular in an automobile. The experience of driving in an automobile can be compared to, but finally quite surpasses, that of galloping on horseback. Huxley writes:

> The automobile is sufficiently small and sufficiently near the ground to be able to compete, as an intoxicating speed-purveyor, with the galloping horse. The inebriating effects of speed are noticeable, on horseback, at about twenty miles an hour, in a car at about sixty. When the car has passed seventy-two, or thereabouts, one begins to feel an unprecedented sensation – a sensation which no man [*sic*] in the days of horses ever felt. It grows intenser with every increase of velocity. (256)

Going sets *To the North* uncannily in motion, and everything in *To the North* is moving. Everything is conducted through multiple velocities in thought and space. There is Cecilia who, opines Lady Waters, 'never seems to be happy when she is not in a train – unless, of course, she is motoring' (15). There is Emmeline's and Peter's travel agency which 'seemed to radiate speed' (144), shooting 'travellers like arrows' (125), an agency whose slogan is 'Move dangerously' (23) and 'go anywhere' (24). There is the 'exalting idea of speed' (135) and hunger for flight in the context of Emmeline and Markie's journey to Paris by plane – 'the acceleration of movement about the aerodrome as though they were about to be shot out of a gun' (135), then the transit like that of 'a pleasure-cruise through this archipelago of the cloud-line, over shadowless depths'. It is in this flight, in particular, that we begin to encounter the sense that Emmeline is unstoppable, tragically and unstoppably elsewhere: she 'was embarked, they were embarked together, no stop was possible' (138). Emmeline, on this climactic trip to Paris, goes beyond Mark Linkwater: 'Travelling at high velocity he had struck something – her absence – head on' (142). His overwhelming sense is 'of having been overshot, of having, in some final soaring flight of her exaltation, been outdistanced' (142). This rapture, this undecidably erotic exaltation, this outdistancing supplement the sense that 'no stop was possible'; they link up, too, with the impression of Emmeline's 'straying faculties', her capacity for being 'ardently elsewhere' (125), her being – as Linkwater says – 'like a cat; always coming and going' (147).

The sense that they '*are* riding for a fall' is translated, in *To the North,* from the arena of horse-riding to the stranger, loopier world of automobiles. For nowhere is the force of going more powerfully inscribed than in the figure of the most 'intoxicating speed-purveyor', the motor car. Browning's ominous but ecstatic poem, 'The Last Ride Together', is transposed into the context of Paris taxis: 'Swerving violently at a corner, the taxi flung Emmeline against Markie, then out of his arms again. "I like Paris taxis," she said, holding on to the window-frame, "they're like the Last Ride Together"' (147).[18] And still within the context of driving, Linkwater will later summarize his fear in the face of Emmeline with the words: 'I can't live at top gear' (183).

But Bowen's text is not concerned with living at top gear. It is concerned with what is *beyond* top gear. Figures of excessive velocity, an uncontainable, dangerous supplement of speed, abound. Accompanying these are fear and terror, a sense of being 'terrified' by speed, and the supplementary sense of fear generated (particularly through Emmeline) by the apparent absence of fear. One night, going back late after having dinner at Markie's, for instance, Emmeline 'shot into gear, accelerated, and the small car went spinning, terrified, up the empty streets to St John's Wood' (50): the syntax suggests that it is the anthropomorphic 'small car' – not Emmeline – who is 'terrified'. On another occasion, there is Julian and Cecilia's drive into Buckinghamshire to visit his niece Pauline at her school, when the speed is such that 'Buckinghamshire was too small, not many times the length of his car; they would soon overshoot the School and run out of the county' (74). Then in Paris, there is the Browningesque taxi: 'Their taxi steered between two lorries, bumped on an island and spun just clear of a bus. Emmeline laughed, seeing Paris spin round, and blinked at the crash of light'

(149). And as all these velocities might suggest, driving is ultimately linked with a kind of insanity, loopy with the thought of being lost, absent, as in Linkwater's recounting of a drive after a party: 'We got into a car to drive a man home to Hertfordshire; coming back we went round in loops, I don't know who was driving: possibly no one' (103).

The setting of *To the North*, whether Paris or London, is one in which 'shadowy trams crashed by' (146) or in which it is possible to be, like Julian Tower, 'hypnotized by the glare and vibration of traffic – long cars nosing like sharks, vans whirring in gear, the high tottering buses' (114). But all these dislocations of driving, the entire network of characters perpetually in flight, all the pervasively and intensively locomotive dimensions of the text, are themselves set adrift within a logic of going which exceeds them – exceeds every figuration, every instantiation. Going drives the text; but going cannot be presented. 'Going' can be understood, finally, in relation to death – not as a way of *arriving* at a sense of what the phrase 'to the north' means, but rather as an attempt to adumbrate what will constantly have been *going on*, the movement of radical estrangement escorting all presence, including that of the reader and reading.

Faced with 'this flood, this impetus that he could not arrest' (185), Mark Linkwater has already told Emmeline: 'The fact is ... one can't live on the top of the Alps.' 'Alps?' replies Emmeline. And then: '"I can't live at top gear," he said, rather more lamely, conscious that half his meaning must go astray' (183). The accumulating movement of metaphors of driving, walking, locomotion ('top gear', 'lamely', 'go astray') in turn dramatizes the ineffaceable, incessant yet inconceivable work of going within – but other to – language, sense and meaning. The notion of 'living at top gear' is necessarily unreadable but still demands to be read: its meaning misses, falls short or overshoots and yet, going astray, it keeps going. Its capacity for going astray is an effect of going, in accordance with a logic which prevents any sense or meaning from ever simply or completely coinciding with itself and consequently prevents any sense or meaning from not being marked by the necessary possibility of going astray.

Living in top gear, in the context of Bowen's novel, would be to go beyond it, to accede to a going beyond going, a movement beyond merely 'speed', a departure from every classical or conventional conception of departure, an overturning and displacing of all established conceptions of going and departure. This would be going *to the north*. It would be necessarily apocalyptic, in accordance with the strictly rhetorical question of Browning's 'The Last Ride Together': 'Who knows but the world may end to-night?' Unpresentable, it can only be figured as an 'unheard of finality, breaking down every control' (243), driving 'as though away from the ashy destruction of everything' (244); it would be a going beyond 'one's last day on earth when fear and all sense of farewell had alike departed and only a very brief transit remained ahead' (140). The movement 'to the north' sets the self apart from itself, launching a departure *of* the self, exceeding any experience of departure, 'seeing the strands of the known snap like paper ribbons'. This is the last drive together:

> Like a shout from the top of a bank, like a loud chord struck on the dark, she saw: 'TO THE NORTH' written black on white, with a long black immovably flying arrow.
>
> Something gave way.
>
> An immense idea of departure – expresses getting steam up and crashing from termini, liners clearing the docks, the shadows of planes rising, caravans winding out into the first dip of the desert – possessed her spirit, now launched like the long arrow. (244)

The deathliness of this final departure, the tragic force of the ending of *To the North*, like the movement of affirmation, the experience of rapture and exaltation, is inscribed within going. 'TO THE NORTH': we will have been left with the impossibility of reading those words, that title, the black on white as well as the supplementary but essential arrow, the still life, immovably flying. For the work of going is a work of difference preventing the very coincidence of 'TO THE NORTH' with itself. Going inscribes itself as what must but cannot be read, as what resists every fixity of sense, in 'TO THE NORTH' or *To the North*. Going is that which, conjoining self and language ('a shout', 'TO THE NORTH', 'her spirit, now launched like the long arrow') and rendering it impossible to conceive the former without the latter, is nevertheless other to them, gone on, gone before, gone away.

To the North ends in unarrested suspense: not only in the suspenseful imminence of collision, in which 'like gnats [Emmeline and Markie] hung in the glare', in other words in the proleptic suspense of 'what was past averting' (245); but also in the suspense of Cecilia's and Julian's waiting back at Oudenarde Road, a suspense the unresting force of which is figured by the kitten Benito: 'Benito was restless tonight: he slipped round the door ajar, a small presence flitting and dark as a thought, a wide wild look over the cushions, something springing and turning and never still' (246). *To the North* closes on a house in motion – a ghostly house which 'seemed still to echo the others' departure' (246) – and in a sudden motion towards the implied necessity of an unthinkable dispossession, an unstoppable homelessness.

If tragedy breaks us up it is not because it comes to us, arrives as something to be encountered and collided with; rather it is, as necessary possibility, that which inhabits every experience, every perception. Such an observation is not made in order to corroborate some loosely Paterian advocacy of the precious experience of 'moments': it is not a question of the preciousness suggested by Cecilia at the end: 'Never forget any moment,' she tells Julian in the midst of the final suspense, 'they are too few' (246). For, despite the belief apparently imputed to Cecilia, there is no moment 'utterly free of oblivion' (246), no moment undivided by going, by the shivering multiplicity of arrivals and departures which themselves belong to no simple present. *To the North* impels a logic of tragedy, pathos and passion on the basis of going, that is to say as irreducible to any self-identity or to any presence, whether psychical or phenomenal. The novel is what happens within the force of this going, this radiance of atoms. Such would be the contribution of *To the North* to a theory of the novel, to the genre of the novel: shivered.

3

Fanatic Immobility

> For the writer, writing is eventful; one might say it is in itself eventfulness. More than any activity, it involves thought, but the thought involved in it is by nature captive, specialized and intense. ... Reading is eventful also. It, too, engages the faculties, so closely that reflection is only possible when the book has been finished and put down. At a first reading one has little but reflexes.[1]

> An act of reading takes place as an event. It is something that happens, with the same inaugural violence, breaking any predictable concatenation, as other events in the real world like birth, copulation, death.[2]

The force of going which we have elaborated in our reading of *To the North* is dramatized by the very structure of *The House in Paris*. Like *The Last September* and *Friends and Relations* before it, *The House in Paris* (1935) is divided into three parts. Parts I and III take place on a Thursday in February, the narration being intersected by that of the chronologically anterior events of Part II. The events of Part II take place over a period of several months, one spring and summer ten years earlier. Far more than with Bowen's earlier novels, however, the tripartite division of *The House in Paris* itself participates in a specific and systematic dissolution of temporality. And although this division might superficially appear to repeat that of other modernist novels such as, for example, Virginia Woolf's *To the Lighthouse* (1927), the structure of Bowen's novel entails a radical disruption of temporality, memory and causality, which Woolf's only begins to explore.[3]

In Part II of *The House in Paris*, a twenty-three-year-old Englishwoman, Karen Michaelis, has a brief and secret love affair with a 'French-English-Jewish man' (89), Max Ebhart. The affair is secret because Karen is engaged to an Englishman, Ray Forrestier, and Max is engaged to a Parisian woman, Naomi Fisher. Karen and Max meet one weekend in Hythe, in Kent, and make love before Max returns to Paris to break off his engagement. After talking to Naomi, Max then has an interview with her mother, during which he slits his wrist and dies. Karen gives birth to Max's child, has it adopted, and marries Ray as previously planned. Parts I and III span one day in a house in Paris owned by Naomi's widowed mother, the manipulative and unnerving Mme Fisher. After the death of her husband, Mme Fisher, with the help of Naomi, had provided lodgings for young English and American women – *'pensionnaires'* – who were staying in Paris to complete their education. Thus, five years before the events of Part II, Karen had been a lodger in the house, where she had met Max, at that time closely associated with Mme Fisher. In Part I, two children meet in Mme Fisher's house. Both children are, coincidentally, in transit between their respective guardians and relatives, and are being looked after for the day by Naomi. One is Leopold, the nine-year-old illegitimate son of Karen and Max who has, since birth, lived in Italy with his American foster-parents, the Grant Moodys. He has come to Paris to meet his mother for what may, paradoxically, be described as the first time. Part I ends and Part III opens with the arrival of a telegram from Karen to say that she will not, after all, be coming to meet Leopold. Part III concerns the after-effects of this telegram and the final arrival of Karen's husband Ray, who takes Leopold away to meet Karen, having decided not to send him back to the Grant Moodys. The other child waiting in the house in Paris is Henrietta Arbuthnot, an eleven-year-old motherless girl who is on her way from England to stay with her grandmother in the south of France. Mme Fisher, by now bedridden, dying or more specifically living a posthumous life, continues nevertheless to exert discreet but violent psychological force on visitors to her house.

With the dark and intricate web of these relationships, Bowen casts a narrative of unprecedented psychic tension. *The House in Paris* is centrally concerned with the terrifying pressures which adults impose on children as they grow – pressures originating most powerfully in the unspoken, in the originless utterance. The novel concerns the haunting of children by their own, and, more importantly, by others' pasts: it offers a telepathological analysis of the cryptic structures of human genealogies. Above all, through the character of Leopold, it presents Bowen's most rigorous and unremittingly clairvoyant elaboration of the structure and effects of psychic trauma. *The House in Paris* is what we propose to call a traumaturgy, both a work and a theory of wounds. It is, we shall argue, a traumaturgy which works as a cicatrix of reading, scarring and skinning over. This is what, in our epigraph to the present chapter, has been called the 'inaugural violence' of reading.

* * *

This chapter is, then, largely concerned to tease out or loosen the thematics and theorizations of injury, of wound, the genealogical injustices committed against Leopold. It is concerned to present a reading of what we might call the damage of Leopold. At the same time, we would wish to distinguish our reading from more conventional thematic or characterological analyses. Leaning on or borrowing from the established techniques of such readings, we shall not only read the damage of Leopold, but also suggest that this work of reading is itself a kind of damage: the work of reading as a work of (self-)wounding, as traumaturgy. In order to elaborate a traumaturgy of reading we shall be working with the notions of crypt and crypt-effect. As we seek to show elsewhere in this study, Bowen's texts are traversed by crypt-effects. Initially elaborated in a primarily psychoanalytical context, the notion of the crypt has become widely used in contemporary literary and critical theory. If we invoke it here, as elsewhere in this study, this is less because it seems to throw explanatory light on Bowen's texts than because her novels seem to promote a rethinking of a currently fashionable critical concept. Briefly, a crypt is a figuration of a secret, especially in relation to refused or impossible mourning. One can, without necessarily ever knowing it, be inhabited by a crypt or crypt-effect. More disturbingly, however, one can be unknowingly inhabited by the crypt or crypt-effect of someone else – by the secret or refused mourning of another. To be inhabited by the crypt of another is to be haunted: such a crypt is a ghost or phantom.[4]

Our reading, which attempts to trace the effects of crypts in *The House in Paris* – the effects of refused or impossible mourning, secrets and transgenerational hauntings – would be reducible neither to psychobiography nor to characterological analysis (we do not, for instance, offer a crypto-analysis of 'Elizabeth Bowen' the author, nor, in any simple sense, of Leopold). Rather, our reading might lead to an acknowledgement of the idea that there is fiction at the origin, that there is no clinical or any other purportedly real context which is not worked over, cut up in advance by fiction, by literarity, by otherness.

* * *

In *The House in Paris,* Leopold is constituted as a person by unknown and unknowable pockets of thought, haunted crypts of his father, his mother, and his own genesis, the act of his own conception. Leopold is explicitly *conceived* in *The House in Paris* in terms of both sexual procreation and cerebration: Leopold, being conceived, is thought. And Leopold is haunted by the secret of his genesis, haunted, in other words, by the thought of himself, immobilized in thought. But if Leopold is subject to loss, injustice, injury, he is also, himself, a loss, an injustice, an injury, a wound or damage to himself: Leopold is a traumaturgy, a work of wounding. It is not only the case that Leopold is haunted by crypt-effects: we would like to suggest that *The House in Paris*, like other Bowen texts, might itself be said to function as a crypt-effect, figuring the spoken and the unspoken. Our account of the crypt-effects of Leopold will involve, above all, the elaboration of a cryptanalysis of reading. The narrative structure of the novel moves from one day back to the events of ten years earlier – events which both determine and, more disquietingly, are determined by that day – and then back to the day in Paris in Part III (the same day but a day of irretrievable difference now); this structure itself presents a damage of linearity, a trauma or wound of narrative. Such a narrative strategy not only overturns, shifts, irreducibly places in abeyance or abyss questions of cause and effect, person and personality, conception and cognition, etc., but also inscribes reading as itself the haunting of a crypt-effect. Events, thoughts, cognition, in Part I of the novel, for example, are at once traversed and riven by what is to be read in Part III. Yet events, thoughts, cognition in Part II occur earlier in historical time, so that the logic of cause and effect is placed in abeyance and becomes a function of reading itself. Reading *The House in Paris* is a kind of wound, or, more accurately, a cicatrice: both a wounding and a scar.

* * *

The trauma of cognition in *The House in Paris* is most clearly evident in a scene of reading early in Part I. Waiting alone in the salon in the house in Paris, Leopold discovers three envelopes in Naomi's handbag. One of the envelopes contains a letter concerning himself written by Marian Grant Moody, 'Aunt Marian': the letter gives Naomi instructions on how to look after Leopold. The second envelope contains a similar letter from Henrietta's grandmother, Mrs Arbuthnot, on how to look after Henrietta. The third envelope, addressed to Naomi in what Leopold recognizes as his mother's handwriting, is empty. Leopold first reads the letter from Marian Grant Moody. The letter is a masterpiece of innuendo, moralistic, self-righteous concern and half-veiled reproach. It is clear that the Grant Moodys are unhappy about Leopold's proposed meeting with his mother, fearful that it will undo all the 'good' they have achieved in raising Leopold. The letter makes it clear that their achievement is due primarily to a massive suppression of knowledge. Naomi is told twice that Leopold has not yet 'received direct sex-instruction' (41). But this explicit acknowledgement of suppression both hints at and suppresses another far more problematic suppression, that of the circumstances of Leopold's birth: the suppression of the biology of reproduction constitutes a displaced suppression of Leopold's illegitimacy and his father's suicide. The psychic and social trauma of this knowledge is what the Grant Moodys 'dread' for Leopold. In order 'to keep his childhood sunny and beautiful' (41) and to prevent him from knowing his own genesis, the Grant Moodys have carefully delimited Leopold's exposure to information as well as his behaviour and conduct generally. Thus the letter lists the petty rules and constricting protocols for the regulation of Leopold: he is to be given certain kinds of food and drink, regardless of 'whatever he may say' (40); he has been warned not to speak to strangers (40); his 'religious sense', which 'seems to be still dormant', is being nurtured by education 'on broad undenominational lines such as God is Love' (41); Naomi is asked to make sure that Leopold has changed his underwear, to check his bowel movements, and to encourage him to masticate (41–2). From the trivial to the physiological to the ethical and spiritual, Leopold's foster-parents constrict and construct his every move and mode of behaviour. In particular, Leopold is formed by prohibitions on knowledge: beneath the protocols for the formation of Leopold runs an anxiety about what Leopold knows – 'Almost any fact [Karen] might mention seems to us still unsuitable' (41).

This letter, a letter which Leopold should not read, which is unsuitable for Leopold, which he should not know, has devastating psychic repercussions:

> The repercussions on Leopold of this letter were such that for some time he seemed to stay quite blank. He sat pulling at his upper lip with his thumb and finger ... staring at what he now saw from the outside. The revulsion threatening him became so frightening that he quickly picked up Mrs Arbuthnot's letter and read it, as though to clap something on to the gash in his mind. (42)

What he sees 'from the outside' is his own life – his life stilled by his relationships with his foster-parents and his non-relationship with his biological parents – a knowledge which splits him, opens up a gash in his mind. The threat of haemorrhaging, of an explosive seepage of the mind, can only be assuaged by the pressure of other words, another letter. Leopold's reading functions as a cicatrice, both a wound and a healing scar. The event of Max's suicide, the unspoken and traumatic scandal which the Grant Moodys' letter silently articulates through its suppressions, is a cerebral gash, a cut, the blood from which – thoughts, emotions, identity itself – must be stemmed by reading another letter. Nothing, however, has been expressed except for a general prohibition on Leopold's knowledge. The cerebral gash is not a result of Leopold's knowledge of Max's suicide: rather, it is a result of the suppression of this knowledge. It is the structure of prohibition, of interdiction, which produces the gash. It is a gash strictly without origin, a gash of what is without origin, the gash of Leopold.

The explosive letter from Marian Grant Moody returns after Leopold has read the letter from Mrs Arbuthnot, by which time he has decided that he cannot return to live with his guardians in Spezia: 'Miasmas crept over all he had done and touched there. He saw himself tricked into living' (44). The sentence immediately following this confirms the very immobilization of his thought, the stilling of his life: 'Then I will not, he thought' (45). The gash of Aunt Marian's letter, the explosive cut, produces stainings, pollutings, poisonously pervading his life in Italy: Leopold's reading of this letter rewrites, with miasmatic intensity, the plot of his life in Spezia. The consequences of that life, above all the letter itself, are gathered as an event – an event of reading, an event of 'inaugural violence' – which produces, in its turn, a termination of life. The miasmatic dissolution of his life in Italy is the result of a violent inaugural reading of the 'fiction' of that life. Correspondingly, *The House in Paris* itself presents a trauma of reading in that the events of Part II indelibly scarify an earlier reading of the chronologically later events of Part I. Leopold's trauma of reading is also the trauma of reading *The House in Paris*.

Finally, Leopold picks up the empty envelope from his mother, an envelope (we have already learnt) traversed by death and the uncertain mobilities of writing: 'dead white and square', the writing on which is 'dynamic and pausing' (39). Reading the letter from Mrs Arbuthnot had been figured as a metaphorical compress of reading, applying words to the gash in Leopold's consciousness. Picking up the envelope from his mother, Leopold presses it to his forehead, literally enacting the figurative compress of reading:

> he began to pace the salon, with his eyes shut, pressing her empty envelope to his forehead as he had once seen a thought-reader do. Then he began to read slowly aloud, as though the words one by one passed under his eyelids: 'Dear Miss Fisher,' he said. (45)

Leopold then 'reads' the text of the missing letter from Karen, until he is interrupted by Henrietta. To Henrietta, re-entering the room after a disturbing meeting with Mme Fisher, Leopold's 'reading' transgresses the conventions both of sanity – conventions already shaken for Henrietta by her interview with Mme Fisher – and of a kind of insane decorum: 'you oughtn't to thought-read letters to someone else', she tells him (59).[5]

* * *

A gash in the mind is a strangely figural embodiment of the potentially traumatic effects of reading and knowing in *The House in Paris*. What both Leopold and his mother Karen simultaneously desire and dread on the other hand, are gashes, cracks, cuts in the order and propriety of social relationships. Leopold is reported to want to 'crack the world by saying some final and frightful thing' (34), and after reading Marian Grant Moody's letter, Leopold wants to become a Shelleyan destructive wind[6] – a 'black wind' or an earthquake or a volcano, destroying the Moodys' villa, 'rushing', 'wrenching', 'tearing', 'cracking', 'erupting', 'showering' (45). Similarly, as a young woman ten years earlier, Karen, like Sydney in *The Hotel*, expresses a desire for revolutionary change. For her parents and their generation, 'change looked like catastrophe, a thing to put a good face on: change meant nothing but loss' (124). Karen's dread, by contrast, concerns what she sees as the rigor-mortified social and political future: 'I wish the Revolution would come soon; I should like to start fresh while I am still young, with everything that I had to depend on gone. I sometimes think it is people like us ... people of consequence, who are unfortunate: we have nothing ahead' (86). Paradoxically, it seems, people of consequence are people without consequences, without the mobilities of change.[7]

Catastrophe does, however, occur in *The House in Paris*. And if Karen and Leopold desire change, they also dread it. One such catastrophe is the death of Karen's Aunt Violet, a death which takes place in Ireland, away from the geographical focus of the novel in England and France, and a death which has a strangely peripheral centrality in the text. Above all, Aunt Violet's death – like, almost, her name – suggests the cataclysmic violence which Karen desires, and suggests that, desired or not, cataclysms occur anyway, revealing 'the crack across the crust of life' (127), a crack which Karen perceives as threatening to 'crack my home' (136). Without desiring the death of Violet, such a death effects the violent change which Karen desires. In the same way, Leopold's disappointment at not meeting his mother 'tears the bearable film off life' (197).

Gashes in *The House in Paris* constitute violent change; but the event of change, the gash or cut or cracking, is also constituted by its consequences, by the seepages and eerie repetitions which such an event produces. The violent gash is also, in a strange mobility, an effect of the uncontainable seepage or miasmatic staining of its consequences. The gash of Leopold's mind is both produced by and a repetition of another gash, the anterior event of Max's suicide, the cutting of his wrist to the artery in the house in Paris. The unspeakable and unspoken event of this incision is not confined to any singular occurrence. Instead, the action of cutting seeps through the text of *The House in Paris* and seeps, in particular, into Leopold's consciousness and actions: as we shall see, Max's suicide is, in a number of ways, configured within and compulsively, cryptically repeated by his illegitimate son. The cutting movements with which Max slashes his wrist to the artery are deceptively still:

while he is talking to Mme Fisher, talking still, Max takes out a penknife and slits his wrist. Max's movements are so 'quiet' that he is able to kill himself in front of Mme Fisher without, so she says, her 'knowledge'. Naomi tells Karen what her mother saw: 'The force he used took so little movement; she said: she only saw him frowning, then blood flowing' (184). This uncanny quietness of mobility at the moment of self-slaughter is characteristic of men in *The House in Paris*. Bowen's novel offers a reversal of the arguably more traditional identification of women with stillness and men with movement.[8] Although the bedridden Mme Fisher is necessarily still, it is the male characters who are presented most decisively as immobile. The condition of male characters in *The House in Paris* is not only to be still, however, but also to employ immobility as a weapon, a strategy of subversion and containment – against movement, time, events, action. When Naomi tries to comfort Leopold, for example, he offers 'simply by staying still, violent resistance to her' (191), and Ray, assaulted by Leopold's insistent questions, takes on a 'fanatic immobility' (222). While Naomi, by contrast, is characterized by her 'over-mobile face' (25) and has 'a way of making straight lines bend and shapes of things fluctuate as though a strong current were flowing over them' (101), Max, in particular, is characterized by a paradoxical immobility. Thus he writes, when he tries to write a letter breaking off his engagement with Naomi, 'straight ahead, immovably' (158), and he exhibits the strange, paradoxically slow movements which constitute the gestures of a frenetic catatonic – 'Something inside his head being at white heat, his movements were more than ever deliberating and slow' (139).[9]

Max's suicide – and his fanatical, suicidal immobility – is, in fact, eerily prefigured, mimed in advance. Thus, for example, when Karen, Naomi and Max meet for lunch in a London hotel, some months before the suicide, the complicating stillness of Max's gestures prefigure the event of his death:

> That nervous, rather forbidding stillness still swung back on him, now and again, like something that he would rather you had not touched. What few gestures he made, from the wrists only, moulded sharp surprising shapes on the air. The turn of his head was polite, attentive, slow. Slowness of movement in a quick-thinking person makes you feel some complication of thought or feeling behind anything that is done. (105)

The 'surprising' concatenation of slowness, a complexity and obscurity of thought processes, and the movement of Max's wrists, prefigure, very precisely, the nature of his suicide. In order to break off his engagement, Max goes to the house in Paris and has an interview with Naomi. During this conversation, Max opens the door of the salon to find Mme Fisher eavesdropping in the hall: 'When he opened the door she smiled and came in calmly, with the quiet manner she has when there is no more to know' (181). Naomi comments that 'Max did not belong to himself. He could do nothing that she had not expected' (182). Two pages later, however, Naomi reports Mme Fisher to have said that Max's suicide 'struck myself, himself, my knowledge of him', and that 'his attack on himself had been, however, so quiet that when it happened she did not understand' (184). Max's suicide, then, is structured in terms of 'knowledge': suicide is the only possibility he has to surprise Mme Fisher. The surprising gesture of Max's wrists in the London hotel encrypts the knowledge of the surprise of suicide. Reading these gestures of Max's wrists earlier in the novel, we can now see, we are unknowingly reading, conceiving, Max's suicide. Max's suicide is encrypted within the very reading of *The House in Paris*.

There is a proleptic concentration on the gestures of Max's wrists, then, a telepathological encoding of his death in his movements, his paradoxical immobility. But Max's suicide is not only prefigured in stillness: it is also refigured in the stillness of his son. In a crucial and powerful passage in Part III of the novel there is a bizarre moment of concentration on Leopold's wrists. Leopold is summoned to his first and only meeting with Mme Fisher who is lying upstairs sick and dying, and, by her own admission, already beyond life, in the house in Paris:

> His blouse-cuffs fell away from his wrists, which she glanced at. Not an object in this unknown room had, since he came in, distracted his eyes a moment, but, sitting still, he knew everything there. Everything, to the last whorl of each shell on the bracket, would stay sealed up, immortal, in an inner room in his consciousness. That her presence ran against him like restless water showed only in the unmovingness of his face. She re-read a known map of thought and passion in miniature. (202)

What Leopold knows and what is known of him is not his knowledge and not knowledge of him. He has never been in this room before: he cannot know it. As Mme Fisher recognizes and signals in her glance at his wrists, Leopold's knowledge of the room is inherited or transferred from his father, and the glance recognizes, too, that it is the gash in Max's wrists, his suicide, which inscribes this encrypted knowing – the knowledge which remains within the inner room in Leopold's consciousness. What is locked up inside the inner room, the tomb-like room of Leopold's consciousness, is Mme Fisher's room. Entombed within Leopold's consciousness, it is also a tomb for Mme Fisher, the room in which she herself admits to leading a posthumous life, to having been dead throughout the ten years since Max's death and Leopold's birth (202). A still life, she is described as being 'like someone cast, still alive, as an effigy for their own tomb' (48). Mme Fisher's figure, her face, is that of a death's head: 'Waxy skin strained over her temples, jaws and cheekbones; grey hair fell in wisps round an unwomanly forehead; her nostrils were wide and looked in the dusk skullish; her mouth was graven round with ironic lines' (47). The tomb or crypt which Leopold is in, Mme Fisher's room, is also the crypt in his mind, the crypt of his mind.

The trauma of this scene, of this reading, will take some time to elaborate, as we seek to trace its reverberations and effects. In the first place, the scene takes us back to the very conception of Leopold. From the beginning of *The House in Paris* it has been clear that the crucial question for Leopold is the question of what he knows. Throughout the novel, Leopold is specifically conceived as an embodiment of knowledge in at least two ways. In the first place, as we shall see, Leopold is explicitly conceived in thought, conceived – in an undecidably tautological way – as a conception.[10] Secondly, he is the mark of an illicit sexual act or sexual knowing which allows others to have knowledge of that act: he is the walking, talking, thinking, conceiving and knowing evidence of an event which should never have happened, and, having happened, should never be known. Everything turns on the knowledge of Leopold – at once knowledge about Leopold and Leopold's knowledge. What he is allowed to know is constantly subject to suppression by others and to repression by himself. But knowledge – that which is to be secreted, suppressed, distorted – is itself empty. It is only the act of hiding, of suppressing, which ascribes to knowledge its significance:

> The mystery about sex comes from confusion and terror: to a mind on which these have not yet settled there is nothing you

> cannot tell. Grown-up people form a secret society, they must have something to hold by; they dare not say to a child: 'There is nothing you do not know here.' (68)

The secret of this secret society is precisely that there is no secret. There is nothing for children to know. The only knowledge that adults can keep from children is that there is nothing that they can't know. Just as the suppression of the facts about sexual reproduction by the Grant Moodys is a displaced suppression of the facts of Leopold's origins, secrets are always displaced suppressions of other secrets. And, paradoxically, the ultimate secret would be that there is no end to this endless displacement except on the condition that there is no secret. Nevertheless, or therefore – undecidably suspended within the cognition of reading – knowledge-effects, like cracks in a tomb, unremittingly fissure the surface tranquillity of the house in Paris.

Mme Fisher's room, then, is a tomb of knowledge. Although this tomb of knowledge – this dead room – is inside Leopold, Leopold is also born inside the tomb of this knowledge, a tomb that he will have to crack in order to live: to contain a tomb in the mind is also to be contained by that tomb. The inner tomb of Leopold's consciousness both contains and is contained by the tomb of Mme Fisher's room, a tomb which its occupant is herself instrumental in making. The evil, uncannily prescient Mme Fisher[11] tells Leopold that he is in a tomb, and that 'To find oneself like a young tree inside a tomb is to discover the power to crack the tomb and grow up to any height' (203). The power to crack the tomb of one's encrypted life, it seems, comes from the knowledge of this encryptment. But it is precisely by imparting *this* knowledge that Mme Fisher in turn participates in the encrypting of Leopold: Leopold's knowledge that he must break out of a tomb is the knowledge that entombs him. Mme Fisher's suggestion that Leopold must crack the tomb of his existence is the suggestion that he must produce a crack, a tear, a cut, a gash, in his life. But this very suggestion, and her entire conversation with Leopold, is ineluctably traversed and haunted by the dead – above all, by the death of Leopold's father. Leopold is unknowingly haunted by the death of Max, a tomb of knowledge constructed, at least initially, by Mme Fisher. And this tomb of knowledge is also, in another sense, Leopold himself. To crack the tomb would also be to crack the tomb which is Leopold's life. The text strongly suggests that to accede to the knowledge of his own encryptment would, for

Leopold, be death: Mme Fisher's commendation to Leopold, like her commendation to Max, is potentially deadly.[12]

* * *

Mme Fisher's commendation not only suggests Leopold's entombment, but also configures him as a tree. Branching out, reading forwards and back from this scene, we find that humans are repeatedly figured in terms of trees and the tree-like. To Henrietta, for example, Leopold is like 'an unconscious strong little tree' and the touch of his arm is 'unknowing as wood' (61). Like other 'growing girls', Henrietta is 'tempted up like plants by the idea that something is happening that [she] will some day know about' (56–7). Naomi is 'like a white wood-carving' (113). Karen tries to imagine she is a tree in order not to think, not to know (155). Leopold stands, in despair, 'one leg writhed round the other like ivy killing a tree' (196), and he holds Henrietta 'as though he were gripping the bole of a tree' (197). Mme Fisher's words fall 'slowly on to Leopold, like cold slow drops detached by their own weight from a tree standing passive, exhausted after rain' (207), and she is like a tree in her illness, 'prey to one creeping growth, the Past, septic with what had happened' (208). Rather than adding 'polish' to the young women who stay in her house, Mme Fisher applies 'emery-friction' to their 'young wood' as a preparation for polish (103). And *The House in Paris* is about Leopold's change of name, from Grant Moody, to, he hopes, Forrestier, a significantly woody name.[13]

People, then, are tree-like. People are repeatedly characterized by a lack of feeling, thought and knowledge, by immobility. And people are potentially subject to creeping, poisoning, strangling by an exterior, parasitic other such as, above all, 'the past'; they are impassive and passive, simply, silently suffering. Mme Fisher's notion of Leopold as a tree growing out of a grave has an irrepressible force in this novel. The grafting of people and trees erupts from the tomb of language, cracking the repressive containment of reason and narrative, forcing itself out of the novel. The repeated figuration of people as trees is wrapped up in that strange dissolution of fictionality which haunts Bowen's writing: rooting people to the spot as trees, particular forms of still life, suggests the fictionality of a person – people as dead wood, as people in books, in the paper of novels. In ways that ineluctably contort and exceed every conventional notion of the organic, reading must grow like a tree out of the tomb of the text (but the tomb of the novel is the tree, the paper, the materiality of the artifact held in the hand – dead wood). The sense that a tree growing out of the grave constitutes an irrational crack in the surface of the text is evoked by Henrietta: 'To begin with, no one would plant a tree in a grave' (226). But in *The House in Paris*, trees, humans, *are* planted in graves, and the tomb of *The House in Paris* is both Max and the tomb that *he* is in. For earlier in the novel, Max himself employs Mme Fisher's metaphor to speak of her effect on him: 'she made me shoot up like a plant in enclosed air' (138). Mme Fisher, as Naomi succinctly puts it, 'was at the root of him' (182).

The tomb of Leopold, then, is (also) the tomb of Max. Not only is this signalled by Mme Fisher's glance towards Leopold's sleeve and his impossible foreknowledge of her room, it is also apparent in his physical features and motions. Leopold's step, for example, is described as his father's: 'he has a step like his father's', comments Mme Fisher (52). Yet if we wish to establish the character of Max's step, the text provides only one description. Heard but not seen, leaving the house in Paris after his self-laceration, his step is described as 'not like his own' (182). Max's step is not like his own because he has started to become other to himself. It is as if, in this figure of his step, Max has already started to become the phantom of himself. His step is other, a step internalized and repeated by his son, Leopold. Leopold is also marked – specifically cut or gashed – in the same way as his father: 'A scar from some operation showed on his neck ... under the jaw' (61) is a scar which on Max is seen as 'a slight cut on his chin' (108).[14] The grave of Max's body, then, is the tomb out of which Leopold must grow, grafted like a tree. And the gash of Max's suicide – as well as the cracks in the world that this produces – is figured in Leopold. Finally, Max's self-laceration also results in the cuts, scars, gashes and cracks which, in accordance with Mme Fisher's advice, Leopold must inflict in order to grow.

Trees, scars, tombs. Such lacerations of the text constitute the thematics of crypt and conception, of reading in *The House in Paris*. Reading reverberates, shivers, with the trauma of these objects. Traumaturgy, the work of reading, is bound up in what is at once the necessary acknowledgement and impossible knowledge of these scars.

* * *

We have suggested that the event of Max's suicide has a number of consequences – most critically its embodiment in Leopold. To talk about the 'consequences' of an event, however, is to imply a conventional notion of event which *The House in Paris* everywhere exceeds. Conventionally conceived, results or consequences necessarily follow from an original and determining event: temporal and logical causality are fundamental to any narrative, to any narratological consideration of the novel, fundamental to what we can 'know' in reading. In Bowen, however, such determining causality is haunted, inscribed within a radical instability and uncertainty, it demands to be determined *otherwise*. This is, in part, what we mean when we refer to Elizabeth Bowen and the dissolution the novel. If *To the North* is exemplary in its exposition of the moment as inhabited in advance by forms of its own departure, *The House in Paris* is a more studied exploration of how events are traversed by their own consequences. The event of Max's suicide overflows, stains, poisons what is to come: the stabbing, cutting, gash of the event of death becomes, in time, its consequences. There is a consistent and pervasive reversal by which events, in *The House in Paris*, are constituted by their consequences. Thus, as we shall seek to show, Max and Karen's sexual intercourse is determined not only by how it is thought, but also, fundamentally, by its results: copulation is *conceived* as Leopold. Moreover, this radical disturbance of causality is further displaced by the strange movements of knowledge, of how people know and are human. Leopold is 'determined' by Max's suicide while the suicide remains unknown to him. Despite the fact that Leopold cannot know, cannot remember Max's suicide, he must repeat the gesture, he must crack the tomb. The suicidal gash in the novel is, at the same time, the encrypted cause and the displaced effect of (unacknowledged or impossible) mourning, the displaced effects of the event and the event itself. *The House in Paris*, then, figures the dissolution of the novel through a dissolution of causal relations, a dissolution of events into consequences, a dissolution of the very space of narrativization, events as cognition. The novel dissolves into eerie, uncontainable and undecidable reading effects.

The most prolonged and explicit consideration of the notion of the event in *The House in Paris* comes in a long interior monologue by Karen (in Part II, Chapter 9, 151–5), as she lies awake in the early hours of the morning after making love to Max (and conceiving Leopold). Karen's post-coital and *cerebral* conception of Leopold concerns the problematics of the structure of the event of 'conception': in this reverie, Leopold is conceived in thought as he is conceived physically. Leopold, being conceived, is thought.

Before they make love and make Leopold, Max warns Karen about the consequences: '"I am supposing", he said, "that you know what you are doing. It will be too late when you ask yourself: What have I done?"' (151). The temporality of Max's question, its unstable sliding between past, present and future, is disseminated throughout *The House in Paris*, both before and after its occurrence. The question concerns not only the social question of illegitimacy, but also the very uncertainty of eventhood, the possibility of knowledge as such. Sex in *The House in Paris* is, like people, determined in terms of a bizarre kind of epistemology: copulation is conception. And in a sense it would be possible to argue that people in this novel are themselves epistemologies, theories of knowledge. When Mme Fisher tells him that Karen does not have any other children, Leopold already knows this: 'But how could she have?' he asks, 'I never thought of another child' (207). According to Leopold's wild improvisatory logic of procreation, a child of his mother can only be conceived in thought: Karen could only have a child on the condition that Leopold had thought (of) him or her. The dissolution of the event comprehends that of *The House in Paris* itself. It is a dissolution based on the aberrations of conception: thought. 'No one knew about Leopold' (219): how is it possible to know Leopold?[15]

Karen asks herself Max's question, lying awake in the night after having made love: 'What have I done? ... Having done as she knew she must she did not think there would be a child: all the same, the idea of you, Leopold, began to be present with her' (151–2).[16] This passage incorporates what is arguably the strangest word in the entire novel: the narrator's unprecedented use of the second-person pronoun in reference to Leopold. Just as the instability of free indirect discourse and its slippage into third-person narration opens up a problematic space of narratorial identity at this point, 'you' opens up a gash in the text.[17] This singular apostrophic figuration of Leopold is an uncanny conception of Leopold in writing. Leopold is constructed as a person, before being born, by this deictic reference: he becomes the preternatural reader of his own text. Copulative embodiment is mapped onto a grammatical conception. Leopold *is* in a copulation of grammar and bodies. Leopold is conceived in thought and in writing, he is figured, given a face and becomes known. But this knowledge becomes legible only on condition that we read a copulative conjunction of the reader with Leopold in *you*.

Karen's monologue continues: 'Naomi and my mother, who would die if they knew, will never know. What they never know will soon never have been. They will never know. I shall die like Aunt Violet wondering what else there was; from this there is no escape for me after all' (152). The sentence 'What they never know will soon never have been' presents a strange double logic which is central to the trauma of cognition in *The House in Paris*. On the one hand, there is the question of how an event can be known after its own time. That is, the event can only be 'known' in the imagination or the memory or in its consequences. To this extent the event can only be known after its time but can never be 'known' after its time in its irreducible eventfulness; the event is irreducible to any 'knowledge'. On the other hand, there is the question of how a secret event loses its singularity as an event on being 'known' by others. Such a formation of knowledge – the necessity and impossibility of cognition, of the very conception of people – determines traumaturgy, reading, in *The House in Paris*. The work of wounding can never be known and never not known.

* * *

On a number of occasions in *The House in Paris*, the structure of the event is figured as the permanent mark which the hands of Max and Karen do not make on the grass. In a critical scene, Max and Karen secretly and silently hold hands while sitting on the grass in the garden of the house of Naomi's recently deceased aunt in London. Before Naomi returns to the garden they lift and unclasp their hands. The mark which their hands have made on the grass – the evidence of their secret love – disappears before Naomi is able to see it. 'Max put his hand on Karen's, pressing it into the grass. Their unexploring, consenting touch lasted; they did not look at each other or at their hands. When their hands had drawn slowly apart, they both watched the flattened grass beginning to spring up again, blade by blade' (120). This momentary effacement is referred to a number of times as a complex figuration of the event, its consequences and the possibility of its being known. The invisible trace, the unknowable consequence of the event of holding hands, traverses *The House in Paris*, a trace marked only in writing. Much of Karen's reverie after making love to Max concerns a consideration of the structure of the trace – in particular, as read through the event of the hands pressing together on the grass. The invisible trace on the grass can only become visible in a displaced representation of the event. An event – holding hands – can become known by the consequences of another event. The relationship between an event and its consequences disseminates. An event can produce consequences – traces – through other events:

> If a child were going to be born, there would still be something that had to be. Tonight would be more then than hours and that lamp. It would have been the hour of my death. I should have to do what I dread, see them know. There would still be something to dread. I should see the hour in the child. I should not have rushed on to nothing. He would be the mark our hands did not leave on the grass, he would be the tamarisks we only half saw. And he would be the I whose bed Naomi sat on, the Max whose sleeve I brushed rain off ... that other we were both looking for. (153)

This dread knowledge would be a kind of death, the time of Karen's death, but the gash of knowledge – Leopold – would also be a future, a posthumous other life for Karen living on in Leopold. The event of the night would then be more than itself, staining the future and becoming its own consequences. But Leopold also stains the past by becoming a hypostasis of other events that have already occurred or a bodily figuration of invisible traces. Leopold is conceived in thought, in particular, as the displaced event of Max's suicide – Karen's action of brushing off the water from Max's sleeve.

The staining of the event by its own – and more disturbingly by other – consequences, the notion that an event is not itself, may also be read specifically through the notions of blurring and effacement. Throughout *The House in Paris*, there are comments on the importance of blurring, of imprecision in description, in language, in thought and in people. Through the thoughts of Karen, Bowen suggests that 'realistic' photographs 'stunned your imagination by *being* exact' (118): unlike her mother Mrs Michaelis, who likes photographs and descriptions to be precise, Karen recognizes the aesthetic value of mystery, vagueness, obscurity. Bowen, however, takes this idea further: 'Without their indistinctness things do not exist; you cannot desire them' (118). There is an irreducible uncertainty here, over the question of whether things only exist because we desire them, or whether things do not exist *and* we do not desire them unless they are indistinct. The thought that objects only exist to the extent that they are indistinct then leads to a reconsideration of the human:

> Blurs and important wrong shapes, ridgy lights, crater darkness making a face unhuman as a map of the moon, Mrs Michaelis, like the camera of her day, denied. She saw what she knew was there. Like the classic camera, she was blind to those accidents that make a face that face, a scene that scene, and float the object, alive, in your desire and ignorance. (118)

Once again, we can discern a refiguring or disfiguring of the event and its consequences in terms of the effacement of knowledge, the dissolution of the novel. Events and objects only come into being through their blurrings. Knowledge itself is a kind of blindness; and desire is inseparable from ignorance.

In a similar way, the love of Max and Karen is disabled both because of its lack of history – lovers need a shared past but Max and Karen 'could remember nothing that they could speak of' (143) – and, even more, because of their different languages:

> Talk between people of different races is serious; that tender silliness lovers employ falls flat. Words are used for their meaning, not for their ring. If she had learnt to dread that kind of talk about art and life, most of all about love, to which literalness is deadly, she would have suffered more. (157)[18]

If literalness is deadly, if less precise language is at once more desirable and more capable of causing suffering, then important near-homophony in this passage rings throughout *The House in Paris*: the repetition of the words 'dread' and 'dead'. 'Dread' repeatedly seems to produce 'dead' – as when Karen and Max say goodbye earlier in the novel: 'they faced each other unwillingly, defiant, dead. ... All your youth, you are dreading more than can happen' (122). The peculiar and peculiarly repeated reverberation of 'dead' within 'dread' is itself like a gash in language: it is as if this near-homophony is itself gouging the body of the text. But the homology of 'dead' and 'dread' is also the gash which the balm of words – the novel itself – attempts to salve. The novel can only salve itself through words but those words themselves produce the gash. Words themselves cicatrize the trauma of *The House in Paris*. Indeed, to 'salve' or 'redeem' itself, language would have to be 'read'. But 'read' is itself figured within dread, contained by the gashed logic of 'dead' and 'dread'. How do we read dread? Is dread itself a kind of reading?[19]

The word 'dread' appears over forty times in *The House in Paris*.[20] Coming, on average, almost once every five pages, the word acts as a kind of *leitmotif*, a scarification of narrative mobility: its occurrence, irrepressible, inevitable, can itself be dreaded. Not only can 'read' and 'dead' be 'read' within 'dread', but this 'dread', it may be suggested, adumbrates the very temporality of the event. 'Dread' suggests a fear of future events, a fear grounded in the present: as such, dread would seem to be the overshadowing of an event of the future materialized in the present. Within dread, temporality is gashed, divided and blurred between the present and the future. But 'dread' is also a fear of what has already happened. Although dread points towards an unknowable event in the future, the subject of dread is caught up in – already dreading, and therefore already experiencing – the event which is dreaded. The end of dread cannot arrive, dread is the deferred arrival of an event which can never be known but only conceived, apprehended, dreaded. But dread has, therefore, always arrived already. Just as the word 'dread' may be seen to contain the word 'dead', so it is marked by death: death is contained in this dread as the 'meaning' of its fear. And the containment of death within dread suggests that death can only be 'experienced' proleptically, as the very adumbration of every event.[21]

Dread may be conceived as at once immobilizing and displacing every traditional notion of the event, even or especially when that event is figured as a cut or gash – a momentary, violent, destructive and irreversible cut in time. This is explicitly expressed at the end of Part I of *The House in Paris*: as Henrietta and Leopold wait for Miss Fisher to come back into the room they both 'dreaded, as she was palpably dreading, her coming in' (65). Dread then determines her entrance as a seepage, an entrance which has always already occurred: 'Miss Fisher's entrance, like anything much dreaded, happened at no one moment; she seeped in round the door. She seemed, *now*, to have been standing between them always, with the telegram shaking in one hand' (65). The arrival of the telegram announcing that Karen will not arrive has always arrived, is now and always. Dread entails an irreducible excess, it exceeds the parameters of the event ('All your youth, you are dreading more than can happen' [122]). It is an excess ineluctably characterized by haunting and absence. As Karen silently tells Ray: 'while [Leopold] is a dread of yours, he is everywhere' (217). The eerie and uncontainable logic of dread, a logic of (d)reading, presents a final figuration of traumaturgy: the work of reading, of the wound, is structured by the temporal and cognitive displacements of dread. The crypt of reading, necessarily promulgated out of an originless 'past', is also the logic of dread which reverses cryptic temporality. In both cases, the work of cognition or reading – what we have characterized as a cicatrice – displaces and disperses itself as event. Traumaturgy, the work of reading, is known now and will never be known.

* * *

At the beginning of Part II of *The House in Paris*, Karen goes to visit her Uncle Bill and Aunt Violet in Ireland, an arrival which opens into a meditation on the event of arrival, on dread and death, on the notion of being born, and of living trapped inside a room, whereby life itself seems once again to be construed as a kind of gash:

> By having come, you already begin to store up the pains of going away. From what you see, there is to be no escape. Untrodden rocky canyons or virgin forests cannot be more entrapping than the inside of a house, which shows you what life is. To come in is as alarming as to be born conscious would be, knowing you are to feel; to look round is like being, still conscious, dead: you see a world without yourself. (77)

The event of arriving, coming in, is determined by its non-presence to itself, its going. This is still life – 'being, still conscious, dead'. Such is the structure of Karen's arrival, but it is also the encrypted arrival of Leopold at the house in Paris, where he arrives to start living as himself – as Leopold Forrestier rather than by his borrowed name, Grant Moody. Before his final undecidable departure with Ray, Leopold is trapped in a house in Paris where he arrives to see his own departure, a house in which he is stillborn, being, still conscious, dead.

4

Dream Wood

> The impression of being in a wood gave place to one of phantasmagoric architecture improbable in London.
>
> (*HD 105*)

> what is the word –
> seeing all this –
> all this this –
> all this this here –
> folly. ...[1]

To provide a description of *The Death of the Heart* (1938) may be likened to relating a dream. *The Death of the Heart* focuses on Portia, a sixteen-year-old orphan, callously described by her sister-in-law Anna as 'the child of an aberration, the child of a panic, the child of an old chap's pitiful sexuality. Conceived among lost hairpins and snapshots of doggies in a Notting Hill Gate flatlet' (246). Her father, Mr Quayne, has an extra-marital affair with a woman called Irene and thereby 'start[s] Portia' (18). His wife ejects him from their house in Dorset, and Quayne spends the remains of his life with Irene and Portia, 'trailing up and down the cold parts of the Riviera' (14), living in 'the back rooms in hotels, or dark flats in villas with no view' (21). He dies. Not long afterwards, Irene also dies, in Switzerland. This leaves Portia, together with a letter from Mr Quayne, which is posthumously forwarded to his son Thomas and wife Anna (who live childless in Windsor Terrace, Regent's Park), requesting that they give the girl a year of '*normal, cheerful* family life' (15).

The Death of the Heart opens, then, with Anna talking in the park with her writer-friend, St Quentin Miller, about the newcomer to Windsor Terrace, the little 'animal', Portia. No one seems to know quite what to do with Portia, who develops a closer attachment to the housekeeper, Matchett, than to either her half-brother Thomas or his wife. Things are made more complicated and, for Anna especially, unpleasant because Portia has been keeping a diary and Anna has had the furtive and dubious privilege of reading it. Although the diary records her private impressions of 'family life' at Windsor Terrace, Portia shows it to Eddie. Eddie is a 'specious' 'little rat' (306), a twenty-three-year-old man who charms Anna, Portia and other women, and comes to be employed by the advertising agency, Quayne and Merrett, of which Thomas is joint owner and controller.

The Death of the Heart traces, in particular, the love that develops between Portia and Eddie. This relationship alters, and intensifies, when Anna and Thomas leave London to spend a few weeks in Capri and Portia is sent to stay with Anna's old governess, Mrs Heccomb. Now widowed, Mrs Heccomb lives with her son and daughter, Dickie and Daphne (both older than Portia), in a house with the whimsically exotic name 'Waikiki', at Seale-on-Sea, in Kent. Eddie comes to visit Waikiki and flirts with Daphne: holding hands with her at the cinema, he is observed by Portia. The relationship between Portia and Eddie – which remains (in mundane terms) sexless – grows steadily more ominous. Soon after she returns to London, Portia is overwhelmed by a double realization, set in motion by an apparently thoughtless question from Anna's friend, St Quentin. In Anna's confidence from the start, he happens to meet Portia in the street and asks: 'How is your diary?' (248) Portia's discovery that Anna has been reading her diary is compounded by the deluded but no less significant conviction that it is Eddie who alerted Anna to the diary's existence. An emotionally explosive meeting between Portia and Eddie, first in Covent Garden and then at his flat, ends with his saying she gives him 'the horrors' (282) and telling her to go away. She leaves. But instead of returning to Windsor Terrace she goes to the Karachi Hotel in Kensington where she throws herself upon the kindly but unwilling Major Eric E.J. Brutt. Brutt is a pathetic survivor from the 1914–18 war who knew Anna slightly in earlier days and, on the basis of a chance meeting at a cinema, not only becomes reacquainted with her but also befriends Portia. In 'unfeeling desperation' (295), Portia wants to stay with him in his attic room at the Karachi. Brutt insists on telephoning Windsor Terrace; Portia lets him do this on condition that Thomas and Anna are told that she is waiting to see 'whether they do the right thing' (304). The right thing may, or may not, be sending Matchett round to the Karachi to fetch her. *The Death of the Heart* ends with Matchett on the verge of going in at the giant front door of the hotel.

It is towards this giant front door that the present essay will journey, in particular insofar as this door figures an opening onto the future, and insofar as it can be identified with what we are proposing to call 'dream wood'. The phrase is used by Anna near the beginning of the novel, when she is recounting to St Quentin the story of Mr Quayne's having to leave his wife for the pregnant Irene: 'He had not got a mind that joins one thing and another up. He had got knit up with Irene in a sort of a dream wood, but the last thing he wanted was to stay in that wood for ever' (19). What is a dream wood? What would it mean to be 'knit up' in one? Does Mr Quayne stay for ever? If so, what would it mean to suppose that Portia is born in a dream wood? And what does all this prompt us to think about the phrase, 'the death of the heart'? These questions provide one avenue of approach in the present chapter – as frigid and strange, perhaps, as the poplars standing up 'like frozen brooms' (16) in the scene in Regent's Park in which this story of Mr Quayne is recounted. Being in a dream wood suggests a strange, fairy-tale collusion of the oneiric and arboreal, commingles anthropomorphism and phantasmagoria, evokes the sense of a wood in a dream, the dreaminess of wood itself, and even the sense of a wood that dreams. It suggests, most strikingly perhaps, the sense of a wood that has been subjected to the transmogrifications and distortions, the surrealism and lunacy of dreams, a wood that may be scarcely recognizable, only partially or barely identifiable. Implanting, grafting and disseminating itself through the present chapter, 'dream wood' – as may already be evident – presupposes multiplicity. 'Knit up', on the other hand, suggests the magical power of Shakespeare's Prospero: 'My high charms work, / And these, mine enemies, are all knit up / In their distractions' (*The Tempest*, III. iii. 88–90).[2] Without knowing, Portia's father gets knit up in a dream wood; perhaps not wanting to, perhaps never realizing that he does, still he must live in it: the dream wood of a still life. The words 'dream wood' are imposed by Anna, with characteristically acerbic detachment, on the still life of another.[3] This prompts slightly different questions: what is a person if he or she lives in the description of another, lives in 'a dream wood' which is the spoken invention, the dream, of another? What is the relation between 'dream wood' and language, speech, reading? Or between 'dream wood' and fiction? *The Death of the Heart* suggests that there is a dream wood in all of us, that we are all in a dream wood, that there can be no conception of a person outside the haunting effects of a dream wood.

In these respects, then, we shall seek to sketch out the logic by which *The Death of the Heart* opens and closes, like a giant front door, on a dream wood. The present chapter focuses on the ways in which *The Death of the Heart*, like other Bowen texts, furnishes a new and different account of human identity. We shall attempt to explore what St Quentin at one point emphatically refers to as 'These *lacunae* in people' (251). Bowen's work can be described as postmodern in its resistance to traditional Western assumptions of what constitutes an ethics and politics of the subject. In chronological terms, this dimension of Bowen's work becomes increasingly articulate and explicit. The gaps or lacunae through which *The Death of the Heart* traces human identity can in part be transposed into the language of contemporary literary and cultural theory. But if the novel inscribes and dramatizes such notions as the metafictional, the immemorial, a radically literary unconscious and the other, it also elaborates more unusual figurations such as the animal, laughter, the heart, furniture, buildings, acting and multiple identity, dream wood.

The Death of the Heart suggests that it is not (and never was) tenable to conceive the human simply in opposition to the animal: human identity is necessarily fractured by forms of an ahuman otherness, inhabited by lacunary forces and effects. Bowen's work suggests that there is nothing essentially human about meaning; there is no meaning which is not traced, and divided from itself in advance, by a logic of non-humanizable otherness. What might conventionally be described as the animal metaphors in *The Death of the Heart* have a doubling force which puts the human necessarily beside itself, displaced and animated differently by conjunction with the putatively animal and by the deflationary economy of laughter. As figures of resemblance, these metaphors generate a sense of laughter which doubles and dislocates, dissolving the very logic of likening and likeness. Bowen's characters are not themselves – they are neither simply human nor simply animal – in the strangeness of these figurations. Similarly, we are not ourselves, nor are we human, in the strangeness of this laughter. Bowen's comedy is the incisive deflation of human sense. As we hope to suggest, both in the course of the present chapter and elsewhere in this book, the force of laughter in Bowen is ultimately indissociable from a logic of 'death', from a dissolution of identity or what (in another context) St Quentin Miller calls 'a convulsion of one's entire nature' (251).[4]

Portia is 'more like an animal' (8) than a child; indeed, Anna says, she must be 'a little monster' (12). By Thomas, however, she is remembered as one who suggested a 'sacred lurking' and who 'stared at him like a kitten that expects to be drowned' (40). When Portia arrives at Windsor Terrace she is 'as black as a little crow, in heavy Swiss mourning chosen by her aunt' (41). Elsewhere, and repeatedly, Portia (like Emmeline in *To the North*) is described in terms of a kitten or cat.[5] Eddie's visits to Windsor Terrace on the other hand are characterized by Matchett as those of someone 'popping in and out like a weasel' (84). According to Portia's diary, in a scene of eerie romance Eddie mimes the uncanny still life of a dead animal: 'he said that if he was a lady's fox fur and I was him, I would certainly stroke his head. While I did, he made himself look as if he had glass eyes, like a fur' (119). Anna, we may recall, is described near the beginning as 'a sardonic bland white duck' (8). We do not know, and Mr Quayne in the midst of his dream wood with Irene evidently does not know either, 'whether he was a big brute or St George' (18). Thomas is on at least one occasion described as 'having an uneasy baited look, like an animal being offered something it does not like' (32). Major Brutt, on the other hand, is merely doglike. Coming uninvited to Windsor Terrace he is left to wait in the study while Thomas talks to other new arrivals in the hall: 'Major Brutt, during the colloquy in the hall, had sat with his knees parted, turning his wrists vaguely, making his cuff-links wink. What he may have heard he shook off, like a dog shaking its ears' (96). Mrs Heccomb, by contrast, is like a bird. As a further instance of the strange pathos which inhabits these non-human animations, we are given Portia's response, following her arrival at Seale-on-Sea, to the bustling preparations of her new hostess: 'Portia saw that all this must be in her honour. It made her sad to think how Matchett would despise Mrs Heccomb's diving and ducking ways, like a nesting water-fowl's' (132). At Waikiki we encounter Clara: 'Clara was a smallish girl with crimped platinum hair, a long nose, a short neck, and the subservient expression of a good white mouse … her head look[ed] as though it were on a tray' (165).[6] Sense grows monstrous. Sense lurks, pops, stares, shakes its ears, ducks and dives, is momentarily subservient, loses itself (as though decapitated) in laughter. The doubling of the animal and of laughter – a laughter which may be painful, even tragic – forecloses any reduction of the figurative or metaphorical here to thinking the animalism of the human as merely resemblance or likeness. Rather it is a question of how laughter disturbs the grounds of being and of likeness, dissolves any opposition *or* identification of the animal and the human. At its most disruptive, laughter in Bowen is the sometimes affirmative, sometimes dreadful, never avoidable convulsion of being. It is, 'like' death, beyond all recognition or likeness.

'Likeness' might here correspond to its exploration in the description of the portrait of Anna produced years ago by Mrs Heccomb and resting on the mantelpiece of Portia's room at Waikiki. This is a pastel-portrait of Anna hugging a kitten to her breast 'in a contraction of unknowing sorrow' (207). It is a 'bad portrait', the work of 'a negative artist', of which we are told: it 'only came alive by electric light'. Yet the most peculiar galvanization of this still life depends on what is not 'like' life at all. For even when it is not 'alive', it is precisely its unlikeness which disturbs:

> Even by day, though, the unlike likeness disturbs one more than it should: *what* is it unlike? Or is it unlike at all – is it the face discovered? The portrait, however feeble, transfixes something passive that stays behind the knowing and living look. No drawing from life just fails: it establishes something more; it admits the unadmitted. (207)

The establishment of 'something more' here might be seen in part as the product of disturbances within the very phrase 'drawing from life'. Drawing from a genealogy that would include Poe's 'The Oval Portrait' and Wilde's *The Picture of Dorian Gray*, the portrait at Waikiki is a 'drawing from life' as at once and undecidably verisimilitude (a drawing based on life); vampirizing or supplanting (a taking away of life); and difference or unlikeness *per se* (a drawing away from life).[7] Such would be the contaminating, non-admissible, eerie power of a figuration (a portrait or still life) which is not so much a likeness but rather a showing, a monstrosity, of what haunts the very self-identity of a face or figure, as an otherness within likeness and beyond it. If a portrait can 'admit the unadmitted', it would seem to let in something which has not yet been made manifest and perhaps never could be. In this respect Bowen's text exploits a kind of ghostly temporality, draws out a ghostly structure of correspondence or likening. Portia's schoolfriend Lilian is presented:

> Portia thought the world of the things Lilian could do – she was said, for instance, to dance and skate very well, and had one time fenced. Otherwise, Lilian claimed to have few pleasures: she was at home as seldom as possible, and when at home was always

> washing her hair. She walked about with the rather fated expression you see in photographs of girls who have subsequently been murdered, but nothing had so far happened to her. (51)

The exposure of a ghostly temporality in this passage consists less in the ominous future hereby brought to overshadow Lilian in the unfolding of the narrative (nothing murderous in fact comes to pass) but more in the bizarre status of this 'fated expression' *per se*. It can only look 'fated' in retrospect, but this time of retrospection does not exist; and yet, to envisage the visage or 'expression' as 'fated' is already to have envisaged Lilian dead. Such would be the haunting temporality of still lives.

What do we become, even (or especially) as lovers or loved ones, in the future memories of others? How does this work of future memorability inscribe itself, as it necessarily must in some sense do, in the so-called present? Such a question engages with a notion of posterity, of living on or surviving oneself, which inhabits all Bowen's still lives, and which we shall elaborate in greater detail in our discussion of *The Little Girls*. This memory-work is also threaded through *The Death of the Heart*, not least by way of the pitiful figure of Major Eric E. J. Brutt. This man with the ludicrously but provocatively 'brutish' name (97) by chance meets again with Anna – and with Portia and Thomas – after watching (unamused) a Marx Brothers film at the Empire. They all go back for a drink at Windsor Terrace: what draws Brutt and Anna Quayne (née Fellowes) together are their memories of a loved one, a man with the avian name of Robert Pidgeon.[8] It is 'nine years plus' (43) since Anna Fellowes and Robert Pidgeon had been 'perfect lovers' (45). In the 'admirably hot and bright' study, Thomas serves drinks:

> Anna could not speak – she thought of her closed years: seeing Robert Pidgeon, now, as a big fly in the amber of this decent man's [i.e., Major Brutt's] memory. Her own memory was all blurs and seams. She started dreading the voice in which she could only say: 'Do you hear anything of him? How much do you see him, these days?' Or else, 'Where is he now, do you know?' (45)

To be a big fly in the amber of another's memory, or to be scratched and encrypted in the 'blurs and seams' of another's memory: such a mode of still life is not only the fate of every love, its strange state of existence in a memory of the future; but it also imposes itself, impacts itself, in the necessity of what can be called a memory of the present. As with our account of 'dread' in the previous chapter (and Anna's experience at this point is itself explicitly a 'dreading'), Bowen's text points towards a notion of temporality that cannot be situated, a notion that does not conform to any comfortable sense or understanding. *The Death of the Heart* explores the 'blurs and seams' that mark every passing moment of experience, forms of scarification which are nevertheless not thinkable, not assimilable to the present or to presence. Like the fated expression in a photograph, the present is inhabited by a ghostly future, the 'memory' of our own 'death'. And this inscription of a memory of the present is not a supplementary or complementary adjunct to the experience of the present. It is a logic of still life which divides the present from itself, just as it divides any notion of past or future as in itself conceivable on the basis of a simple, undivided present.

We might say that this otherness within the present, this unpresentable or immemorial marking of every experience of the present, is a necessary condition of love. It may seem unarguable that one of the primary concerns of Bowen's *The Death of the Heart* (as of other texts here being read as still lives) is the portrayal of what are conventionally regarded as various kinds of selfishness and egotism (Anna's, Thomas's, Eddie's). In this respect, Bowen's writing may be read as a satire of precisely these aspects of the individual and social. Such a reading might readily meet with the phantasmagoric posthumous approval of Dr Johnson, who famously defined satire as a work (strictly, a poem) 'in which wickedness or folly is censured'. Analysis of *The Death of the Heart* in terms of satire and social comedy can do much to illuminate the extraordinary power and intensity of Bowen's work, particularly in relation to that work's most readily recognizable sociopolitical articulations. This, however, is only to go part of the way. Our interest here is in something more disruptive, and concerns rather the ways in which Bowen's writing displaces the very grounds of traditional satire and social comedy. We would suggest that Bowen's work prompts a different conception of social space, and indeed of the ways in which the Johnsonian notions of 'wickedness' and 'folly' may be thought. This is not simply to propose that the selfishness and egotism of various Bowen characters is ambiguous – it could no doubt be argued that Eddie is 'wicked' but also has his good points, etc. Rather, it is to gesture towards a quite different kind of logic and ethics. It is to signal the force and value of that which in some sense both precedes and circumscribes notions of self, subject, ego, codes of individual ethics and morality. We are concerned, that is to say, with another notion of satire (and with another notion of 'folly' as well), with a kind of satire *before* the social and individual, and thus before and beyond the traditional ethics or morality with which they are identified. A Johnsonian ethics of reading – a 'moralistic' reading – would, we believe, tend to eschew what seems to us a more radical and disruptive dimension of Bowen's writing, namely its concern with an otherness which precedes, haunts, solicits the very possibility of self-identity and individuality, memory and the present, the social and the human.

Love would only be possible, then, on condition of an asocial otherness, and we would argue that it is with this conception of love that Bowen's writing is most intensively and passionately engaged. It is in this context that we might try to consider the title of Bowen's novel, in which Wordsworth's 'the human heart by which we live' undergoes a strange work of translation and transformation. The title-phrase, 'the death of the heart', does not occur in the text itself. Yet it pervades the novel in a multiplicity irreducible to the fixity of a particular sense or reference. In this respect the death of the heart can be intimately identified with the notion of still lives. The 'death of the heart' mimes the ceaseless arresting of 'still lives', just as 'still lives' imposes on the notion of the death of the heart its own logic of a radical literarity and uncanny survival.

Bowen's text offers a consistent demystification of the Wordsworthian 'human heart' at least insofar as that heart is identified with spontaneity, sincerity, instinct, truth, virtue and love. *The Death of the Heart* works with a conventional language of broken hearts, but never rests with it.[9] Certainly one of 'these *lacunae* in people' is more than once figured as that of the heart. Matchett, for example, tells Portia about the death of Mrs Quayne, at the residence at which Matchett was formerly housekeeper: '"Oh, I did feel upset, with death in the house and all that change coming. But that was the most I felt. I didn't feel a thing here." With a dry unflinching movement, Matchett pressed a cuffed hand under her bust' (77). Later, Eddie spots Portia at Covent Garden:

> Then he saw Portia, waiting at the one corner he did not think they had said. Her patient grip on her small case, her head turning, the thin chilly stretch of her arms between short sleeves and

> short gloves struck straight where his heart should be – but the shaft bent inside him. (273)

It is not, however, a matter of the text figuring a simple death or absence of the heart: rather the text multiplies and undecidably suspends the readings of its title. Similarly, this suspension would not be that of a mere negativity or indeterminacy: rather it would be a cardiac arrest that ceaselessly sets off another rhythm, sets other hearts beating, regenerates and degenerates, starts reading over again. Above all it would open the heart to death and writing, to a literarity, theatricality, fictionality and otherness of the heart. Sitting with Anna and Thomas at Windsor Terrace wondering how to respond to Portia's relayed message from the Karachi, St Quentin declares: 'Look where we all three are. Utterly disabused, and yet we can't decide anything. This evening the pure in heart have simply got us on toast' (310). The force of 'utterly' and 'pure' here is necessarily equivocal, partly on account of the accompanying, paradoxical recognition that they 'can't decide anything', and partly because any final determination of what might be involved in the cannibalistic oddity of being had 'on toast' is left in suspense by the novel's abrupt ending. What is 'pure in heart' in Bowen's text cannot, in any case, be identified with the purity or truth of spontaneity or intuition: after all, as we are told earlier, 'nine out of ten things you do direct from the heart are the wrong thing' (56). Instead the text obliges us to associate 'whatever feeling is in the heart' with that strange 'unwritten poetry [that] twists the hearts of people' (123); with the theatrical, fantastical twists and turns of what Bowen calls 'arabesques of the heart' (271); with the uncanniness of sensing the heart as other, as, for instance, at the Karachi when Brutt is faced by Portia: they do not touch and yet 'he felt her knocking through him like another heart outside his own ribs' (295). If there is the comic outrage and cannibalistic impropriety of the 'pure in heart', arrested cardiographically on the threshold of the Karachi Hotel, suspended in the imminence of an arrival which never completely takes place and therefore never stops taking place, this heart will always have been worked over in advance by forms of impurity and expropriation, by patterns and compulsions which prompt us to conceive the heart as inhabited by its own 'death', the death of the heart. There is nothing absolutely pure about the pure in heart, nor any absolute originality, nothing ever to be truly heartfelt – even in dream wood.

Portia is in church, meditating on how Eddie had been 'unwittingly caricatured by someone [Mr Bursely] who does not know him at all'. She sits, 'in imitation of Mrs Heccomb' by keeping her gloves on, with 'wrists crossed on her knee':

> she wondered whether a feeling could spring straight from the heart, be imperative, without being original. (But if love were original, if it were the unique device of two unique spirits, its importance would not be granted; it could not make a great common law felt. The strongest compulsions we feel throughout life are no more than compulsions to repeat a pattern: the pattern is not of our own device.) (169)

This is the law of love, and the law that governs Bowen's work, in a Bowenesque parenthesis sealed by the other: there is no imperative, no originality, no feeling that springs straight from the heart except insofar as it is granted, compelled, patterned by otherness, by what is 'not of our own device'.

This might also be a helpful context in which to situate Bowen's concern with acting and drama. 'Original' feelings are always in advance 'in imitation'; unwitting or unconscious caricature (an abyssal kind of self-satire) marks every identity; the theatrical and dramatic inscribes every social relation, every experience of the self. St Quentin suggests, in his writerly and quasi-Shakespearean fashion, that 'the world's really a stage' (310): this should be understood in the most exacting sense, namely that there is imitation, theatre, drama at the origin, or rather before the origin, before the very first stage, prior to any staging of the self or of social relations. This is not to suggest a simple aestheticizing of selfhood or experience: the notions of imitation and drama here are forms of otherness acting at the very *heart* of identity, setting identity going, setting identity beside itself, slowly but surely beating itself to death.

It is through this radically non-experiential logic of imitation and acting, theatre and drama, that Bowen's work can be read as the elucidation of a theory of multiple identity, a multiplicity itself sketched, staged, haunted by otherness. That is to say, more than simply a satire or critique of selfishness or egotism, *The Death of the Heart* dramatizes the logic of what cannot be assimilated or reduced to self-identity, and proposes a proliferation without original or origin. Anna plays patroness (or ex-patroness) to Eddie:

> 'You can make your own way – after all, you are very clever.'
> 'So they all say,' said Eddie, grinning at her.
> 'Well, we'll just have to think. We've got to be realistic.'
> 'You're so right,' said Eddie, glancing into a mirror. (64)

The glance in abyss: nothing will ever allow the realism of this glance to coincide with itself, or reduce the constitutive disturbance of an otherness which haunts the very possibility of likeness in self-reflection.[10] The comedy of this glance reflects what is at once the irony of the abyss and the abyss of irony. Any notion of being self-identical, single, individual, is dispersed in the kind of palpable and generative multiplicity which Eddie later explicitly associates with Shakespeare. As he tells Portia, in the fitting context of tea at Madame Tussaud's:

> Why am I ever with anybody but you? Whenever I talk to other people, they jeer in their minds and think I am being dramatic. Well, *I* am dramatic – why not? I am dramatic. The whole of Shakespeare is about me. All the others, of course, feel that too, which is why they are all dead nuts on Shakespeare. But because I show it when they haven't got the nerve to, they all jump on me. Blast their silly faces – (101–2)

A sense of the constitutively dramatic, and of irreducibly polymorphous literary identities, is something that all people 'feel'. We *are* dramatic. Only a lack of 'nerve' prevents people from showing it – though they show it anyway, through a kind of sublimated madness, the passion and enthusiasm of their still life 'silly faces', being 'dead nuts on Shakespeare'.

Of course, there is a conventional reading of the 'dream wood' of *The Death of the Heart*, in which Eddie is a dangerously, brutally selfish individual who is aware of his 'horrible power' (214) and who becomes frightened by what Portia sees as his capacity to 'stay alone in [him]self':

> 'You stay alone in yourself, you stay alone in yourself!'
> Eddie, white as a stone, said: *'You must let go of me.'* (215)

This exchange happens in a dream wood – the wood in which they go for a walk during the weekend that Eddie spends at Waikiki (210–17). Here he tells her: 'You and I are enough to break anyone's heart – how can we not break our own? We are as drowned in this wood as though we were in the sea' (216). Conventional instances, then, of a breaking or death of the heart and a romantic dreamlike wood: 'But that wood was where I kissed you' (275), as Portia later reproaches him. The romantic fantasy that marks Portia's experience with Eddie in the wood seems to involve what is earlier described as 'that closeness one most often feels in a dream' (59).

The Death of the Heart, then, is pervaded by forms of 'dream wood', some more readily recognizable than others. Not only is there the dream wood in which old Mr Quayne gets 'knit up', the inescapable 'forest' of which Portia dreams (141), or the dream wood in which she and Eddie kiss. There is also, for example, the dream wood within the house on Windsor Terrace itself, where 'the windows framed panoramas of wet trees' and 'the room looked high and faint in rainy afternoon light' (253). It is here, we may recall, that Portia shuts her eyes and feels a dream-like 'immunity of sleep, of anaesthesia': 'She saw that tree she saw when the train stopped [in Switzerland] for no reason; she saw in her nerves, equally near and distant, the wet trees out there in the park' (256–7).[11] And then there is the equally strange dream wood of Major Brutt's room at the Karachi, a room in which Portia's attention fastens on the Major's shoes. Brutt explains that he cleans them himself, that he's 'always been rather fussy': 'She looked at the row of shoes, all on their trees. "No wonder they look so nice: they look like chestnuts"' (296).[12] Beyond these figurations, however, 'dream wood' designates a condition of being and a form of relationship (with others and with the past). Both individually and in relation to one another, people in *The Death of the Heart* are in a dream wood. Thus we can read, in a dream wood, the interrelations of Mr Quayne and Irene, Anna and Robert Pidgeon, Anna and Thomas, Thomas and Major Brutt, Thomas and Portia, Portia and Anna, Portia and her father, Portia and Eddie, Portia and Major Brutt, Portia and Matchett, St Quentin and (from his writerly perspective) all the others. But such a 'dream wood' is not assimilable to individual self-consciousness, identity or experience. And it is in accordance with a notion of dream wood resistant to identity, to individual possession or mastery, that we wish to describe *The Death of the Heart* itself. In other words, we would like, in the remaining pages of this chapter, to offer a reading of *The Death of the Heart* as itself a dream wood, and of 'dream wood' as the condition of reading this text. 'Dream wood', we suggest, would designate a space which haunts every romantic or social relation, including every form of auto-affection. 'Dream wood' concerns a preoriginary fictionality, a fundamental dislocation of experience; it marks a dreamlike displacement of the self and an opening onto the phantasmagoric multiplicity of otherness. This may be terrifying but it is also inescapable. It is the condition of life and love in Bowen's text: it precedes and succeeds us.

If dream wood concerns 'that closeness one most often feels in a dream', it is the closeness of being beside oneself, it is the dislocation of proximity itself, a recognition that in dreams we are all unavoidably mad. Dream wood – that is, *The Death of the Heart* – does not, however, suggest a simple falling into madness or giving ourselves over to the utopian realm of some romantic fantasy or irrationalism. Dream wood is more precisely atopian, to be traced in a past which was never present and in the very opening of the future. As a dream would, dream wood articulates the logic of still lives and of the death of the heart. In other words it is the pattern of what is not our own, the admitting of the unadmitted, the memory-work of blurs and seams, being in amber, being 'dead nuts', disseminated within the presence of the present, within the instant of living, the moment of a heartbeat. It is in these terms that *The Death of the Heart*, like Bowen's other novels, adumbrates another ethics, another thinking of the social and political, an ethics and a thinking neither governed by nor reducible to a logic of presence or identity, of mastery or possession.

Dream wood cannot be appropriated or mastered. In this respect we could suggest that it can be neither entered nor left. How should we draw, or draw from, the still life of this scene? If, as we have suggested in our reading of *The House in Paris*, people are woody, people are trees, the paper of books, dream wood, what is there to see, in the leaf-veins of our nerves? Dream wood is at once gigantic and microscopic, phantasmagoric. Strange tracks, dream-grafts, unknown trees, unadmitted looks, dreadful voices, laughter, concealed structures, columns: writing. There is no individual, no identity, which is not inhabited by this dream wood. As St Quentin says, just after his comment about being on toast:

> Not that there is, really, one neat unhaunted man. I swear that each of us keeps, battened down inside himself, a sort of lunatic giant – impossible socially, but full-scale – and that it's the knockings and batterings we sometimes hear in each other that keeps

> our intercourse from utter banality. Portia hears these the whole time. (310)

The Death of the Heart figures the necessity of such a 'lunatic giant' as that which cannot be assimilated or reduced to the self: it is 'battened down' under dream wood which can never be ours. This lunatic giant is necessarily knit up with other figurations which we have discussed – the unadmitted and inadmissible, the monstrous and the undecidably animal, the alterity of love, laughter, the heart, acting and multiple identity, in short all these '*lacunae* in people'.

In an essay called 'Coming to London' (1956), Elizabeth Bowen describes Regent's Park as 'seeming something out of (or in) a book' (*MT* 89). The Bowenesque parenthesis is crucial: it renders at once more precise and more undecidable the sense of what it might mean to be living out of (or in) a book. What is a book? How is it framed? What are its boundaries? Are we 'in' it or 'out of' it? What does it mean to read a book, to read into it, or for a reader to be '*in* a novel' (*LG* 78)? What kind of thing is a book? Should we try to describe it in spatial, architectural metaphors, as a sort of structure or edifice? Or in terms of a hallucinatory aurality, as a soundtrack of so many sounds and voices? Or visually and materially, as a black-and-white still life, a largely paper product made from trees? *The Death of the Heart* is a dream wood, constructed of dream wood. But it is a dream wood of lacunae, a space or structure which, being lacunary, is neither complete nor even continuous and consistent with itself. A lacuna is 'a gap or hiatus', but also 'a cavity: a depression in a pitted surface'.[13] In this way it is related to 'lacunar' which is defined as 'a sunken panel or coffer in a ceiling or a soffit: a ceiling containing these' (*Chambers*). What is lacunary might include something sunken in the underside of a stairway, archway or entablature; but it could also be the ceiling itself. This logic of the lacuna, like that of the cicatrix, engages with both that which is hidden and that which hides. The ceiling, and the sealing, of dream wood.

The Death of the Heart, then, is a dream wood structure of which it is not possible to know whether one is inside or outside it, or how to judge what is lacunary about it. Even the furniture of this uncanny building would be composed of dream wood. Dream wood furniture is itself undecidably lacunary: it concerns that force of furniture which traverses the human, inscribing itself in the heart as that which lives on, as that which must – but cannot – be anthropomorphized.

As Matchett tells Portia, explaining her reasons for following the furniture from Mrs Quayne's house to Regent's Park:

> 'It seemed to me proper. I hadn't the heart, either, to let that furniture go: I wouldn't have known myself. It was that that kept me at Mrs Quayne's. I was sorry to leave those marbles I'd got so nice, but those had to stop and I put them out of my mind.'
>
> 'The furniture would have missed you?'
>
> 'Furniture's knowing all right. Not much gets past the things in a room, I daresay, and chairs and tables don't go to the grave so soon. Every time I take the soft cloth to that stuff in the drawing-room, I could say, "Well, you know a bit more." My goodness, when I got here and saw all Mrs Quayne's stuff where Mrs Thomas had put it – if I'd have been a silly, I should have said it gave me quite a look. Well, it didn't speak, and I didn't.' (81)

What makes this furniture dream wood is, above all, its quasi-hallucinatory, unspoken rapport with Matchett and with the past. It is 'the past', too, which furnishes Matchett and Portia with their own dream wood. And it is Anna's conviction of their being 'knit up' in such a dream wood that in turn justifies sending Matchett to fetch Portia from the Karachi. As Anna tells Thomas, Matchett and Portia 'talk about the past':

> 'The past?' said Thomas. 'What do you mean? Why?'
>
> 'Their great mutual past – your father, naturally.'
>
> 'What makes you think that?'
>
> 'Their being so knit up. They sometimes look like each other. What other subject – except of course, love – gives people that sort of obsessed look? Talk like that is one climax the whole time. It's a trance; it's a vice; it's a sort of complete world. Portia may have defaulted lately because of Eddie. But Matchett will never let that drop; it's her *raison d'être*, apart from the furniture.' (311–12)

'Knit up': Matchett would thus be the wood, the match for Portia, and vice versa, they 'look like' and match each other, in a 'trance', they enclose and seal the other, in 'a sort of complete world'.

Such enclosure, sealing or completion is, however, itself lacunary. Partly this is an effect of the haunting differences to be tracked everywhere in dream wood, to be traced in the force of furniture, the past, the death of the heart. Ultimately, as we shall try to show, this lacunation has to do with the way Bowen's novel ends. If *The Death of the Heart* is a dream wood structure, are we inside or outside it? The undecidability of this question, we would suggest, is figured by Matchett and Portia, two figures matching, enclosing and sealing the other, in a lacunary and phantasmagoric architectonics. Matchett is variously decribed as 'a vaseful of memory', a 'living arch' (77), 'a wall' (79) for Portia. Just as Portia's name can be associated with a gateway or entrance, Matchett is described as 'an arch' (77).[14] Like a 'statue' (77), 'monolithic' (231), Matchett is 'the woman with the big stony apron', 'a caryatid' (312) – the 'female figure used instead of a column to support an entablature' (*Chambers*).[15] Is such an architectonics – at once the construction and knowledge of dream wood – to be conceived from the inside or the outside? In the abruptness of its ending, *The Death of the Heart* simultaneously figures – and traces an approach towards – an uncanny edifice which is necessarily unfinished, a *folly* both in the architectural sense of a building that is by definition exorbitant and 'left unfinished' (*Chambers*) and in the Johnsonian sense of a kind of madness or deficiency in understanding. This is not to suggest that *The Death of the Heart* is 'merely' a work of madness or intellectual folly; it is rather to indicate another space of literature as such, and of Bowen's work in particular. It is to approach a theory of the novel as dream wood.

The literary text is a folly: it is by definition linked to madness, to being 'dead nuts', to what is exorbitant and what resists being finished. Such a folly cannot be appropriated, made 'our own' or made 'human'. It concerns the unpresentable. It is at once affirmation and dissolution. This would be the oneiric folly on the threshold of which our reading must ceaselessly stop and start. The eerie threshold thus configured would be the opening of dream wood – highlighted in the novel's 'closing' account of a 'portentous' and dreamlike colossus, a double edifice 'of great height', 'connected by arches'. This is the Karachi Hotel, with its portico of columns and its strange double giant doors:

> The Karachi Hotel consists of two Kensington houses, of great height, of a style at once portentous and brittle, knocked into one – or, rather, not knocked, the structure might hardly stand it, but connected by arches at key points. Of the two giant front doors under the portico, one has been glazed and sealed up; the other up to midnight, yields to pressure on a round brass knob. (285)

We are left, then, on the threshold of dream wood, borne up by Matchett, the woman whose power of speech mixes Brontë's Nelly Dean and Joyce's Molly Bloom. We are left with the unfinished movement of being sent towards a strange place and not arriving, with a sense of what Matchett calls 'going off to where I've got no idea' (316). Just as Matchett is dispatched in a taxi to an unknown destination, so we are embarked on the unforeseeable and uncanny trajectory of reading *The Death of the Heart*. We are left caught up in a figuration of what we have called *going*, that is to say with a sense of movement which is not properly thinkable, a sense of arrival which is at the same time non-arrival, an unfinished movement which is undecidable, at once affirmative and traced by death.[16] For Molly Bloom's double 'yes', we have Matchett's insistent 'Well, I don't know, I'm sure' (318). Identifying a 'sort of joy' in the opening of 'all hearts', in the undecidability of what never arrives, in the sense that (to adopt Major Brutt's words) 'You can't foresee anything' (262), *The Death of the Heart* closes, without closing, and thus opens, without ceasing, on the threshold:

> Through the glass door, Matchett saw lights, chairs, pillars – but there was no buttons, no one. She thought: 'Well, what a place!' Ignoring the bell, because this place was public, she pushed on the brass knob with an air of authority. (318)

What grounds this, or any, 'air of authority'? Has the taxi-driver 'brought [Matchett] wrong' (318) or not? Does Matchett fetch Portia? Is sending Matchett to fetch Portia 'the right thing' (304) to do or not?

To be fetched or seized, to be brought or called forth, to be with Matchett and Portia, 'knit up' in a dream wood, 'knit up' in 'the past': this figuration finally concerns the very possibility of reading *The Death of the Heart* as a whole, the completion of a reading, the end of the book. The threshold of the ending suspends our reading: so long as this suspension is maintained, we remain 'knit up' in the dream wood of reading. But this maintenance is itself lacunary, phantasmagoric, a folly: the undecidability of the ending of *The Death of the Heart* ceaselessly starts reading over again. Thus we can speculate, look ahead, go beyond, 'out of' the book and decide: yes, Matchett fetches Portia, yes, this is 'the right thing', yes, they will be united, they will be – because they *already* are – 'knit up' together. To read in this way is indeed to be 'knit up'. But to be 'knit up' in the dream wood of this ending is, paradoxically, to be identified with 'the past', to disavow the present of reading and to eschew the judgement – always still to come – of what is 'right'. Dream wood: it is in the ceaseless, ghostly and affirmative force of this undecidability that *The Death of the Heart* at once leaves us as readers, and stages, 'with an air of authority', the dissolution of the novel.

5
Sheer Kink

> Anywhere, or at any time, with anyone, one may be seized by the suspicion of being alien.
>
> (*TR* 19)

> Daniel George, who read the novel in manuscript for Cape, wrote about her characteristic contortion – at its most noticeable in this novel – in his report. So far from seeing it as affected, or deliberately high-flown, he saw it as the extreme of colloquialism: she wrote so colloquially, he said, 'that unless the reader is lucky enough to coincide with her in placing a stress on the key word of a sentence, he may be baffled completely'.[1]

The setting of *The Heat of the Day* (1948) is wartime London, the events mostly taking place between 1940 and 1942. The protagonist, Stella Rodney, is employed in 'secret, exacting, not unimportant' (26) intelligence work. Her son Roderick, who is in the Army, comes in the course of the narrative to inherit from a cousin Francis (whom he has never met) Mount Morris, an Irish country house. Parentless, brotherless, husbandless, Stella is having an affair with Robert Kelway, also working in intelligence. She is approached by another intelligence man, called Harrison, who tries to persuade her that Kelway is actually a spy, a traitor to his country, and that she might do well to drop him and take up Harrison instead. She does not submit to this bizarre form of blackmail – although its twisted effects might be seen to culminate in Stella's later offering herself to Harrison and being refused. But the seeds of Bowenesque uncertainty have been sown. Kelway is 'like a young man in Technicolor' (114). His enigmatic nature is paralleled by his family home, Holme Dene, where his mother lives with his sister Ernestine and the children of another sister, Anne and Peter. Holme Dene – which Stella and Robert visit in the midst of her uncertainty regarding him – is a house full of things that seem 'like touring scenery' (121), inhabited by people for whom 'Mum is the word' (113) and who appear to Stella 'suspended in the middle of nothing' (114). Eventually Stella confronts her lover with the explicit suggestion that he is 'passing information to the enemy' (189). Kelway for a while passionately denies the charge but later acknowledges its truth. Convinced the authorities are closing in on him, after a final meeting with Stella at night in her Mayfair apartment, he tries to leave by the skylight. His death is officially recorded as 'misadventure, outcome of a crazy midnight escapade on a roof' (301). Harrison in the meantime has disappeared without trace. The closing pages of the novel shift rapidly from the end of 1942 through to 1944. Harrison turns up again in London and visits Stella; but in an oddly inconsequential climax or resolution to the novel, we discover that she is shortly to marry someone else, the 'cousin of a cousin' (321).

Apparently marginal to this narrative are two other characters. First there is Stella's cousin Nettie, who used to live at Mount Morris but who has since been transferred, for mental health reasons, to a 'home' called Wistaria Lodge. Cousin Nettie is important because, while representing a derangement threatening the apparently established, 'normal' orders of the world of the novel, she is also a figure of health and benignity. Roderick's visit to Wistaria Lodge, for example, may allow him to gain a more informed, clearer understanding of his family and its history, but the presence in Bowen's novel of this woman with 'the eyes of an often-rebuked clairvoyante' (207) is also more pervasive than this. Cousin Nettie provokes a powerful and affirmative destabilization of those assumptions of self and meaning, of society and order, that are elsewhere shown as so coercive and constraining. Second, and in significant respects supplementing this force, there is Louie Lewis, the seemingly 'moron' (14) young woman who happens to meet Harrison in the opening chapter of the novel and becomes inadvertently woven into the story of Stella and Harrison. Louie's husband, Tom, is out fighting in Italy. In his absence she finds company in other men as well as in a girlfriend called Connie. The potentially tragic effect of the discovery, near the end of the novel, that Louie is pregnant by a man other than her husband is uncannily overcome by the arrival of a telegram: Tom has been killed in the fighting. *The Heat of the Day* ends, as it begins, with a scene involving Louie: she is with her baby, who is named Thomas Victor in what seems to be at once a strange celebration of her dead husband and a cryptic tribute to Stella's first husband, Victor. The novel closes with Louie out in the country with Thomas Victor, observing the flight overhead of three swans 'disappearing in the direction of the west' (330).

* * *

As we have argued earlier in this study, Bowen's novels disturb, analyse, alter the very grounds of characterization. In particular, they derange the ways that – both in works of literary realism and in so-called real life – we distinguish between what is dramatic and what is non-dramatic. More visibly and more sharply even than in the work of Henry James, we would suggest, Bowen's writing – and its bizarre omniscient narrator – metamorphoses the very form of the novel into the stony clarity or still life of something like a post-modern Elizabethan drama. *The Heat of the Day* stages a generic dissolution of the novel. This has to do with its uncannily dramatic qualities – and above all with the ways in which Bowen's omniscient narrator enacts a Browningesque proliferation of dramatic personae, embodies a telepathic network of multiple voices and identities. In order to elaborate further this question of the extraordinary force of drama in Bowen's work, we propose to read *The Heat of the Day* alongside its most striking Shakespearean intertext, *Hamlet*.[2]

Earlier in this study, borrowing a phrase from a character in *To the North* (60), we suggested that Bowen, like Shakespeare, affirms the obvious. It is not simply that these writers give us a forceful sense of real life, that they (in Hamlet's abyssally ironic or abyssally metatheatrical words) 'hold the mirror up to nature', that they show us life and prompt us to whisper, admiringly, 'How true'. More importantly, we would like to suggest that the writings of Bowen and Shakespeare relentlessly affirm that there is no real life, no nature, no truth and indeed no self not fundamentally haunted by effects of fiction, drama, multiplicity and death. References to Shakespeare's plays, whether in the form of narratorial allusions or in discussions between characters, are woven throughout Bowen's work: her novels are demonstrably and powerfully Shakespearean. But we would argue that the correspondences between these writers entail a rereading and displacement of intertextual relations which would allow us to appreciate not only Bowen's work as Shakespearean, but also Shakespeare's work as importantly Bowenesque. Such a co-implication of Bowen and Shakespeare would participate in a narrative of intertextual relations governed by the kind of logic which the present chapter will attempt to trace: reading as 'rereading', as the necessary reconstruction of what never happened, as chiastic diplopia, double-vision or 'hallucination'; narrative – including any presentation and unfolding of 'character', any narrative of the self, or of love, or of intertextual relations – as dissolving knots, gloves, ties, knitting. In short, it is a matter of what we shall describe as sheer kink.

* * *

Spy story, love story, ghost story: *The Heat of the Day* gathers all these together. And yet, threading in and out, it constantly transpires to have pulled out, gone away, lost its head, buried and sealed itself, elsewhere. In the beginning was sheer kink.

In the end, Roderick questions his mother about Robert's death, expressing his anxiety that she should or could wait 'on and on and on for something, something that in a flash would give what Robert did and what happened enormous meaning like there is in a play of Shakespeare's' (300). This reference to 'enormous meaning' in Shakespeare would seem to be inhabited by an enormous irony, a kind of hyperbolic, disseminating irony which at once parodies and dissolves the very possibility of enormous Shakespearean meaning. It is ironic first because it comes shortly after a citation from *Hamlet* (Hamlet's last words, 'The rest is silence'), which occurs while Stella is negotiating the delicate business of telling her son about Robert's death and explaining that he had been a traitor. She hesitates yet recognizes the need to tell: 'It would have been easy to recline, to become suffused by indifference, to be thankful that all was over – but it was not, yet; the rest was not yet ready to be silence' (298). Both Bowen's and Shakespeare's texts might be seen as suggesting that the rest is not silence, that there is no such thing as silence, that the silence of a suffused indifference is no conclusion, or that silence is never at rest, least of all if we are being invited to think about it as enormously meaningful. Secondly, Roderick's remark is ironic because it is so seemingly innocent – not only from the characterological perspective of a twenty-year-old who is able to believe in something as clichéd and obscurantist as 'enormous meaning' in the works of the Bard, but also from the narratological perspective in which Roderick cannot have known that his mother was, apparently, in her thoughts quoting

Hamlet. His remark demonstrates an instance of dramaturgic or textual telepathy, of ironic telepathy or telepathy in the abyss.[3] In this respect, the darkness of *Hamlet* and of the uncanny, even appalling silence that punctuates and envelops it, necessarily marks our reading of Roderick's use of the cliché. The hollow-sounding phrase about enormous meaning in Shakespeare is haunted, to be thought differently, as an effect of his mother's thought.

The sheer kink of enormous meaning. As we shall try to suggest, correspondences between Bowen and Shakespeare are most intensive not at the general 'bardic' level of 'enormous meaning' suggested by Roderick, but rather at the micro-level of transient words or phrases. Moreover analysis of such micro-level correspondences underscores the ways in which the writings of Shakespeare and Bowen put all assumptions about 'meaning' in question. Bowen's novels and Shakespeare's plays have in common a radical capacity for deranging the value of sense and meaning in general: in this, again, their critical power is precisely in the affirmation of 'the obvious', even if this obviousness may be both terrifying and ecstatic, inextricably bound up with madness and death.

* * *

'I appeared to be up against sheer kink' (136), says Harrison. 'Sheer': adjective, 'bright', 'thin', 'pure', 'mere', 'downright', 'vertical or very nearly'. Also, a noun, 'sheer' as 'a very thin fabric' (*Chambers*). 'Kink': noun, 'A short twist or curl in a rope, thread, hair, wire, or the like, at which it is bent upon itself' (*OED*). For the first dated appearance of the word in such a sense, the Oxford English Dictionary gives 1678 (Phillips): '[Kink] is when a Rope which should run smooth in the Block, hath got a little turn, and runs as it were double.' But 'kink', too, it should be stressed, as 'a mental twist: a crick: a whim: an imperfection' (*Chambers*). All of these senses cross over, fold into one another, get knit up, knotted and undone, snipped off, started up again elsewhere, in *The Heat of the Day*. Proliferating in all that links a text with weaving or knitting (Latin *texere, textum*, 'to weave') and in all that binds narrative to notions of unfolding and to the analysis of threads and lines, *The Heat of the Day* is sheer kink. Such proliferations may be seen as variously and heterogeneously figured in the text, for example, in 'the unflickering velocity of Mrs Kelway's knitting' (252), her needles 'flying along –

smoothly, lightly, apparently under their own volition' (109); in Robert's tie, in the strange timing of its being done up and undone and the impossibility of judging it (102–3, 271); in the string around a parcel which might or might not have been posted (127, 134, 169); in the 'absolute disconnexion' (209) attending Nettie's woolwork; in all the stories, the narratives and metanarratives, micro-narratives and grand, stagey narratives, 'knitted together' (99).

The operations of sheer kink are suggested by the pervasive undecidability of madness and reason, acting and not acting, in Cousin Nettie. Over everything hangs that 'sidelong glitter of reason, the uncanny hint of sanity' (215) dramatized by her. Over everything hovers that necessary possibility, the constitutive haunting, of some other (unmasterable, unassimilable) kind of 'volition', and of the 'absolute disconnexion' figured by Nettie's woolwork: 'she at once set out, with stork's-beak scissors, sedulously to snip off straggles of wool from the rough side. But the scissors, out of some impish volition of their own, kept returning to peck, pick, hover destructively over the finished part' (209). Nettie is the Ophelia of Bowen's novel or, doubling and kinking that, the Hamlet.[4] As Roderick, threaded into the choral embroidery of the Bowenesque narrator, wonders: 'Hamlet had got away with it; why should not she? But there had been doubts about Hamlet, Roderick understood; and, as for Cousin Nettie, could anybody who voluntarily espoused Wistaria Lodge be *quite* normal? – but then again, normal: what was that?' (215).

Just as *The Heat of the Day* casts the uncanniness of Cousin Nettie and of the still life she leads at Wistaria Lodge as a glitter that both inhabits and disrupts any conception of the 'normal', so the novel weaves a narrative that is at once interminable and multiple in itself – weaving and woven out of sheer kink.

* * *

There are only stories, only conversations, knitted together or grafted onto others: there is no metanarrative, no metaconversation, that exists outside the knitting and knotting of sheer kink. This logic governs the work of Bowen, of Shakespeare, of their intertextual relations, and of any critical discourse which is necessarily knitted into them, up in them, out of them, in turn. It is a logic of what in another context in Bowen's novel is called 'sheer "otherness"' (318); it is delirious knotting and undoing, ecstatic mental twisting, irreversible chiasmatic asymmetry, never simply separable from dream or madness, or from the very invention of the self. For there is no agent, even double agent, to which the operations of 'sheer kink' can be assigned. There is no subject who might, even in principle, supervise or determine its workings. Nor can any linearity of narrative escape it. Rather it figures a dissolution of identity, the dissolution of the subject and of the novel, the impossibility for narratives and narratees ever to coincide with themselves. Talking, story-telling, reading and deciphering in the abyss: there are only lines to go on, lines which nevertheless in their very knotting up, or in their very extremities, turn up something different, lead elsewhere. As Harrison puts it, in the context of what Stella calls his 'line of business': 'Go right out on one thing ... and immediately something else opens up' (136).

Investigating Stella Rodney, Harrison is confronted with the coincidence of a woman who has 'turned up in two different stories' (135) – the story of the love affair with Robert Kelway, and the story involving Cousin Francis, at whose funeral Stella sees Harrison for the first time. Harrison is checking out two *lines* (is Robert Kelway's treachery a question of a woman or money?) or – doubling this without simply repeating it – 'killing two birds with the same stone' (135). He tells her:

> 'Frankly, after the showings of the check-up, I wrote you off, crossed out "*cherchez la femme*" and switched to money. I'd made the switch, I may tell you, some weeks before we buried the old boy. In fact, I had made that switch long enough ago to have found that there wasn't anything along *that* line, either. No, I appeared to be up against sheer kink.'
>
> 'What kink?'
>
> 'There I'd thought you might help me.' (135–6)

Sheer kink is a spy story in which investigator and investigated, teller and told, intelligence work and conversations and 'conversations about conversations' (63), are all disentanglably woven into and out of one another. As Stella goes on to tell Harrison: 'Below one level, everybody's horribly alike. You succeed in making a spy of me' (138). Sheer kink is a spy story which is also love story, a knitting and knotting of stories that leaves no notion of love standing free of the radically dispossessing power of the dramatic and the fictive. Bowen's novel suggests that love is fundamentally *affected* by the impossibility of knowing how far one's own behaviour – and the behaviour of one's lover – is 'merely' acting, merely 'the appearance of love' (191), and the impossibility of extricating the recognition of such an impossibility from a sense of spying and fiction, a logic of fictional espionage.[5] Beyond this and more importantly, however, *The Heat of the Day* actually *affirms* this radically dispossessing power of the dramatic and fictive: it embraces and elaborates the generative possibilities of undecidable identity and of an erotics of this undecidability. Like other Bowen novels, *The Heat of the Day* relentlessly picks up, picks at, undoes assumptions of personal identity, and thus undoes the values of all constructions of the individual, social, political, erotic and ethical on which they rest. As Stella puts it: 'What is anyone? Mad, divided, undoing what they do' (287). Or as her son asks, in a question which is not merely rhetorical but which implies an inevitable sense of the addressor as alien: 'You do really think I am a person?' (300).[6]

An essential and invisible thread running through all of this is the work of 'death'. For sheer kink is at the same time a ghost story, a tying and weaving of stories of espionage and love which are constantly untied and unwoven, retied and rewoven through trance, madness and hallucination, the constant and non-assimilable power of the dead, of the cryptic, telepathic and uncanny. The sheer kink of *The Heat of the Day* concerns the experience of reading and the reading of experience. In other words it concerns a ghostly doubling, coming back or revenance, as a work of what we propose to call the retrolexic, a work of rereading or re-experiencing which can neither help to constitute a more accurate 'original' reading nor indeed, by the very necessity of this doubling, even coincide with itself. It is a work of rereading or re-experiencing which cannot be snipped free of the imperative of, among other things, remembering what never happened. In this way the retrolexic engages with a demand for reading back, for 'rereading backwards', for a rereading which at once doubles and obliterates any 'first reading'. It is the immemorial logic whereby 'One could only suppose that the apparently forgotten beginning of any story was unforgettable.' It is the demand imposed by a sense of the *written*, but a sense that takes the form of 'the lost first sheet of a letter or missing first pages of a book' (133). It is a demand which, while figuring the starting-point of reading or experience, cannot itself be situated.[7]

* * *

Love is sheer kink. The lovers Robert and Stella, we are told, knitted together the stories of their experiences into the larger story of their love: 'In the two years following 1940 he and she had grown into living together in every way but that of sharing a roof. Soon they could both conjecture the ins and outs of each other's days, and of evenings which had to be spent apart they knitted together the stories when they met' (99). Love is the interweaving, the fabrication of 'a common memory' which, while rendering everything 'no more than simulacra', is itself a common memory of what was never experienced, of what never happened:

> His experience and hers became harder and harder to tell apart, everything gathered behind them into a common memory – though singly each of them might, must, exist, decide, act; all things done alone came to be no more than simulacra of behaviour: they waited to live again till they were together, then took living up from where they left it off. Then their doubled awareness, their interlocking feeling acted on, intensified what was round them – nothing they saw, knew, or told one another remained trifling; everything came to be woven into the continuous narrative of love. (99)

The sheer kink of such continuity, the linearity and unfolding of this narrative constitutes the abyssal irony of Bowen's novel. No continuity exists, except as a hallucination it is that very narrative's force to have dissolved. The strangeness of 'hallucination' here may be understood in relation to the occurrence of that word in Bowen's short story 'Mysterious Kôr', in which Arthur poses the haunting rhetorical question, 'A game's a game, but what's a hallucination?'(*CS* 738).[8] 'There is', as Bowen delicately puts it in a 1960 Preface to Virginia Woolf's *Orlando*, 'a touch of hallucination about "reality"' (*MT* 135). The love story of Stella and Robert is to be in reverse, like a glove which, once turned inside out, can no longer be worn except with the truly disarming uncertainty of whether the hand is inside or out.[9] It is a story which is never finished and which at the same time undoes itself. Sheer kink is not a stop, not an end: it is indeed kink precisely because it fails to stop – it is necessarily *not* a knot. Linked to the logic of *going*, sheer kink would be, above all, that which prevents any arrest, any final or irrevocable knotting, any univocality or stoppage of sense.

Robert tells Stella on their last meeting, just before his death: 'Don't quarrel now, at the end, or it will undo everything from the beginning. You'll have to re-read me backwards, figure me out – you will have years to do that in, if you want to. You will be the one who will have to see: things may go in a way which may show I was not wrong' (270). This violent invocation of 'years' in which to 're-read' seems in turn to be telepathically, cryptically picked up and reiterated by someone who never heard it. For it is Roderick who, near the end of the novel, remarks on the 'fifty years' (299) it might take him to work out what has happened: he 'couldn't bear to think of [his mother] waiting on and on and on for something, something that in a flash would give what Robert did and what happened enormous meaning like there is in a play of Shakespeare's' (300).

Rereading backwards: the sheer kink of this scenario (what could ironically be called its enormous or abyssal meaning) would have to be understood as working in at least two directions – backwards into a nonexistent past and forwards into an unthinkable future. These two directions, it may be stressed, conduct us to no synthesis, to no present or final reading, but only to further multiplications and relays, knittings up, snippings off and reconstitutions, graftings and hoverings. They involve the radical disruption of a classical, linear temporality, dissolving the very possibility of narrative.

This rereading backwards, then, is inescapably oriented towards the future. The re-reading of what had once, like a hallucination, been presented as a 'continuous narrative of love' has no stop. This narrative of love is by definition interminable, irresolvable, constitutively open to a movement of rereading which can be called ghostly precisely in the sense that, as Stella tells Harrison in the closing pages, 'What's unfinished haunts one; what's unhealed haunts one' (321). The love story of Robert and Stella is definitively cryptic: any understanding of Robert's 'treachery' is undone by his death, disordered by the eerie imperative to remember or reconstruct what never happened. Love cannot be dissociated from a non-existent past, from a past which is always still to come. This is suggested by Robert when, in his final minutes with her, he says: 'best of all, Stella, if you can come to remember what never happened, to live most in the one hour we never had' (288). And it is suggested by Stella when she tells Harrison, at *their* final meeting, that 'one goes on hearing what [the dead] said, piecing and repiecing it together to try and make out something they had not time to say – possibly even had not had time to know' (317).

This impossible past is also at work in the cryptic transmissions from one generation to the next. Roderick's future is inscribed by the dead – by his father, 'the defeated Victor', by Robert, 'the unadmitted stepfather' (312), and by all that he has inherited from Cousin Francis, the man he never met. It is in relation to determining the significance of these dead that Roderick explicitly acknowledges the logic 'that nothing might *be* possible to finish' (312). It is in this context that he considers making a will:

> By a written will one made subject some other person – but he saw that what worked most on the world, on him, were the unapprehendable inner wills of the dead. Death could not estimate what it left behind it. Robert's had left grief – what more, if there had been anything more, Roderick's mother had not told him. Roderick reflected that, as things were, there would be nobody but his mother to be *his* heir, either. (313)

It is sheer kink, this narrative directed towards the remembering of what never happened, towards the inheritance of what cannot be estimated – oriented and determined by 'the unapprehendable inner wills of the dead'. Sheer kink also, it may seem, this figuration of the mother who is heir to her own son. (But isn't this, in a sense, what writing is? – Not only, as Plato and others would say, an orphan, but also the childless mother?)

Finally, as regards the inescapable orientation towards the future, there is the inextricable knitting together of the individual and the national, the personal and political, which characterizes Kelway's treachery and deception. Why does Kelway 'betray' his 'country'? His own account of this is itself subject to the effects of what Bowen calls 'rereading', reading as interminable, not least because of its explicit engagement with politico-historical concepts which remain still to be analysed. Robert and Stella are 'the creatures of history' (194) in a conventional sense; but they are also creatures of a movement of going which entails deferral and rereading.[10] In particular, Kelway's account of international politics – while itself specifically tied to the period of the Second World War – is open to rereading, to reading otherwise. For Kelway 'there are no more countries left; nothing but names' (267). For him words like 'betrayal', 'freedom' and 'democracy' belong to a language that is simply 'dead currency'. To believe in 'democracy' is, he suggests, just to be 'kidded along from the cradle to the grave': 'Look at your free people – mice let loose in the middle of the Sahara' (268). To construe Kelway's account in ideologically categorical terms, 'merely' as a voicing of German Fascism, would be to elide its strangeness and obliquity. Rather, in its very equivocality and fragmentariness, it implies the possibilities of quite different readings. It is a part of the sheer kink of Bowen's novel that this would include a reading that would accord with the shivering and dissolution of the conceptual grounds of 'democracy' inherent in the argument of the present study. For what Bowen's still lives lead us towards, among other things, is an acknowledgement of what could be called the unpresentable of democracy itself, especially insofar as democracy is conceived on the basis of a set of highly problematic assumptions about individuality, identity and the authority of the self. Bowen's work calls for another kind of thinking about notions of self and identity, a kind of thinking that would leave dramatically in abeyance the very attribution of identity to a self, the very notion of a unitary self, the very equation of identity-as-authority.[11] It would be a kind of thinking necessarily concerned to affirm and keep before it the undecidable force of the question posed by the alien Roderick which we cited earlier ('You do really think I am a person?'), a question which marks all of Bowen's novels and which finds its most candid expression in *Eva Trout*: 'What *is* a person? Is it true, there is not more than one of each?' (*ET*, 193).

In this way *The Heat of the Day* points towards the possibility of another thinking of the political as such, by way of notions of radical difference within the very construction of the individual, social and democratic. Bowen's novel works towards an affirmation of the undecidability of identity, and towards an ethics and an erotics of such an affirmation. Such an affirmation would be explicitly historical in its articulation and its elaboration. It is inscribed in the very title, 'the heat of the day', insofar as this phrase ties the fate of the text's protagonists to that of the historical space in which they live. Thus Bowen identifies the twentieth century as 'a clear-sightedly helpless progress towards disaster' in which 'The fateful course of [Stella's] fatalistic century seemed more and more her own: together had she and it arrived at the testing extremities of their noonday' (134). This sense of the fatalistic or presciently disastrous may be seen to highlight the importance of the kind of different thinking of the political, and of identity, promoted by Bowen's texts.

* * *

Rereading 'love': *The Heat of the Day* is characterized by asymmetrical forms of reversal and the retrolexic. Together with the forms of reversion and rereading already noted, one might consider the 'man in secret ... being a sort of celebrity in reverse' (279); the retrospective notion of 'what nerve, what nerve in reverse' newspaper headlines must have 'struck on' (275) in the 'traitor' Kelway; and the sense of reversal, in Stella's mind, of Robert and Harrison, whereby 'It seemed to her it was Robert who had been the Harrison' (275), a sense of reversal intensified by the revelation that Harrison's forename was Robert as well (321). But these forms and operations of retrolexia belong to no simple present. The retrolexic does not conform to a conception of time as rectilinear, as a 'continuous narrative' unfolding. Rather, the retrolexia of this love story involve the devastating logic of what cannot be known but cannot be forgotten; they concern a retrospection on what can only ever be ghostly, unlived.

The Heat of the Day is blitz-writing. Nowhere is this more evident, more uncannily 'transparent', than in Chapter 5, which gives an account of the 'unprecedented autumn' (96) of September 1940 – 'That heady autumn of the first London air raids' (90) – and the beginning of the love story of Stella and Robert. The origins of their romance are inscribed – in a catching of breath – within a world which is hallucinatory, 'more than a dream' yet 'tideless, hypnotic, futureless' (100), a kind of 'shock-stopped' (99) world marked by 'the unstopping phantasmagoric streaming' (91) of life by day, the deathliness of night, 'the charred freshness of every morning' (93), the telepathic force of war whereby 'the wall between the living and the living became less solid as the wall between the living and the dead thinned', such that 'in that September transparency people became transparent, only to be located by the just darker flicker of their hearts' (92).[12] This is the blitz-writing of a London in which 'everybody ... was in love' (92), a world inextricable from fiction and telepathy, from life as fiction, from fiction as telepathy; it focuses a hypnotic, more than dream-like 'psychic London' populated by the 'unknown dead' (92), inhabited by the sense of an 'unknownness' which can never be 'mended' (92), haunted by the 'torn-off senses' (91) of what could never be experienced. From 1942 the narrative looks back on a cryptic, ghostly world: 'The lovers had for two years possessed a hermetic world, which, like the ideal book about nothing, stayed itself on itself by its inner force' (90).

The origins of this love story, the origins of the relationship between Stella Rodney and Robert Kelway, lie here – in a blitz-riven fictionality and absence, in an exchange of words which are never exchanged, in the phantom of an exchange which can never be known or forgotten:

> both having caught a breath, they fixed their eyes expectantly on each other's lips. Both waited, both spoke at once, unheard.
>
> Overhead, an enemy plane had been dragging, drumming slowly round in the pool of night, drawing up bursts of gunfire – nosing, pausing, turning, fascinated by the point for its intent. The barrage banged, coughed, retched; in here [where Stella and Robert are standing, speaking, unheard] the lights in the mirrors rocked. Now down a shaft of anticipating silence the bomb swung whistling. With a shock of detonation, still to be heard, the four walls of in here yawped in then bellied out; bottles danced on glass; a distortion ran through the view. The detonation dulled off into the cataracting roar of a split building: direct hit, somewhere else.
>
> It was the demolition of an entire moment: he and she stood at attention till the glissade stopped. (95–96)

Still lives. This moment of demolition, this demolition of a moment, bears a significance which can never be either known or forgotten. It figures the sheer kink at the origin of their love, at the very start of their love story: 'What they *had* both been saying, or been on the point of saying, neither of them ever now were to know. Most first words have the nature of being trifling; theirs from having been lost began to have the significance of a lost clue' (96).

* * *

'Enormous meaning' in *The Heat of the Day,* as in Shakespeare's *Hamlet,* is concerned with silence, with the unspoken and the unspeakable; with the uncanny, telepathy, and an associated logic of alien, doubled and multiple identities; with a sense of drama and fiction, ghostliness and hallucination.[13] Like Shakespeare's, Bowen's writing operates through multiple knittings of 'fiction', 'books' and 'acting', on the one hand, and 'life' on the other. *The Heat of the Day* works with those 'rules of fiction, with which life to be credible must comply' (140). There is no 'life' and no 'real' which is not marked by the undecidably fictitious or 'half-fictitious' (166); by senses of being 'inside the pages of a book' (97) or in a drama or 'thriller' (190); by generative uncertainties of what is acting and what is not acting; by the demands of participating in a story or concatenation of stories which has no simple origin or present.

* * *

Like Shakespeare's plays, Bowen's novels have an aesthetic density, force and range which hang, suspended in their own strange atmospheres: it is as if every paragraph of a Bowen text, even every sentence, is already overhead, in the air – already floating or in flight. We shall move towards a conclusion here by attempting a final performance of the kind of micro-level analysis which Bowen's work, in common with Shakespeare's, seems to demand. Any attempt to unfold a critical narrative of Shakespeare and Bowen would, as we have tried to indicate, be sheer kink: it irresistibly conducts us into that uncanny, radically literary and erotic space within which, for example, Bowen's writing restages Shakespeare's as powerfully Bowenesque, as well as vice versa. Any critical account of the work of these writers, and of their intertextual relations, can only be supervised by a logic of sheer kink, can lead only to sheer kink. But let us in any case – as Horatio would say – go to it.

We will focus on a single example, that of unfolding *per se*, in other words the question of what it is, to 'unfold'. Our analysis will, to begin with, confine itself specifically to the question of unfolding a narrative, a tale or account. Like Shakespeare's *Hamlet, The Heat of the Day* is marked by forms of silence, the unspoken and unspeakable, by the unfolding of what remains enfolded or concealed, an unknotting which is only a more compounded knotting up. This dimension of Shakespeare's play is suggested most hauntingly when the Ghost tells Hamlet:

> But that I am forbid
> To tell the secrets of my prison-house,
> I could a tale unfold whose lightest word
> Would harrow up thy soul, freeze thy young blood,
> Make thy two eyes like stars start from their spheres,
> Thy knotted and combined locks to part,

> And each particular hair to stand an end
> Like quills upon the fretful porpentine.
>
> (I.v.13–20)

The Heat of the Day picks up the smallest, lightest words of the Ghost's speech, grafting or weaving them into the unquiet nodal point of the narrative, when Robert and his sister Ernestine meet Stella at Euston Station, on her return from Mount Morris, and they drive off in a chauffeur-driven hire-car. Ernestine's greeting in the dark interior of the car ushers in the strangeness of this scene: 'How-d'you-do, Mrs Rodney? You must be dead' (182). Stella is intent, by now, on asking her lover directly whether or not he is a spy. The principal topic of conversation in the car is, appropriately, lying. It gets underway with Ernestine's remarking, 'In any case, ask no questions and you'll get told no lies. – Don't you, Mrs Rodney, find that to be a golden rule?' (185) The question, already disturbingly rhetorical, quickly gets tangled up: how should Stella answer? How could she? Robert intervenes, Ernestine 'rap[s] out', a family argument begins – precisely concerning familial silence and the telepathic (their mother, says Ernestine, 'of course is practically able to read thoughts' [186]). Then Ernestine tries to move the conversation on:

> 'However, do by all means let us change the subject – whoever began it?'
>
> [Robert:] 'You did.'
>
> 'No, I don't think anyone did,' said Stella. 'It was *plus fort que nous*; it was in the air.'
>
> 'Possibly you, Stella, brought it back from Ireland on you, like a cold or flu?. ... Oh, all right, then, perhaps not. In that case you must mean this is a haunted car.'
>
> 'Hired cars of this type could some pretty curious tales unfold, I shouldn't wonder,' said Ernestine. (186)

No tale is unfolded, however: there is only this kinked enfolding of *Hamlet*. For such a cryptic scenario, there is apparently no language, not even a vocabulary of silence: 'no other vocabulary, least of all that of silence, at once offered itself' (187). *The Heat of the Day* unfolds and enfolds itself here, unfolds and enfolds a relation to Shakespeare's *Hamlet*. It knots itself up in the still life of this 'still uncertain' atmosphere, this 'cushioned darkness' (187), this ghostly scene of treachery and revelation, of what is unspeakable yet '*plus fort que nous*' – 'in the air'. In this cryptic, undecidably motivated, unanswerable citation from the Ghost's speech, *The Heat of the Day* enfolds the unfolding both of the 'continuous narrative' of itself and of a relation to Shakespeare's drama.

After Ernestine is dropped off at Gloucester Road Station, Stella in the darkness of the car at last explicitly confronts him:

> 'Two months ago, now, nearly two months ago, somebody (to give you an example) came to me with a story about you. They said you were passing information to the enemy. ...'
> 'I *what*?' he said blankly. (188–9)[14]

The story is a story, sheer talk, a tale, it is a blank, a lie, 'brainspun': in denying the story as 'crazy, brainspun, out of a thriller' (190), Robert in turn tells such a story himself. Here, then, is the spinning out, the doubling and unfolding of a thriller or love story. Out of this incident in the haunted car will come, eventually, the revelation of Robert's treachery and the need to begin again, to reread everything backwards. Truth is to be (adopting another phrase from Horatio) truly delivered. But what is the truth? What kinds of truth does *The Heat of the Day* unfold? It unfolds the logic of sheer kink, a necessity of rereading and retrolexia which suspends every conventional conception of fiction and history, of literature and criticism, of presenting a narrative, a tale or account.

Finally, what *The Heat of the Day* unfolds has to do with the question of identity, the question of unfolding not only narratives but also people. It is a question of the unfolding of *ourselves*. To provide a last twist for *The Heat of the Day*, we would like to suggest that the protagonist is not, after all, Stella Rodney, but Louie Lewis. This twist would consist not least in a sense of 'protagonist' as itself a multiple identity, bound up with fiction, drama and hallucination. As Louie says to her friend Connie, very near the end: 'Well, I *am*, only, aren't I – just one of many?. ... I've sometimes thought that myself' (323–4). Connie finds Louie's statement troubling: it seems she wants to dismiss it as 'complacency' but also recognizes in her friend a kind of 'sublimity' (324). We would argue that this curious combination of complacency and sublimity is precisely Shakespearean and can be linked up with what we have explored earlier in this study concerning myriad-mindedness and an essential multiplicity of self.

We might conclude by trying to describe retrolexically, and a little differently, what the works of Shakespeare and Bowen share with respect to notions of multiple identity, acting, fiction. These preoccupations could be said to figure the very cutting edge of *style*: what the novels of Bowen and the plays of Shakespeare share are points of style, styles of thought, styles of presenting the thought of others. What makes Bowen's writing Shakespearean and Shakespeare's Bowenesque is among other things a certain force of speechifying, in particular, the quality of what might be called rhetorical departure. What these writers share is a certain style of *presenting people*. In an essay on 'Shakespeare's Centrality', S. L. Goldberg argues that 'Even when English poets have used a special poetical diction, their best verse, significantly, is that which creates the tones and inflexions of a person actively thinking, feeling and speaking in that diction'.[15] 'What really distinguishes dramatic writing', he suggests, and what accounts at least in part for the 'greatness' of Shakespeare, is 'the created sense of a person on whose lips or in whose mind the words are alive'.[16] In conventional terms, the poetic and dramatic power of Bowen's writing is Shakespearean precisely in its capacity to create a sense of what John Bayley has called the 'extreme livingness' of people's (voiced or unvoiced) speech.[17] It is what Goldberg calls this 'created sense of a person' which links the writings of Bowen and Shakespeare. This 'created sense of a person' involves the immediacy and disjunctiveness of rhetorical departure, a force of speechifying which is perhaps inseparable from what – in the passage cited in an epigraph to the present chapter – Daniel George evokes as 'the extreme of colloquialism'. Shakespeare and Bowen pose an 'extreme of colloquialism', of speaking together, of speech. Colloquially speaking, Shakespeare and Bowen present persons. But what is a person?

'"Who's there?" "Nay, answer me. Stand and unfold yourself"' (I. i. 1–2): shocks of abruptness, the stony clarity of speech in the dark.

Retrolexically Bernardo's 'Who's there?' and Francisco's response ('Nay ...') prove to have been prompted by the mutual apprehensions of a ghost, to have been traversed by death and by a ghostliness of addressee (and addressor). From the opening words of *Hamlet*, as with *The Heat of the Day*, any question of identity or of an unfolding of the self is necessarily phantomized in this way by the ghostly and undecidable. Like the unfolding of a narrative, any unfolding of the self is governed by sheer kink. And this question of identity ('Who's there?') and of unfolding the self is, in Shakespeare and in Bowen, already by definition enfolded within the multiple identity of the (omniscient) dramatist-narrator. In strangely similar ways, both Shakespeare's drama and Bowen's novel entail a style of speechifying that permits rhetorical departures, a speechifying that can be defined *as* rhetorical departure. Examples are everywhere, for they are the very *manner* of Shakespearean or Bowenesque writing; but a further instance in the opening lines of Shakespeare's play would be Francisco's: ''Tis bitter cold, / And I am sick at heart' (I. i. 8–9). Francisco's words are unwanted, unprepared-for, even superfluous – but this is rhetorical departure, this spontaneous elaboration of a person, this abruptly taking off into the delirium of speechifying, the creation of a person who is 'sick at heart'.

What makes Bowenesque omniscient narration in certain respects stranger and more disruptive than the figuration of the Shakespearean dramatist is the degree to which it involves a multiplicity which is also explicitly dramatized by characters themselves in turn. Bowenesque narration involves an embodiment of multiple identity eerily miming, doubling and proliferating that of her characters. Louie Lewis's sense of being 'just one of many' is exemplary in this respect. The Bowenesque narrator is indissociable from the logic of such multiplicity. Telepathically we are given, for example, the effect on Louie Lewis of thinking of Stella Rodney's gloves:

> Louie felt herself entered by what was foreign. She exclaimed in thought, 'Oh no, I wouldn't be *her*!' at the very moment when she most nearly was. Think, now, what the air was charged with night and day. ... You did not know what you might not be tuning in to, you could not say what you might not be picking up: affected, infected you were at every turn. (247–8)

Tuning in to Louie tuning in to Stella, tuning out of Louie in to 'you', the Bowenesque narrator – inhabiting 'the air' – picks up, affects, infects at every turn. One could say that, both in *The Heat of the Day* and throughout Bowen's other novels, the generative uncertainty of where this omniscient narrator stops and starts – of tonal and pronominal border-crossings (of 'he', 'she', 'we', 'our', 'they', 'their', 'you', 'your') – constitutes the dynamic model and rhythm, the very grammar of still lives. In many ways, this structure of Bowenesque omniscient narration actually permits a greater fluidity and mobility than does the form of Shakespearean drama. The voicing of the irreducible multiplicity of self is more formally at liberty, more properly at large, in Bowen's writing. The delirious boldness of her thought or writing – thought or writing which does not belong, which is not and never could be recuperable to the singularity of a self-identical thinker or writer – takes place as a bizarre disjunctiveness, tuning in, tuning out. Taking off at every turn, rhetorical departure is mimicry in the abyss, a flight of thought or words surprising, unprepared for.

* * *

Decapitated, one might say. A notion of decapitation would apply to the senses of voice, the takings off and rhetorical departures which characterize Bowenesque narration. Decapitation could thus be seen as a governing figure – or, more precisely a governing *disfigurant* – of Bowen's writing in general. Such would be the manner whereby the works of Shakespeare and Bowen are peopled.[18] Bowen and Shakespeare: the speechifying of decapitated heads, rhetorical departures and mimicry in the abyss. Decapitated, last but not least, at the level of syntax – in reading over, or as Hamlet says, 'on the supervise, no leisure bated' (V.ii.23).

* * *

The extraordinary relationship between Louie Lewis and her friend Connie works through apparent counterpointing. Connie is the practical, pragmatic one, Louie the dreamy, even mad one. Off her head, it is Louie who, like a bird, seems 'to have no sense'. But Louie and Connie also join up, reverse roles, they are doubled and knit up. Halfway through the novel they have a conversation about a newspaper report on the migration of birds. 'Why did it put them in?' asks Louie. Connie replies:

> 'Because they do keep on doing what they always did do, I should imagine. They go to show how Nature pursues her course under any circumstances. Birds like that wouldn't notice there was a war – you might say they were lucky to have no sense. Airman complained how he got in among a pack of birds flying only the other day; decapitated, he said he shouldn't wonder if many of them were. But who's to say *I* don't get decapitated any one of

> these fine nights; and I do have sense and I do have to worry, so where does that get me?' (154)

'Decapitated, he said he …': to read over this without hesitation – in Hamlet's words 'on the supervise, no leisure bated' – is to undergo the syntactical, still-life fascination of what is elsewhere construed as the undecidable presence or absence of a comma in the phrase 'Charles I walked and talked half an hour after his head was cut off.'[19]

Connie's syntax prompts not only the 'senseless' sense of a decapitated airman speaking, but also, in her final rhetorical question, a 'senseless' sense of herself: where that does get her is, in effect, precisely decapitated. But Connie's syntax also articulates a more general sense of the importance of decapitation in writing or speaking, in reading or listening. For there *is* decapitation, in particular there is a logic of decapitation at work in all literary texts and literary criticism. Bowen's writing can be seen to engage with this at numerous levels and in various registers. In *The Heat of the Day,* decapitation would be especially appropriate to the notion of blitz-writing, as we have tried to describe it, and to a sense of the London wartime experience itself as 'heady and disembodied' (*MT* 95). More generally – both in *The Heat of the Day* and in other novels – decapitation would be a governing trope or disfigurant for the analysis of Bowenesque syntax, haunting the sense and order of every sentence: in this respect, phrases such as 'decapitated, he said he' or (in *The Little Girls*) 'an infuriated Chinese warrior's decapitated head' (27) or a statement such as 'Charles I walked and talked half an hour after his head was cut off' are merely exemplary. Again, decapitation would be a fundamental critical term for the conception and theorization of Bowenesque narration itself – that is to say, for the 'senseless' strangeness of a speaking, bodiless, omniscient narrator. Presenting persons presupposes the decapitational logic not only of tuning in then cutting off: it also engages with a recognition that personal identity itself is decisively *cut* with drama and fiction, constitutionally haunted and deranged by the 'senseless' sense of mimicry in the abyss and losing one's head. In conventional terms, decapitation offers itself, also, as a basis for a conception of the very *portrayal* of character, to the extent that the very notion of character portrayal implies the presentation of a head. In this manner we are led to what might be called the very scaffold of literary criticism, to the thought of characterization itself as a form of decapitation, as necessarily engaged with a ghostly or senseless sense of each and every character having, like Clara in *The Death of the Heart* (165), their head presented on a tray.[20] And finally, decapitation would unfold as a governing trope or disfigurant of narrative itself. Thus, in *The Heat of the Day*, it would figure, for example, the very origin of the love story of Stella and Robert, the very instant of unfolding. As we are summarily told, in Chapter 5: 'The top had been knocked off their first meeting' (96).

* * *

The configuration of aircraft, birds and decapitation to which Connie's statement refers is eerily reversed, cut and edited, knitted and knotted up in the final sentences of *The Heat of the Day*. Husbandless, parentless, heir to her own son, called Tom, Louie pushes him in the pram through the stillness and solitude of the Kent countryside:

> No other soul passed; not a sheep, even, was cropping anywhere near by. A minute or two ago our homecoming bombers, invisibly high up, had droned over: the baby had not stirred – every day she saw him growing more like Tom. But now there began another sound – she turned and looked up into the air behind her. She gathered Tom quickly out of the pram and held him up, hoping he too might see, and perhaps remember. Three swans were flying a straight flight. They passed overhead, disappearing in the direction of the west. (330)

'Remember': inscription of the impossible, the immemorial, gathering the baby 'hoping he too might see, and perhaps remember'.

Overhead, over one's head, without one's head, without sense: the decapitating, breathtaking, convulsive sense of another kind of kink – as 'A fit or paroxysm, as of laughter or coughing, that for the moment catches the breath' (*OED*). Extraordinary exhilaration, the dissolving force of the Bowen text, momentarily held up, decapitated.[21] Isn't that what a title, a heading, an ending is? *The Heat of the Day*: sheer kink. Going, flying, heading off.

6
Obelisk

> The obelisk having no approaches is taken away.
>
> (*TN* 99)

> The futility of the heated inner speed, the alternate racing to nowhere and coming to dead stops, made him guy himself.
>
> (*HD* 14)

If only YOU had been here!

Throughout this study we have sought to engage not only with a rereading of Bowen's work but also with the indissociable question of how to write about that work. In other words, how might we present the novels or still lives of Elizabeth Bowen in critically appropriate ways? What sorts of critical concepts and vocabulary do the novels themselves prompt? What kinds of critical and theoretical thinking does Bowen's work seem to call for?

A World of Love (1955) has been regarded as the most mannered of all Bowen's novels.[1] We consider it rather as, alongside *The House in Paris*, her most intense and compact. It also marks an eloquent and subtle shift in the unfolding of the Bowen *oeuvre*. In this novel, perhaps more than in any of those preceding, attention is concentrated not only on the intricate configurations of the past within the present, but also on the sense of what is dedicated, transferred, bequeathed to the future. *A World of Love* is set almost entirely in and around an Irish country house called Montefort, in the post-1945 years, during a period of extremely hot weather. It concerns the immediate family who live there – Fred and Lilia Danby and their two daughters Jane and Maud – as well as Lilia's cousin Antonia, the owner of Montefort, who is currently staying there on a visit from London.

The narrative focuses on Jane's discovering in the attics a bundle of love letters written by Guy – a man who died in the Great War, and who had been Lilia's fiancé and Antonia's beloved cousin. To whom were, or are, these letters addressed? *A World of Love* explores this question, in the first place by tracing the effects of these letters, read *or* unread, on the inhabitants of Montefort. In this way it serves to suggest how far experiences and events, people and what happens to them, are consistently and inescapably determined by forms of trans-generational haunting. The past is haunting. But the radicalism of *A World of Love* (as of other later Bowen texts) is that it presents a world haunted by a past which is unrememberable or which never existed. This haunting scenario is not confined to the lives of the inhabitants of Montefort, but explicitly concerns the question of how we should conceive the events of the twentieth century, and more generally traces the need for a theory of memory – and a conception of history – appropriate to two world wars, the Holocaust and the atomic or nuclear age. Such a conception or theory is inextricably linked to the text's presentation of love, and not least to the romantic encounter between Jane and Richard Priam with which the novel closes.

Finally, *A World of Love* both explores and embodies the effects of Guy's love letters in relation to the future and in relation to future readers, up to and even beyond ourselves. Expectant of the notion of posterity central to Bowen's next novel, *The Little Girls*, *A World of Love* elaborates the question of addressees of the future. The letters which form the dramatic heart and narrative core of *A World of Love* are almost completely absent: they are hardly quoted at all, apart from a few words and an indication that they are signed with a 'G' tied up in a quite unthinkable 'knot' (42). The novel unfolds the possible remnants of this absence, this epistolary and ghostly death of the heart. In doing so, we would suggest, it affects the world of literary criticism and literary theory in general. As we shall attempt to show, criticism and theory are themselves inscribed by what *A World of Love* presents to us: a passion of writing and writing of passion fusing in what we propose to call 'thermo-writing'; a logic of the immemorial and cryptic; a ghostly epistolarity and an unmasterable, even laughable, convulsive relation to the future; the curiosity and effacement of an obelisk.

* * *

This is the primary effect of *A World of Love*, as of other Bowen texts: to vivify and draw out the sense that there is no real, no experience, which is not fundamentally marked by otherness and fictionality. It is not a matter of suggesting that everything is 'in' a book, or that everything happens *as if* it is 'in' a book. On the contrary, *A World of Love* shows how notions of fiction, of the written or novelistic, are at work in the very constitution of the world, experience, the present, and so forth. *A World of Love* is metafictional in the strong sense: it not only draws attention to its own status and strange existence as writing, as text or fiction, but also, and more importantly, displaces, translates, transforms the very conception of the referential and 'the real'.[2] How does this happen? Everything is in play – from the title, and from the first sentence, onwards. It is the question of a world of love:

> The sun rose on a landscape still pale with the heat of the day before. There was no haze, but a sort of coppery burnish out of the air lit on flowing fields, rocks, the face of the one house and the cliff of limestone overhanging the river. The river gorge cut deep through the uplands. This light at this hour, so unfamiliar, brought into being a new world – painted, expectant, empty, intense. (9)

These opening four sentences arrest the text in the heat of the day of another novel, another world. The opening four sentences of *A World of Love* establish the uncanniness of every dawn: they insinuate the unfamiliarity of every daybreak as bringing into being 'a new world'. And this is writing which remarks *itself*, underscores the strangeness of its own existence by referring the 'real' to a labour of art and artifice ('coppery burnish', 'painted'), to the ineluctable modalities of the anthropomorphic and phantasmagoric ('pale', 'flowing', 'face', 'gorge', 'expectant'), to effects of citation and literarity. The first sentence of *A World of Love* incorporates the title of Bowen's previous novel, itself already a citation, 'the heat of the day': the writing stages the force of a certain self-remarking or self-referentiality, incorporation, encryptment or enflasking, melting and dissolution.

In attempting to render a sense of the specificity and intensity of writing in *A World of Love*, we will speak, in the present chapter, of thermo-writing. This neologism is justified by the language of the novel itself in various ways. *A World of Love* is a thermodynamic text. As with the description of the local town Clonmore, *A World of Love* could be said to generate the 'glare' and glaze of 'a picture postcard such as one might receive from Hell' (88). 'Thermo-writing' refers to heat, both to a work of enflasking and preservation, and to melting and evaporation. Bowen's novel effects a discandying and dissolution of events and identities, places and experiences, in heat. Heat is the very atmosphere and climatic condition of this text and of its reading. The atmosphere is 'spattered' with sun, of 'a brightness quite insupportable' (10). The heat seems to become 'more dreadful day after day' (12). Out of doors the buildings are 'sunstruck' and 'the heat [stands] over the land like a white-hot sword' (20).[3] Everything is 'shimmers' and 'glare' (43), 'clamped under a burning-glass' (84). Inside Montefort itself all is centred on the 'ravenous range' in the kitchen – with its 'roaring' (21) flames and 'massive heat' (121). Sometimes in highly 'peculiar' (20) ways, heat determines the inhabitants of Montefort as well. While the demonic Maud is specifically characterized by an 'overheating' (22) of her blood, her mother is the sort of person who can blithely point out to Antonia: 'I lie sleepless, sometimes, picturing you in flames' (12). More literally and intensively than any other Bowen novel, *A World of Love* appears to accord with a dictum from her 'Notes on Writing a Novel' (1945): 'There must be combustion. Plot depends for its movement on internal combustion' (*MT* 39). The very narrative of *A World of Love* is clamped to burn, in particular through 'the beginning of burning, smouldering' (40) signified by Jane's discovery of Guy's love letters up in the 'stuffy', 'baking' (27) attics. And the dissolution or evaporation of the heat in which the narrative is enveloped coincides quite precisely with the close of the novel, when rain starts falling in 'far-apart tepid drops' (148).

Above all, to speak of *A World of Love* as thermo-writing is to suggest the ways in which individual identity and experience, as well as the relations between individuals, are themselves inscribed. It is in the context of thermo-writing that we may understand not only the physical heat of the novel and the 'internal combustion' of its narrative, but also the heat of desire, love and passion. This is most crucially true in the case of Jane. It is she whose desires are specifically ignited by (Guy's) writing and who is, more generally, characterized in the language of heat. Jane's relation to the world is like that of 'someone bidden to enter an already overcrowded and overcharged room': the 'passions and politics' of the world around her, including that of her family, bear the apocalyptic sense that 'too much had been going on for too long' (34).[4] In response to this, we are told, Jane 'did what she could by adding no further heat' (35). But this is merely a mirage. What figures the necessary supplement of heat, both for Jane and for the world around her, is precisely *writing*, in the form of the inflammatory power of a bundle of love letters. Guy's letters constitute the inescapable supplement of 'further heat'. In this way they suggest the extent to which any desire or intent – here Jane's 'adding no further heat' – is subject to the uncanny and unforeseeable effects of writing.

Writing – or thermo-writing – is disruptively at work in the very conception of who we are and what happens to us. Let us spell out the implications of this as clearly as possible: *A World of Love* not only suggests that writing (in the form, above all, of Guy's letters) can determine, disrupt, metamorphose the identity of its addressee, but also works with a notion of writing which resists any kind of conventional understanding or appropriation. One way of trying to figure this strangeness of writing in *A World of Love* is by way of the notions of citation and self-remarking. Thermo-writing, then, refers also to that force of writing which generates itself out of citation and self-remarking, a capacity for citation which constantly carries writing ahead of itself. In other words, thermo-writing highlights the necessary dependence of the real or of the referent on effects of writing and citation: *A World of Love* suggests, relentlessly and unstoppably, that there is no real, no reality or experience which is not affected by a work of the 'fictitious' (58), the 'novel'-like (94) and 'theatrical' (56), by 'counterfeit notions of reality' (67) and 'the art of reviving the life-illusion' (89). But this force of dependence, the temporality of this thermo-writing or citationality, is not assimilable to any simple present. The phrase 'the heat of the day' (*WL* 9), for example, does not lead back to the book-title (or even, which is just as legitimately proposed, to the entirety of the text designated by that title) as to some simple origin: any reading of 'the heat of the day' is caught up in a work of citation and intertextuality which moves both forward and back, which is retrolexic and irreducibly generative.[5] *The Heat of the Day* cites *A World of Love*, as well as vice versa, but this forward-and-back cannot be contained by a rectilinear temporality: thermo-writing upsets it. Thermo-writing marks 'the heat of the day' – whether in the Bible, in Bowen or elsewhere – as already a citation, as conditioned by a logic of citation which itself has no simple origin or present, neither past nor future.[6] In this respect the phrase 'the heat of the day' corresponds to the aphoristic, citational and ghostly quality of desire and love figured by our opening quotation from *A World of Love*, virtually the only citation from Guy's love letters: *'If only YOU had been here!'* (48) Such an aphoristic and citational desire (the very language of desire) inscribes and traverses us. In this way thermo-writing concerns that which does not coincide with itself and which prevents us from ever coinciding with ourselves. Inscribing the power of the unremembered or unrememberable past, this writing inhabits the experience of the present and conditions every conception either of ourselves or of our relation to others; and it is drawn by the future, especially insofar as it is linked to monumentalization and preservation.

Self-remarking is again marked in the fourth sentence of *A World of Love*: 'This light at this hour, so unfamiliar, brought into being a new world – painted, expectant, empty, intense.' The reference to 'a new world' is an invocation, citation or enflasking of the title of the text, 'a world of love', and of its epigraph. Likewise the 'expectant' is already a citation. It too invokes the epigraph, the words of Thomas Traherne: 'There is in us a world of Love to somewhat, though we know not what in the world that should be. ... Do you not feel yourself drawn by the expectation and desire of some Great Thing?'[7] *A World of Love* begins in citation, at the same time as beginning by bringing into being 'a new world'. This world is neither real nor unreal, neither realistic nor unrealistic, neither novel nor un-novel, neither new nor familiar; it is self-remarking or citational in ways which are not traceable to any original, to any origin or source which would not in turn be citational. It begins (in) a world of love. There is no presentation in this text which is not next to or multiplied in itself: all the world is staged, enflasked, generated and conflagrated by a work of difference. This difference is marked – even in the opening sentences of the novel – in polymorphous and inescapably perverse ways: in citation and self-referentiality, in anthropomorphism and other forms of the putatively non-literal, in allusions to other art forms such as painting, sculpture and drama, in terms of memory and expectation. None of these, however, would terminate analysis, for each would be lit up by difference or otherness in turn.

The opening into, of and after 'a world of love' continues:

> The month was June, of a summer almost unknown; for this was a country accustomed to late wakenings, to daybreaks humid and overcast. At all times open and great with distance, the land this morning seemed to enlarge again, throwing the mountains back almost out of view in the south of Ireland's amazement at being cloudless. Out in front of the house, on a rise of rough grass, somewhat surprisingly stood an obelisk. (9)

Shadowy forms of anthropomorphism continue to be cast in this 'new world' – 'a country accustomed', 'the land ... throwing', 'Ireland's amazement', the obelisk which 'stood'. But at the same time there is no one present: the scene is eerily 'expectant' but 'empty': there is no one to be surprised at how the obelisk 'surprisingly stood'. The opening of *A World of Love* is unpeopled; it is haunted presentation, the presentation of thermo-writing.

What is the narrative perspective of such an opening? Let us leave that question to stand for a while, like an obelisk.

* * *

A World of Love generates a heat, a smouldering, a claustrophobic burning stasis, a torpidity and lassitude which is both ecstatic (beside itself) and phantasmagoric. The thermo-writing of *A World of Love* is writing beside itself, writing in which human identity, the conception of the self as single and self-identical, is set irrevocably, ecstatically, phantasmagorically adrift. In this world we don't know who we are, or when or where, it's so hot it's impossible to live in it, it's a thermal world of living on, still living but living in a kind of 'ecstasy of lassitude' (22) or trance. The thermal currents of temporality shift strangely. This is a hypnopoetics in which there is an 'almost total irrelevance of Time, in the abstract' (21). In the heat of this world, this text, it's as if we never wake up, no one wakes up, even if one passes or is 'sent on out of one deep dream into another ... more near perhaps to the waking hour' (132). Will there be a 'waking hour'? Are we awake? Or are we rather dreaming, remembering the future?

'Nerve-racking ghastly endless sublime weather! No, I can't simply live in it, can't take it. What's it meant for? Something has got to happen' (24), says Antonia. Living without living, living without being able to take it. In this ghastly endless weather, in this strange thermo-world, all the inhabitants are living without living, in a dream, other than themselves. Jane is 'like a boy-actor' who 'belong[s] to some other time' (10). She is 'all the time somewhere else', in a 'trance' (26). Her twelve-year-old sister Maud meanwhile is never not demonic, never unaccompanied by her uncanny familiar or 'dream companion' (94), the 'non-dimensional Gay David' (142). Lilia, their mother, experiences and responds to the heat of the day 'like a waxen lady with clockwork breathing' (32). She lives on, uncertain of whether she is alive or dead. Wanting to hear how she is, Antonia prompts: 'So you mean now you're dead.' To which Lilia hotly retorts: 'In this heat how can I know what I am?' (12) Like other remarks which Lilia makes, there is the uneasy evocation here of speaking 'in a dead voice' (18). 'The recognition of death', as we come to discover, 'may remain uncertain' (44).

Uncertain, uncertainty. This is what marks the writing throughout. Inscribed here, cryptically, will be the entire drama of expectation, the drama of every expectation. Uncertainty, in particular, concerning the thought of being-in-memory-of-oneself or rather being-in-memory-of-the-other, that is to say uncertainty concerning the distinctions between being alive and being dead, between living as a living death and death as a *modus vivendi*, as a mode of survival or living on. 'You're far too quick to assume that people are dead' (37), Antonia tells Jane: it is this assumption which *A World of Love* renders most vividly uncertain.

The thermal world of this novel is engendered under the roof, built up within the house called Montefort, between Antonia and Lilia, between Lilia and her husband, between these three and the younger generation, Jane and Maud. Of Lilia and Fred's marriage and their coming to live at Montefort, Antonia the owner thinks: 'something monstrous seemed to her to be under her own roof. These two engendered a climate; the air around them felt to her sultry, overintensified, strange; one could barely breathe it' (18). This rarefied world of barely breatheable air, this rarefied discourse of trancelike heat spells, beyond everything else, an uncertain concatenation of otherness, expectation and death. Shimmering, tottering, suspended, the house and its surroundings, the world of the writing itself, are caught, caked, spelt over by this concatenation. Jane goes out into the back yard:

> The slate roofs sent shimmers up; the red doors, ajar, all seemed caught by a spell in the act of opening; white outbuildings tottered there in the glare. Grass which had seeded between the cobbles parched and, dying, deadened her steps: a visible silence filled the place – long it was since anyone had been here. Slime had greenly caked in the empty trough, and the unprecedented loneliness of the afternoon looked out, as through eyelets cut in a mask, from the archways of the forsaken dovecot. Not a straw stirred, or was there to stir, in the kennel; and above her something other than clouds was missing from the uninhabited sky.

> Nothing was to be known. One was on the verge, however, possibly, of more. (43)

In the phantasmagoric world of this thermo-writing 'something other than clouds was missing from the uninhabited sky'. We would like to suggest that what is figured here is the sense of a crypt, the world as crypt, a crypt of love. As with other Bowen novels, *A World of Love* presents a world of the cryptic and ghostly. It engages the force and effects of refused or impossible mourning, the force and effects of being traced, tracked, inhabited by the dead, by the unknown presence or unreadable 'love' of the dead.

The 'central' character in *A World of Love* is, as in other Bowen texts, absent: dead. Guy – Lilia's fiancé, Antonia's first cousin and first love, Fred's 'illegitimate cousin' (15) – was one of the generation 'mown down' (44) in the First World War. It is in the figure of Guy that the work of crypts and crypt-effects is most clearly located. It is the power of Guy's erotic survival that haunts the other characters – Antonia, Lilia, but also Jane and, less directly, Fred and (most enigmatically of all perhaps) the twelve-year-old Maud. It is Guy, above all, who embodies a refusal or impossibility of mourning. By being 'mown down', killed 'so abruptly' (44), Guy provokes the intensity of a 'blasphemous incredulity' (45) in response to his death and thus seems to fail or refuse to die. Such incredulity amounts to asking oneself, '*was* dissolution possible so abruptly, unmeaningly and soon? And if not dissolution, instead, what?' (44) To Antonia, it seems 'unlike him to be killed ... unlike him to be dead': she is sure that 'he had not envisaged that' (45). In order to die, it seems, death must be envisaged, given a face, figured or thought – Guy is left in a kind of suspense, and he leaves those behind in a state of strange suspension as well: Antonia, Lilia and Fred are 'incomplete' (45). For Antonia and Lilia especially, there is a pervasive sense of what is described as 'the annihilating need left behind by Guy' (76); but Guy has not simply or properly *left*. In particular through love – through what the text calls (in the context of Guy and Lilia) 'that idealization undoomed' (14) – Guy lives on. And insofar as it also bears the 'sense of [the] unlived lives' (45) of all who were obliterated, subjected to holocaustic 'dissolution' (44) by two world wars, the haunting 'lease' (45) of the 'not-dead' Guy can be traced as a figuration of the immemorial – of what can be neither remembered nor forgotten. This immemorialism, we would suggest, is the very space of the novel, and is indissociable from a sense of its cryptic or cryptaesthetic power.[8]

The sense of Guy as living on, as not yet 'done with life', as one of 'the not-dead' (45), as a figuring of death itself as an implausible fiction or 'invented story' (44–5), undoubtedly haunts particular characters, such as Antonia and Lilia. More generally, however, it pervades the narration itself. It marks the Bowen narration as what might be called *omniscience in mourning*. To theorize the narrative perspective of the omniscient narrator in *A World of Love* entails a recognition of the essential or constitutive force of death and mourning. This is not simply a matter of mournful, lugubrious or mortally-inflected tonalities of narration, but more strangely it is a question of a sense of mourning for omniscient narration *itself* – a sense precisely of an impossible mourning, of an omniscience which marks and thereby commemorates and mourns the very impossibility of itself. No longer an omniscient narrator but rather omniscience-in-mourning: *A World of Love*, then, presents the dissolution of the figure of the omniscient narrator into a kind of narratorial crypt-effect.

Bowen's narrator, a multi-personality like any omniscient narrator, speaks a royal 'we' undecidably encrypted in a work of mourning and living on, appearing to accept death and mourning but at the same moment refusing them, appearing to refuse a world of ghosts and a language of the ghostly but (very much in the manner of Henry James's *The Turn of the Screw* or *The Jolly Corner*) by that very negation or refusal, encoding and encrypting them. The narrative 'we' (designated by 'us' and 'our') – as in the following passage – flickers in ghostly fashion between the living and the dead, between a rejection of sharing the dead's isolation and an uncertainty of being able to recognize death in the first place. This flickering is a tracing of omniscience-in-mourning:

> Obstinate rememberers of the dead seem to queer themselves or show some signs of a malady; in part they come to share the dead's isolation, which it is not in their power to break down – for *the rest of us* [our emphasis], so necessary is it to let the dead go that we expect they may be glad to be gone. ... But the recognition of death may remain uncertain, and while that is so nothing is signed and sealed. *Our* [our emphasis] sense of finality is less hard-and-fast: two wars have raised their query to it. Something has challenged the law of nature: it is hard ... not to sense the contribution of the apparently cut-off life, hard not to ask, but *was* dissolution possible so abruptly, unmeaningly and soon? And if not dissolution, instead, what? (44)

Undecidably shifting between a presentation of the thoughts of Antonia and a presentation of those of a detached narrator, this passage also shifts between a sense of 'us' and 'our' as both living and not living. Suggesting that the very identity of the narrator (however ghostly or telepathic) is not 'signed and sealed', this passage seems to challenge what it calls 'the law of nature' and to motion us towards the notion of a narratorial voice which is itself haunted both by dissolution and by a sense of the uncertain *remains* of dissolution.

The uncertainty of death, and especially that of Guy, both the uncertainty of Guy and of his death, focuses the cryptic energy of the narrative. To the extent that this is identified with a kind of secret, it is concentrated most powerfully on the moment in London, at that 'dreadful station ... full of nothing but draught and darkness and echoes – Charing Cross' (91), when Lilia says farewell to Guy for what will turn out to be the last time, and when she is shocked to discover Antonia there for the same reason, and when, finally but most mysteriously, both women are encouraged to suppose that there is yet another woman, yet another 'last-moment comer': if she came 'who was she; if not, what was she not? ... Better uncertainty; best no answer' (96), thinks Lilia. The secrecy of what is uncertain or cannot be known is focused above all on the question of the identity (or the bizarre signification of the *non*-identity or *non*-being) of the other 'last-moment comer'. But it is also suggested by the pervasive sense that Guy 'had stirred up too much' (97); and that, scattering round him an excess of promises, he leaves hauntingly unanswered or unanswerable the question: 'And if not dissolution, instead, what?'

Like the *not* of 'not dissolution' and of 'what was she not?', it is the notion of not being 'any ghost' (45) that at once haunts and dissolves our sense of Guy, dissolves and haunts the very space of reading. On the one hand, the uncertainty of Guy and the uncertain recognition of his death involves the claim – specifically made on at least two occasions (45, 77) – that Guy is not a ghost. On the other hand, it involves a sequence of events or experiences in which Guy is indeed evoked as *coming back*. Ghostlike but not a ghost, he comes back to Antonia one night as she is standing in the doorway, in a still-life moment of 'quickened stillness', when suddenly 'time again was into the clutch of herself and Guy' (77). On another occasion he comes back to Lilia in the garden: 'something more than human was at intensity. In depth, dead-still, branches screened the doorway – of whom was this the ghost in the afternoon?' (97). 'I saw Guy' (99), affirms Lilia, a little later. And finally Guy comes to Jane, the sixteen-year-old who is (as the text in various ways emphasizes) his impossible, inexistent or phantom daughter. For instance, at a dinner party at a neighbouring and 'unusually banal Irish castle' (57): 'there *had* been an entrance' (68), we are told, Guy 'was *at* the party' (69): Jane '*saw* Guy' (70). The cryptic series of hauntings which structures the narrative culminates in Jane's speculation that she 'could be a medium ... without knowing' or else that she could be 'bewitched' (120). And it makes way in turn for the summing up in Antonia's thought: Guy 'came back, through Jane, to be let go. It was high time' (135).

* * *

The cryptic structure of Bowen's text is specifically an effect of *writing* or, in the senses in which we have been describing it, thermo-writing. It is generated and determined by a 'packet of letters' (27) discovered in the 'inflammable' (40), 'baking' (27) attics, love letters written by Guy but without specific dates and without a named addressee. The contents of these letters remain more or less entirely unknown. The most extensive quotation from them comprises the undecidably commemorative and abyssally ironic words, '"*I thought" ... "if only YOU had been here!*"' (48). Still, these letters 'in' *A World of Love* create a world, the world of the text's title: a world of love is created by a discontinuous and fragmentary series of texts which, nevertheless, are most extensively cited only in order to designate the absence of any and every reader ('YOU!'). The transgenerational force of the crypt in *A World of Love* is inextricably bound up with effects of writing and textuality, with *effects* of an absence and ghostliness which correspond to the notion of the uncertain remnants of dissolution.

Guy's letters indeed determine their addressee: from the very start, for example, we are told that these letters 'found [Jane] rather than she them' (27). They are destined to find addressees in Jane, Antonia, Lilia and others in turn. 'These letters, all in the same hand, were headed by day-names only – "Tuesday", "Saturday", and so on. They had been removed from their envelopes; nothing showed where they had been written or when posted' (33). The letters, as Jane points out, 'have no beginnings ... they simply begin' (42). Beginning without beginning. Like *A World of Love*. It is a question of being a reader. It is a question of (in the words of Antonia)

'Falling in love with a love letter' (39). In other words it is a matter of identifying ourselves in fiction and as a fiction – for, as the serial effect of the narrative suggests, the letters are always capable of addressing themselves to another and thus are necessarily always destined to the other in general. As readers of *A World of Love,* we become in turn readers in a world of love, readers drawn towards the expectation of a world of love. We identify ourselves as the addressee of the love letter called *A World of Love* while at the same time recognizing that this text traverses us, addressing itself beyond us and our deaths as readers, addressing – in a ghostly, double sense – readers of the future.

What are the implications of this logic of missives? There is no identification which is not fictive. Identity is a matter of radical play. The acceptance of being the addressee, this determination of oneself as lover (in other words of oneself as loving *reader*) will have been playing – and it remains uncertain that there is anything else besides playing. Nothing can be cordoned off from the igneous if undecidable force of playing, from a cryptic sense of *playing*. Playing is a matter not only of life or death but also of life *and* death – their very illiquation. As the text suggests, querying and thereby skewing the relation between the living Jane and the dead Guy: 'which of them, dead man and living girl, had been the player, and which the played-with?' (119). Engaged and determined by Guy's letters, Jane is the 'medium' through which the crypt or phantom-effect of Guy is transmitted. In these terms we are invited to suppose that the cryptic force figured by 'Guy' is finally 'to be let go' by what is signified in the extraordinary last seven words of the text, which describe the meeting of two strangers, Jane Danby and Richard Priam, at Shannon airport: 'They no sooner looked but they loved' (149). But the romantic, eerie force of this love-at-first-sight is also to declare the very absence of such 'first sight': it is only to the extent that Jane is determined by the crypt of Guy, it is only on the basis of a crypt, it is only on the basis of the fictionality, citationality and radical play of missives, that there is love.[9]

* * *

It may not come as a surprise, then, that we should wish to stress that this ending, like other endings of Bowen novels, is not really an ending at all. 'There is in us a world of Love to somewhat, though we know not what in the world that should be': this world is a crypt-effect, but one which is specifically oriented towards the future. It is a question of the sense of 'expectation' evoked in the epigraph, in what we might describe as that highly Wordsworthian passage of Traherne: 'There is in us a world of Love to somewhat, though we know not what in the world that should be. ... Do you not feel yourself drawn by the expectation and desire of some Great Thing?'[10] What makes the novel's exploration of a crypt-structure or crypt-effect so astonishing is that it is concerned not only with crypts as buried *history* (however secret, uncertain or unspeakable) but also with what can be called crypts of the future, not only with a haunting by the past and the dead but also with a haunting by expectation and what is yet to be.

Insofar as Guy figures a ghost, for example, this is a ghost not only of the past but also of the future. Thus we read the thoughts of Lilia in the haunted garden: Guy 'had not finished with them, nor they with themselves, nor they with each other: not memories was it but *expectations* which haunted Montefort' (97; our emphasis). It is the haunting expectation, for example, of what 'grew like a danger' (54) in Jane, shortly before she receives her invitation to dinner at the castle. It is the haunting expectation of what '*was* about to take place' (102), as Lilia puts it on another occasion, sitting 'as white as a ghost' (98), in the ghostly garden. In referring to the idea that 'one's lookings-forward are really memories' (147), to a kind of impossible space of 'remembering the future', the text remarks its own structure as a missive and as a strange performative. There is much in this narrative to do with presentiment and premonition, with expectation, with something great that is about to happen. There is much to do with the notion of being called or summoned. Jane, for example, just before finding the letters, 'imagined she heard a call': it is 'that inexplicable feeling of being summoned' (27). And there is the 'unlocatable' 'call or calling' (77) which Antonia hears, when standing in the doorway.

This is not simply superstition (though that there is no such thing as 'simply superstition' is in part the critical power and conceptual rigour of Bowen's, as of George Eliot's or Henry James's, thought): it is also a figuration of the novel itself. Expectations are *realized* within the text. Guy's love letters determine – they 'prove' the capacity for texts to create – their addressees. In this instance or example, then, *A World of Love* describes and inscribes its own potentiality as a call, as a love letter and as a performative. This, however, would only be on condition of recognizing that its call is a call from the immemorial, from what is absolutely other, from an otherness which calls and traverses it, that *A World of Love* never arrives at its destination, that its arrival and its reading is always to come. The novel thus suggests that love itself is constitutively linked to the future: a world of love is a world of the immemorial, the very opening of the future.

'If only YOU had been here!': these words are consigned to flames. The thermo-writing of *A World of Love* is finally figured in the burning of those letters out of which its narrative is generated. The fact that, in the Montefort servant Kathie's words, 'Fire's the finish' (122) suggests that any reading of this novel is an encounter both with dissolution and with the uncertain remains of dissolution.[11] In the destruction or dissolution of Guy's letters the novel can be seen to present a mise-en-abyme of its own dissolution. In this way *A World of Love* addresses itself to a reading of the uncertain vestiges of dissolution. These vestiges – which are cryptic, fictive, futuristic – can only become thinkable with the dissolution of the novel.

* * *

P.S. Still there? The immemorialism of an obelisk. Lilia remarks, for the benefit of Harris the chauffeur, who has been admiring it:

> 'I wish I could remember its origin – surely it must have had one, didn't it, Fred?'
>
> 'Chap put it up in memory of himself,' said he, with a glance at the thing, for the first time struck by it.
>
> 'What, while he was still alive?' marvelled Lilia. 'Rather peculiar, surely? What was his name?'
>
> 'Couldn't tell you.' (137)

'I wish I could remember....' The very insistence on the necessity of an origin for the obelisk signals not only uncertainty, the sense of something doubtful or spurious, but also the uncanniness of an obelisk *without* origin, the thought of an originless or pre-originary obelisk.

The text goes on to suggest that Antonia, at least, knows the name of the person who had the obelisk put up; but this name is never supplied by the text. The obelisk, figuring both dissolution and the uncertain remains of dissolution, remains anonymous.

The reality of the obelisk, like an 'enlarged photograph' (132) of itself.

What is an obelisk? For example, what is the obelisk of *A World of Love*, the obelisk of its omniscient narrator, the obelisk of 'Elizabeth Bowen'?

÷

Obelisk

1. A tapering shaft or column of stone, square or rectangular in section, and usually monolithic and finished with a pyramidal apex. ...
2. A straight horizontal stroke, either simple (–), or with a dot above and one below (÷), used in ancient manuscripts to point out a spurious, corrupt, doubtful, or superfluous word or passage ...

(*OED*).

÷

What if the obelisk, the word 'obelisk', is itself an obelisk – spurious, corrupt, doubtful, superfluous? Can there be reading without an obelisk?

Of course it is possible to identify apparent obelisks in the text, such as the curious reference to 'Guy David's Hole' (46)[12] – where 'Guy' has, seemingly, stepped in for 'Gay', in other words substituted for the name of Maud Danby's demonic 'familiar', Gay David. As an obelisk, what might it *not* signify? Does this obeliskine confusion of Guy and Gay David not point, in obeliskine fashion, to a certain relationship between the two, however arbitrary or cryptic?

But what if 'Guy' were itself, even before this determination, an obelisk? The laughable phallus or laughable obelisk of 'Guy': 'guy' as 'man' or 'odd figure'; 'guy' as what is 'used to steady anything, or hold it in position'; and 'guy', finally, as 'a joke' (*Chambers*). In which case, perhaps, as Jane at one point supposes, his letters never existed but were (like thermo-writing) – before ever being present or possessed – 'stolen away by evaporation' (119).

As real as a fictional photograph or letter, there is this obelisk. Cold stone, a deathly monument. Deathly, but also a basis for the sense of some 'terrible joke' (124) – enough to cause us, like Kathie, to rip our arms apart in laughter, to be convulsed in laughter, to vomit laughter. Laughter that is 'mortified', 'tormenting', 'teasing' (124).

But where would we stop? In other words, how should we read 'obelisk'? This, you may remember, is what first catches the eye: Jane's apprehension gathered, like an obelisk,

> into a peak: the inner course of her life was about to change, and the cause was somewhere in the room. ... Her nerves, tuned up by the hot night, waited, though not in fear. What was to happen? She began to undress, looking around her, partly expectant and partly docile – there *were* the letters, on the top of her desk. She went across and stood weighing them in her hand, distantly wondering – how much had shrivelled to this little? Then the word 'obelisk' caught her eye. (33–4)

7

Trance

> Bowen characters are in transit *consciously.*
>
> (*MT* 286)

> What makes the 'miracle' of reading ... even more singular is that here the stone and the tomb not only contain a cadaverous emptiness that must be animated, but they also constitute the presence – hidden though it is – of what must appear.[1]

The Little Girls (1963) presents Bowen's most sustained, most hilarious and devastating analysis of the work of the past on people's lives: the transition of the past into the present. But it also concerns posterity, 'those coming after' or 'succeeding generations' (*Chambers*), and the attempt by the living to live among them. It concerns the attempt by the living, the transitory, to live on after their own deaths, to remain in their remains, to be left, after their leaving, in what is left of them. *The Little Girls* moves on from *A World of Love* with its concerns about the uncertain remains of dissolution, and focuses more specifically on what is involved in this attempt to live on.

Three women in their late fifties or early sixties – Dinah Delacroix, Clare Burkin-Jones and Sheila Artworth (aka Dicey, Mumbo and Sheikie) – meet for the first time since their schoolgirl friendship ended, at the beginning of the First World War. They meet, at Dinah's instigation, to find and exhume (163) a coffer which they had, as schoolgirls, filled with mementoes and buried in the grounds of their school to await posterity. As with a number of Bowen's earlier novels, the narrative is divided into three parts. Part I involves the successful attempt by Dinah to find or disinter her two schoolfriends after almost fifty years. Dinah, by now, has been married and widowed, and has two grown-up sons. Clare, once briefly married to 'Mr Wrong', is now single and a successful businesswoman, the owner of a chain of novelty gift shops called 'Mopsie Pye'. Sheila has married into a prominent family of estate agents in Southstone, on the south coast of England. (Bowen's consistent fascination with houses appears, as it will do again in *Eva Trout*, in the figure of the estate-agent, or here the estate-agent's wife). Part II returns to the summer of 1914, and the three friends' final term together at school in Southstone before the summer break and dispersal following the start of the First World War. This section concerns the little girls' burial of the coffer containing mementoes, together with a letter written to posterity in what is comically known as 'Unknown Language'. Part III returns to the present and focuses on the exhumation of the coffer: 'We are posterity, now' (63), as Dinah earlier puts it. They locate the coffer only to find it empty, however, after which Dinah suffers a physical and emotional collapse, leaving her 'unlivingly still', struck down by a 'sickness' of 'indifference' (199). Across this narrative is woven an intricate, intensive study of the disinterment and transience of the past. More radically, though, the novel investigates the foundations of the past and of temporality *per se*: it investigates *going*, the very possibility of transition, movement in terms of what we propose to call trance.[2] In this chapter, we shall begin to translate conventional senses of trance as a 'dazed, abstracted, ecstatic or exalted state' (*Chambers*), a form of catalepsy or 'interior quietness', into forms of reading, forms of posterity. Trance signifies both a condition of reading and the entrancing movements into and away from that condition; the condition of posterity and the uncanny mobilities of temporality and being which posterity entails.

* * *

The Little Girls, we can begin by suggesting, is a transitional novel, a novel at once transitory and in transit. It seems to involve a movement away from earlier work and to lead towards Bowen's final great novel, *Eva Trout*. But to describe *The Little Girls* as transitional, as transitory or ephemeral, would seem to conform to the judgements and evaluations of what we have characterized at various points in this study as conventional Bowen criticism. *The Little Girls* has often been read as Bowen's most achieved failure. Hermione Lee, for example, is particularly scathing, and provides an exemplary statement of the case against the novel:

> Such 'meaning' as there is appears in fragmentary and diffused form and is presented in a manner which is without depth or res-

> onance. Not only does the novel record an unlikely and whimsical situation, which is dressed up with awkward attempts at comedy, uneasy ventures into symbolism and contrived literary allusions ... but it also feels dubious and illusive. Elizabeth Bowen has decided, at this point, to forgo the controlled, elaborate commentary and the sharp, minute, inward presentation of character which her novels displayed. This narrative has, from the start, a provisional, indeterminate air.[3]

Lee's comments, representative and accurate in their own terms, should be read through the extraordinary and peculiar texture of Bowen's prose in *The Little Girls*. We would like to suggest not only that *The Little Girls* contains many reading pleasures, but also that it represents a powerful engagement with those questions of reading, of identity and the dissolution of the novel, with which the present study is concerned. *The Little Girls* indeed challenges precisely the kinds of assumptions which lie behind Lee's negative appraisal of the novel's 'fragmentary and diffused form', its 'unlikely and whimsical situation', its awkwardness and uneasiness, its 'contrived literary allusions', its feeling of being 'dubious and illusive', its 'provisional, indeterminate air'. The accuracy of such descriptions depends upon an entire conceptual edifice of critical, aesthetic and ideological presuppositions which *The Little Girls* itself places in abeyance.

The question of the transitional nature of *The Little Girls* is bound up, above all, with the question of its being 'dated' and thus transitory or ephemeral. Part of the reason for the limited critical interest in the novels of Elizabeth Bowen in the twenty years since her death, their marginal position in the institutions of literature and criticism, is their apparent susceptibility to precisely this charge. And no novel by Bowen seems so dated, so out of date, so temporally recursive and so stuck in its time, as *The Little Girls*. To suggest that a novel is 'dated' is to suggest that it is transitory because its discursive strategies are fixed within the parameters of a certain historical period – here the early sixties: it is to suggest that the novel is transitory because it does not translate to later times. An account of *The Little Girls* as dated might point to all the ephemeral bric-à-brac collected in the novel, the sheer transience of the objects of mass culture to which it refers: it is a novel about the collection of such objects. The novel as novelty – and like the contents of novelty gift shops, the contents of such novels carry with them a weight of pathos generated by their built-in redundancy, or designed obsolescence.[4] *The Little Girls*, we would argue, is indeed transitory, transient, dated, but more than this it presents a powerful exhumation of the presuppositions inhabiting these terms. Thus *The Little Girls* explores what Dinah calls 'the prefabricated feeling racket'. It explores the ways in which the 'complications' attached to, for example, sex and love, are dated. As Dinah says, 'so many of these fanciful ways people have of keeping themselves going, at such endless expense of time and money, seem not only unnecessary but dated' (168). In a disruptive but characteristic way the novel here, then, inscribes the notion of what is dated precisely in terms of what is happening now, of how people 'keep themselves going'. It suggests the extent to which – for the world of Bowen's penultimate novel – the present itself is already 'dated'. *The Little Girls* is about the transitory nature of novels – about how in some sense they are anything but still lives. It is about novels as language in transit and about trance and entrancement, the transitions and what we shall call the 'revenants' of reading.[5]

The Little Girls is concerned with the disinterment of the past, as well as with burying things for the future. It is also a transitional novel in specifically intertextual terms: it involves the burial of words to be exhumed by *Eva Trout*. *The Little Girls* 'contains', for example, not only the subtitle to *Eva Trout* ('changing scenes' [113])[6] but also, and more curiously, 'a gun' buried in a coffer to await posterity. When the little girls' coffer is disinterred, it is found to be empty: the gun has disappeared. It reappears, however, in *Eva Trout*, as the gun with which Jeremy kills his mother.[7] This is another instance of the curious Bowenesque movements forward and back between novels that we have noted before – the strange intertextual, even prefabricated imbrications of these novels, their elaboration within a logic of transition and trance.

* * *

The climax to the narrative of *The Little Girls*, then, is the anticlimax – the unearthing of the buried coffer only to find it empty. Fifty years earlier, the girls had buried it 'for posterity'. Dinah has unknowingly built her life on the possibility of an ultimate return – in posterity – to the past or an ultimate return *of* the past, the past as ghost or revenant, and this discovery of a void in the past results, eventually, in her collapse. She becomes a kind of living corpse, 'unlivingly still' (199). She becomes a physical simulacrum of posterity, at the same time as suggesting that posterity is itself a simulacrum of life. Posterity involves the notion of living on, the illusion that what is living might be immortal, that what is dead is somehow alive. The coffer which the girls bury is specifically designed to allow for an encryptment of their still living or still lives, to allow posterity to 'know' their lives (not their deaths). Finding the coffer to be empty, with the consequence that both the past and her notion of posterity is illusory, Dinah supplements her own body for posterity. Still life, in *The Little Girls*, is living in posterity, posthumous living, the life of the dead or the inhabitation of the living by the dead.

The specificity of posterity in *The Little Girls* concerns its inflection of the relationship between posterity and reading. That is to say *The Little Girls* offers a theory of the novel in terms of its reception in posterity. It inscribes itself for and within posterity, as transitory, ephemeral. It is concerned with the impossible transitions of death into life and life into immortality, the impossible transitions of posterity. In this reading, posterity opens up the coffer of *The Little Girls*, with all its hoarded remains, its mementoes, secret mascots, its bric-à-brac and unreadable language – its letters 'to' posterity – only to find it empty. And to find a novel empty is to find it unreadable, like the letter deposited in the coffer written in blood and in Unknown Language, or like another letter, also in Unknown Language, from Clare to her father, which arrives too late, after his death.[8] Unknown Language is designed to remain unknown, not only now, but for ever. Indeed, it would be simpler if, as one of the little girls suggests, 'by then' – by the time of the arrival of posterity – 'They may have no language' (117). The letter written by Clare in Unknown Language and buried in the coffer has no addressee and will never be read. And her other letter in Unknown Language arrives too late. Clare's letter to her father is written in the language of posterity: it is both unreadable in the present, and indeed the time of its reading is indefinitely deferred. To write a letter in the language of posterity is to write a letter ostensibly resisting the very possibility of posterity, resisting any reading in the future by those coming after.

One final configuration of posterity is suggested by the two books that Dinah takes with her when she goes to meet Clare for the first time in fifty years: *In Memoriam* and *The Midwich Cuckoos* (45). Showing an ironic but exuberant disregard for Tennysonian pathos, Dinah goes to meet Clare in memory of their friendship, in memory of the little girls that they were and that have died. But she also goes in order to exhume those little girls, to animate the parasitic past within the present. *The Midwich Cuckoos*, John Wyndham's 1957 novel about the inhabitation of children by aliens, is later given to Frank, Dinah's friend, who has just become a grandfather and who is already nervous about children. Frank has a 'conspiracy complex', believing that 'some terrible Hostile Race ... is at any moment going to begin to be born' (196–7).[9] The thoughtless but appropriate gift in turn gives us a sense of the haunting power of children in *The Little Girls*: children are not only (as so often in Bowen) terrifying simulacra of adults, but also alien inhabitations by the past, ghostly and disruptive transitions. Even more than in *The House in Paris* and *The Death of the Heart*, children in *The Little Girls* are aliens, people in transit. What makes the aliens so frightening and powerful in *The Midwich Cuckoos* is the fact that they are indistinguishable from children: they are children. On the one hand, *The Little Girls* suggests that we are all potentially inhabited by these terrifying aliens – by ourselves as children, our past as children. On the other hand it suggests that, while they cannot be forgotten, these alien identities cannot be returned to, and cannot return. The children by whom we are inhabited and haunted are immemorial.

* * *

Within the collapse of the past, the bathetic exhumation of the buried coffer, both posterity and the very possibility of the future collapse. For Dinah, the empty coffer means that she is homeless, that her home has 'run away': 'Everything has. *Now* it has, you see. Nothing's real any more. ... We saw there was nothing *there*. So, where am I now?' (163).[10] The disclosure of the emptiness of the coffer does not simply suggest an allegory of the emptiness of the 'past'. Rather, it suggests the dissolution of posterity, which is to say the dissolution of reading: the text appears as a ghost of reading within a scenario of dissolution and unreadability. The emptiness of the box figures the final emptiness, the illusion, of the past's hold on the present, the dissolution of any assurance of any future that might guarantee a present.

To acknowledge the void of the past is to acknowledge that the past is a question of reading or, to be more accurate, of rereading, retrolexia, revenance. If there is no possibility of 'going back' to the past, if there is only what George Orwell in *Nineteen Eighty-four* calls 'an endless present',[11] and therefore no past, no history, only an eternally suspended present, anamnesis, then to 'have' a memory is a matter of constant rereading. *The Little Girls* evokes this notion of double reading in Part II of the novel. In particular, its final pages both present and provoke a double reading of the relationship between Clare's father, Major Burkin-Jones, and Dinah's mother, Mrs Piggott. During a beach party given to celebrate the birthday of one of Dinah's school friends, Burkin-Jones comes to say goodbye to Mrs Piggott: he is leaving for the war in which he will die. Through a series of glances and gestures, unspoken endearments and intangible inflections, the two adults express the extent of their desire and despair. Dinah, present at this parting, can hardly guess at the intimacies of the scene, but her (re)actions nevertheless register the mobilities of desire:

> Still not far away from them he had stopped, turned and was standing. They saw him. He saw them, calmly and with great clarity. Was there more he wanted, could there be anything else? Mrs Piggott, though moving no more than he did, may have sent some wordless inquiry. He said: 'Just good-bye.' His eyes rested on their alike faces. 'God bless you,' he said to them – turned, and this time was gone.
>
> 'Mother?'
>
> 'Yes?'
>
> 'Why did he say that? He said –'
>
> 'I know, darling.'
>
> 'What made him? He –'
>
> 'I don't know, darling.'
>
> 'He never –'
>
> 'Oh, Dicey – *Dicey*!'
>
> So the child fell silent, sometimes rubbing her cheek slowly against the tussore of the coat sleeve, sometimes rolling her face round against it and breathing into it, with a low loving continuous snuffling sound. Where the warmth of the breath made its way through the stuff moisture remained. (132)

Although Dinah cannot 'know', cannot read, the meanings of adult words and gestures, her body registers the force of this intimate exchange. The auto-affective intimacies and polymorphous sensualities of this little girl – wrapping herself in her own breath and warmth, rubbing and rolling, lovingly snuffling – interpret the inarticulate language of adult desire. Dinah, then, is 'reading' the scene of an illicit love through her body. If Dinah effects a double reading of the scene, she also provides a model of reading. We can hardly guess at the intimacies involved, and nowhere is this affair made explicit or its significance explicated. Instead, we must sense, through, if necessary, our reading bodies (our stilled lives, our trance), the untold reverberations, the nuances and infinitesimal torsions of the scene. And just as the cognitive occlusions of childhood – the equivocal ignorances explored by Bowen in all of her novels – produce meanings deferred and disseminated throughout a life, the childhood section of *The Little Girls* (Part II) resonates soundlessly but resoundingly as it is continuously reread, through Parts I and III. Reading, in *The Little Girls*, then, is double both in the sense of necessitating retrolexia or revenance and in the sense of engaging a dissolution of the Cartesian duality of mind and body.

But what might it mean to read with one's body? To read, we can say, is to be 'in' a book, 'in' a novel. The most explicit scene of reading in *The Little Girls* appears in Part II when Dinah's mother, Mrs Piggott, is reading a novel in the presence of Clare: 'To disturb Mrs Piggott once she was *in* a novel', we learn, 'was known to be more or less impossible'. This is not least because in reading Mrs Piggott takes on the properties of a human simulacrum:

> But for the periodic flicker as she turned a page, Mrs Piggott, diagonal on the sofa, might have been a waxwork. Clare, at a halt with the puzzle, took a contemplative look at her through the curtains. The scarlet, brand-new novel, held up, masked its wholly-commanded reader's face. Though nominally she was 'lying' on the sofa, the upper part of the body of Mrs Piggott was all but vertical, thanks to cushions – her attitude being one of startled attention, sustained rapture and, in a way, devotion to duty. The more flowing remainder of her *was* horizontal: feet, crossed at the ankles, pointing up at the end. She was as oblivious of all parts of her person as she was of herself. As for her surroundings, they were nowhere. Feverel Cottage, the sofa, the time of day not merely did not exist for Mrs Piggott, they did *not* exist. This gave Clare, as part of them, an annihilated feeling. She burned with envy of anything's having the power to make *this* happen. Oh, to be as destructive as a story! (78)

Stories both destroy and create people. Mrs Piggott is 'oblivious', in a trance, in a novel and entranced by it. She is in a state of 'sustained rapture': both her person and her 'self' are consigned to oblivion. Bowen's precise delineation of the figure of reading, the figuration of the reader, the figure of the reader *in* a novel, *in* reading, points up the significance of the body, from head to feet, in reading. It furnishes the basis for a Bowenesque somatics of reading. Put simply, we can say that to read is to be figured both in and by a novel. But the fictionality or 'lying' of the reader in this description, her immobile figuration as a waxwork, a representation of a person, suggests in turn an uncanny figuration of ourselves as readers. To read is to put on a mask: the novel masks the person. This figure of the mask in reading – 'The scarlet, brand-new novel, held up, masked its wholly-commanded reader's face' – is repeated when Clare reads out the letter written in 'Unknown Language': 'The reader's mask was reflected, monkish, over the lit scroll' (116). A reader becomes a person precisely through this inhabitation of the mask. A person, as its Latin etymology (*persona*) suggests, is a mask. The identity of the subject is the simulacrum of a figure over the face, like a book masking the reader reading. By becoming entranced by a book, being *in* a novel, Mrs Piggott annihilates the world, but constitutes herself as a person, a mask.[12] And to be a person is inseparable from being oblivious of one's person, to be a person is inseparable from oblivion: in reading, Mrs Piggott 'was oblivious of all parts of her person as she was of herself'.

* * *

To suggest that the past has to be read, that it is a construction of reading, is not to say that the present is in any sense more 'real'. As we have tried to suggest in a number of ways throughout this study, Bowen's writing ceaselessly defers, departs from, displaces the presence of the present. Any notion of the present in *The Little Girls* is inextricably bound up with trance. Parts I and III both open with descriptions of entrancement. These openings not only emphasize the trance of the present, its constitutive displacement or transition, but also indicate important parallels between shopping for 'prefabricated feelings', and the collection and burial of such things. Indeed, part of the force of *The Little Girls* is to suggest that a person is constructed, a face made, by collections of arbitrarily chosen, but 'symbolic', objects.[13] *The Little Girls* fabricates dissolutions of time, in particular through its complex representations of bric-à-brac. Bric-à-brac clutters, lines, crowds the novel: *The Little Girls* is a work of bric-à-brac. One of the characteristic rhetorical strategies of the novel is the inventory or list. Examples would include the contents of Dinah's garden (17), the china of Mrs Piggott's drawing-room (76–7), the contents of a second-hand shop called 'Curios' (100), the free samples collected by Sheila (108), etc. It might be appropriate to draw up an arbitrary, disordered and incomplete inventory or *bricolage* of bric-à-brac in the novel, a kind of meta-bric-à-brac list or conceptual shopping list for *The Little Girls*: on the next page the reader will find a novel shopping list which can be used for browsing through the confused store of words, phrases, and sentences of the novel in search of a bargain or the truly *useful* buy.[14]

Linked to such ubiquity of bric-à-brac is the notion of prefabrication. Both concern identities – whether it be the identity of coffers or gift shops, memories or lives – as made up out of objects which originate elsewhere. Most powerfully and explicitly, *The Little Girls* presents a critique of personal identity, of a person, in terms of prefabrication: 'what anyone thinks they feel', says Dinah after finding the coffer empty, 'is sheer fabrication' (167). This fabrication, we then learn, is in fact prefabrication:

> People are glad to feel anything that's already been fabricated for them *to* feel, haven't you noticed? And those things have been fabricated for them by people who in the first place fabricated them for themselves. There's a tremendous market for prefabricated feelings: customers simply can't snap them up fast enough. They feel they carry some guarantee. Nothing's so fishy to most people as any kind of feeling they've never heard of. (167)

Coffers, novelty gift shops, novels, but also minds, memories, are cluttered with objects designed to generate 'feelings'. And Dinah's demystification of consumer society presents the paradox of the postmodern simulacrum: in postmodernism, the simulacrum is only ever the copy of a copy.[15] There is an indefinite deferral back to a past which is empty, like a coffer. Fabricated objects, and the feelings that they produce, are always already copies, prefabrications.

Part I of *The Little Girls* opens in the cave in which Dinah is preparing to entomb, with the help of Frank, the symbolic possessions of her friends and neighbours for posterity. Dinah, in a trance, is unknowingly repeating her girlhood entombment for posterity:

Novel Shopping-list: Cut out and Keep

Bric-à-brac in *The Little Girls*

(1) A collection of possessions left for posterity

(2) The contents of Clare's novelty gift shops

(3) The china bowls, figures, etc., which clutter Mrs Piggott's sitting-room and later Dinah's bedroom

(4) The cluttered coffer of consciousness, thoughts, emotions, memories

(5) The various idiosyncrasies which make up a person or personality

(6) A cluttered world in which the living have to make space for themselves amongst the clutter of the dead*

(7) The past

(8) Cultural artifacts

(9) The contents of novels

(10) Language

* Phonetically, of course, the coffer is overdetermined as coffin, a tomb. (See 158, 234 on the coffer as a tomb.) Indeed, from the first, burial of the dead has been suggested: when Dinah tells Frank that she has a 'predisposition to bury things,' he replies 'Not me, I hope' (22). Parallels between, for example, the coffer and novelty gift shops (see 139, where Clare 'mines' objects from a box), or between cluttered rooms and cluttered lives (see 145), are suggested repeatedly in *The Little Girls*. And the homology of the novelty gift shop and the novel can hardly go unnoticed.

> Across the uneven rock floor, facing the steps, was either a shallow cave or a deep recess – or, possibly, unadorned grotto? – now fronted by looped-back tarpaulin curtains. Within were trestles, across which boards had been placed; and a woman, intent on what she was doing to the point of trance, could be seen in back-view, moving her hands about among the objects crowding the rough table. (9)

This tranced state, a state in which the subject is taken outside herself, is produced by the eerie power of objects. Objects in Bowen's novels function in shifting and unstable ways. In *The Little Girls*, they function, above all, as displaced simulacra of life: they live on for us in posterity, representing our idiosyncrasies, idiosyncrasies which themselves make up our identities.[16] In representing our lives for posterity, objects make up our lives: not only do they represent the idiosyncrasies which constitute our identities, but in some sense they *are* those identities. At the same time and by the same token, they also entrance the subject, set the subject beside itself.

The grotto at the beginning of the novel returns, as 'Blue Grotto', the name of the house built on the grounds of the garden in which the first coffer was buried – the prefabricated name of a prefabricated house. But it also returns, implicitly, at the opening to Part III. The descriptions which introduce the narrative present (that is, the contemporary setting of Parts I and III) are like entrances to grottos, crypts, entrancements leading to caves full of collections of objects which produce feelings. Novels are like grottos full of the nicknacks to be found in novelty gift shops,[17] or like caves (or coffers) full of countless arbitrarily chosen objects, each one 'symbolic' of someone's prefabricated emotions, left for posterity, for reading. Deceptively compact on the outside, novels are entrances designed to entrance, like the entrance to Clare's novelty gift shop at the beginning of Part III:

> The length no less than the glitter of the perspective made the shop surprising to enter, after the smallness (stylish though that had been rendered) of the street-frontage. ... The wares were some grouped, some spread, in measured profusion. Some dangled, even, a little above the eye, and were a-twirl, at the moment, in the current of air from the door. Nor was any of this in vain. When Dinah entered, five or six gazing persons were moving

> about in a tranced state which looked like culminating in buying. (137)

The twin entrances to Parts I and III of *The Little Girls* suggest that reading is indissociable from a hypnotic fascination of objects: they are at once introductions and entrancements. Reading is being entranced – both entered and transported, taken out of oneself.[18] This suggests a crucial equivocation, an equivocation which we have suggested earlier, in our reading of the threshold of *The Death of the Heart*: readers enter books only to be entered by them. As we enter the novel and enter its present, we are entranced by the profuse and glittering bric-à-brac of prefabricated emotions that meet our eyes. We open a book as we might enter Clare's shop, to find it larger than it looks on the outside, full of entrancing objects, unstable and floating, a-twirl from the breath of air which reading produces in its entrance, its trance.

* * *

Nowhere is *The Little Girls* so unstable, so transitional and intriguingly ephemeral as in its naming, its designating of persons. It is here, most of all, that the novel threatens mannerism and what Hermione Lee calls 'whimsy'. This is not only due to the inclusion of childish nicknames – Dicey, Mumbo, Sheikie – but, more importantly, because of a pervasive anxiety of naming. To discriminate between the three women/little girls themselves, for example, the text repeatedly picks up an epithet from the preceding dialogue or from the surrounding situation. Thus we have designations such as 'she who thought she hated to wait' (Dinah; 44–5), 'the lovely dancer' (Sheila; 93), 'the joke's maker' (Clare; 111), 'the frivolous one' (Dinah; 139), 'the about-to-depart one' (Clare; 176), 'the miserable one' (Dinah; 179), 'the unsubdued one' (Dinah; 211). Other disconcerting denominations include, for example, that of a minor character, Mrs Coral, whose granddaughter is named Coralie, and whose name seems to be echoed in the first pages of the novel where 'corollas' (17) are mentioned and where Dinah gives Mrs Coral a rose called a 'Caroline Testout' (18). Similarly, there is an undecidably motivated economy of naming in Dinah's friend Frank (Major Wilkins), and Dinah's houseboy Francis. And given the intrinsic diciness of names, their proximity to mumbo-jumbo, no designation in the novel is as frankly ephemeral or shaky as that of Sheila's married name, Artworth.[19]

The climactic, indeed apocalyptic moment of *The Little Girls* is itself an encrypted drama of naming. It occurs when the three women, Dinah, Clare and Sheila, go to dig up their coffer: 'we are posterity now', Dinah has told the others, and so they go to disinter the past. The coffer, buried in the grounds of their school fifty years earlier, is now in the grounds of a private house. At the moment that the women unbury the coffer and find it empty, the owner of the house turns on some lights and 'render[s] apocalyptic' this moment of uncovering (158).[20] As the owner comes out to investigate the disturbance in his garden, Dinah goes forward to meet him, introduces herself and points to her two friends: 'She invited his attention into the thicket, in which her friends rather oddly stood like a non-matching pair of caryatids in transit' (159). This second showing-forth – a showing-forth in which identities remain hidden – is itself revealingly in transit. The reference to the caryatid recalls, without quite matching, Matchett in the closing pages of *The Death of the Heart* (*DH* 312). As architectural figures of women used as columns to support a frieze or entablature, these caryatids are ironic supplements or parerga to the prefabricated architecture of the house which has been built on the grounds of the school, and to its garden furniture: 'As the garden descended, a statuette of Pan or some unknown faun, a white scrolled Regency garden seat and a shell-shaped bird-bath floated one after another on the illuminated darkness' (158). The two women become postmodern classical kitsch – stranded out of context, like the objects left for posterity in the girls' coffer, clues to be deciphered, letters written in Unknown Language. That the caryatids – Clare and Sheila – are *in transit* suggests that they have been caught momentarily, instantaneously, in motion, but also that they are out of place here, like the Regency seat and Pan, on their way across or through, but not belonging to this place or time. Clare and Sheila: the non-matching caryatids of still lives.

But these caryatids have other reverberations, further linguistic depths – as if, with the empty coffer, *The Little Girls* is offering reading an alternative hoard, a word-hoard to be disinterred from the coffin of 'dead' language. Caryatid is from the Greek καρυάτιδες, the priestesses of Artemis at Καρύαι. The Latin name for Artemis is Diana. The caryatids, Clare and Sheila, are votives of Dinah, who changed her name from Diana.[21] Concealed within the phrase 'caryatids in transit', then, is a specific invocation of Clare and Sheila as

Dinah's votives, and this allegorizing of people, this figuring of people as figures, statues, should, by now, be no surprise to us. The apocalyptic figuration of people as statues reveals nothing. In place of the contents of the coffer, then, what we find, once we disinter 'caryatids in transit', what is revealed by the apocalyptic light thrown on the scene, is not so much a name, as an irreducibly proliferating network of naming. The language of *The Little Girls* is not simply, like the coffer, empty. Rather it is empty in another sense, in the sense of a tautology that never stops differing: what we find when we dig up *The Little Girls* is a strictly uncontainable series of words. 'Inside' the novel, buried within the words, within the innermost coffer, is the name 'Dinah' – in transit. This would be the trance of the novel and the dissolution of reading. The solution of reading would be a dissolution of naming. But in claiming that the secret of *The Little Girls*, what is buried in its centre, its so-called 'meaning', is this naming, we claim nothing, we make an empty claim. The entrance of reading is a trance in which we are taken across, beyond and into, only to find that we are back where we started, in transit.

The presentation of Clare and Sheila as statues attending Dinah is later complemented by a sense that Dinah is herself a kind of statue: this is what she becomes in the last chapter of the novel, when she lies 'unlivingly still' on her bed and is attended by Sheila and Clare in turn. But Dinah is also an uncanny simulacrum in another sense: discovered collapsed on the sofa by Francis as he returns from a 'psychological French film, *avant garde*' (205), Dinah seems herself to be part of an *avant garde* movie: 'I thought I was still looking at that film' (206) as he later tells Roland Delacroix. In her unliving stillness, Dinah becomes an *avant garde* movie, an artifact made for posterity.[22] As Coralie, the young granddaughter of Mrs Coral, puts it, Dinah is 'disfigured for life *and* her mind gone' (217). Becoming a figure, a statuesque and immobile simulacrum of a person, Dinah has been disfigured for life.

* * *

Temporal transitions, transports, trances, can take the form of what we call 'memory'. As other critics have noted, Bowen's last three novels in particular are retrospective: they are concerned above all with the past and its memories.[23] *The Little Girls* is about the multiple instabilities of memory. And it is about the concatenations of memory with posterity, the past and prefabrication. Early on in the novel, Clare and Sheila meet for the first time in almost fifty years. For Sheila, this meeting brings the past back: 'with you sitting there opposite, I quite distinctly see you the way you were. You so bring yourself back that it's like a conjuring trick' (31). The Clare of the past, the little girl, is 'brought back' by the adult, contemporary Clare: like hocus-pocus or mumbo-jumbo, Clare is haunted by her past, she is a revenant of herself. By contrast, Clare finds that seeing Sheila occludes her memory of her friend:

> '*You*, on the contrary, do the vanishing trick! To me what you've done's the opposite way round. You still are (in some way?) like enough what you were to make me actually 'see' you the way you were *less* clearly than I – for instance – did an hour ago, on the way here. (31)

In this case, the coincidence of the past with the present actually functions to erase the past. Instead of being constructed by the present, the past vanishes, dissolves.

It is not only for Sheila that Clare is haunted: Clare is *consciously* (in transit) haunted by her past. This is made clear in Part I, Chapter 4, when Clare is standing on the staircase of Dinah's house, looking out through a window at a swing. This triggers the memory of a swing on which she, Dinah and Sheila played almost fifty years before. The text specifically excludes the words 'memory', 'remember', 'haunting', 'the past' here, by eliding the time between then and now, and by suggesting that Clare's action of looking at the swing is itself in the past. The present is engulfed: the present is dissolved as the swing of the past swings into it. Clare's being haunted by the past makes her a ghost for Dinah's friend Frank.[24] Seeing her at this moment, he is haunted by the past of another:

> on the halfway landing, someone or something stood looking out. Like anything at a height it appeared to float, though manifestly it was solid. The apparition (for such in effect it was) not so much scared the man as angered his nerves. If ever he saw a ghost, he had often said, he would stand no nonsense. He was not required, however, to stand anything: the impervious non-ghost affronted him by not turning round. It remained in backview, its thick overpowering stillness giving it an air not only of regardlessness of all time but of being in possession of this place. Loose about the house. ... 'Mumbo-jumbo!' he shouted to himself, internally, silently and violently. (55)

This vision of Clare as a ghost haunted by the past is haunting, and Frank, unnerved, hurries out of the house. His cry of 'Mumbo-jumbo!' is unknowingly accurate: what he 'sees' is Clare haunted by her childhood, a past in which she was called by her nickname, Mumbo.[25] Moreover, 'mumbo-jumbo' reminds us of Clare's novelty shops, full of mumbo-jumbo products for prefabricated feelings. What is finally haunting in this scene is the prefabrication of mumbo-jumbo itself: determined by the hauntedness of another, Frank's 'internally shouted' 'Mumbo-jumbo!' is itself a prefabrication.

Memory in *The Little Girls*, then, has to do with effects of haunting, mumbo-jumbo, vanishing and conjuring tricks. It involves a revenance of the present (Sheila remembering Clare), the dissolution of the past (Clare remembering Sheila), the effacement of the present (Clare recapturing herself on a swing), and the haunting solidity of the apparition of another. Nowhere are such eerie and disruptive dimensions of memory more clearly projected than in Dinah. Memory for Dinah is dissolute. It functions as *déjà vu*, as a sensation or prefabricated 'feeling'. Such remembering disrupts every distinction between the past and the present:

> 'I've been having the most extraordinary sensation! Yes, and I still am, it's still going on! Because, to remember something all in a flash, so completely that it's not "then" but "now", surely is a sensation, isn't it? I do know it's far, far more than a mere memory! One's right back into it again, right in the middle. It's happening round one. Not only that but it's never *not* been happening. It's – it's absorbing!' (22)

The force of Dinah's 'experience' of the past – memory – is to suggest that the past is itself a construct of 'sensations' rather than a number of points along a linear continuum. In a sense – precisely, in a sensation – there is no past: it is in memory – what is 'happening round one' – that the illusion of a linear temporality is constructed. As Clare comments, Dinah 'never had any memory' (39). Instead, Dinah's absorbing desire to disinter her school friends is, according to Clare, 'some sort of attack, with regard to us – call it a seizure' (39). Rather than memories, Dinah has seizures. Dinah's memories *are* seizures.

* * *

One of these seizures is her memory of *Macbeth*, a play which is, for Dinah, 'full of particles of sadness which are seldom noticed – deluded expectations, harmless things come to dreadful ends' (209). Most specifically, she tells Sheila: 'Macbeth is the one I'm sorriest for. ... He'd done an irrevocable thing' (210). Dinah is haunted by the cryptic possibility that having done the terrible, irrevocable thing, one doesn't know it: she is afraid that 'one can miss without knowing what one misses ... without even knowing that one *is* missing' (144). She fears that one could 'fear that one *had* done an irrevocable thing, without knowing exactly what it was' (210). The thing is doubly irrevocable, both because it can no longer be remedied, and because it cannot be remembered. It is both irrevocable and irrecoverable. The 'thing' is immemorial. When the bottom is knocked out of the past, there is only the sensation of the irrevocable, the irrevocable sensation. Now the past is presented as having never happened: 'It's all gone, was it ever there?' cries Dinah, 'No, never there. Nothing. No, no, no ...' (221).

Dinah's ultimate seizure bears witness to the dreadful sense that the past cannot be known and cannot be spoken: it is irrevocable, it cannot be recalled, it is no longer vocable. A conventional reading might describe the narrative of *The Little Girls* as a tracing of the necessary moral development of Dinah away from a fixation on the past towards an acceptance of the past as past, as finished. Throughout the novel, Clare has resisted Dinah's attempts to resuscitate their girlhood friendship. The closing words of the text, however, record a conversation in which Dinah at last refuses to name Clare as a little girl. As Clare enters the bedroom, Dinah wakes:

> The sleeper stirred. She sighed. She raised herself on an elbow, saying:
> 'Who's there?'
> 'Mumbo'.
> 'Not Mumbo. Clare. Clare, where have you been?' (237).

A conventional reading would point to certain remarks earlier in the novel which present an ethical obligation to escape one's fixation on the past: 'It might be better to have no pictures of places which are gone. Let them go completely' (169), for example.[26] Our reading, however, would suggest that things only exist by becoming immemorial and that the name is irrevocable. The name Mumbo, like that of

Romeo, cannot be revoked.[27] But the name is also that which is irrevocable, consigned to oblivion, it is beyond recall. The name cannot be evoked except by being called from the dead as a revenant. Names – Diana, Dinah, Dicey (Piggott, Delacroix); Clare, Mumbo (Burkin-Jones, Wrong, Burkin-Jones); Sheila, Sheikie (Beaker, Artworth); Frank, Francis; Coral, Caroline, Corallie, corolla; caryatid, Artemis, Diana, Dinah – are irrevocable, in transit, raising themselves in the trance of reading.

* * *

And, waking from the trance of reading, we would ask: who's there? Elbow?

8
Convulsions

> The word 'convulsive', which I use to describe the only beauty which should concern us, would lose any meaning in my eyes were it to be conceived in motion and not at the exact expiration of this motion. There can be no beauty at all, as far as I am concerned – convulsive beauty – except at the cost of affirming the reciprocal relations linking the object seen in its motion and in its repose.[1]

BEING STILL

Eva Trout (1969) is about mouths, which is to say about what happens in and through mouths and what does not happen – stuttering, sneezing, coughing, yawning, laughing, crying, breathing, swallowing, speaking or being dumb. *Eva Trout* is also about the ways in which these mouth-events infect or affect whatever is contiguous with the mouth – the face, the ear, the eye. Insofar as writing is conceived in terms of the monumental and immobile, to describe the face is to fix it, to still it. But the living face is constantly set in motion by a smile, a spoken word, a sneeze, a yawn, a twitch, a blink of the eyes. Even at rest or in sleep the face cannot be still, caressed as it is by the mobilities of breathing and the reflexes of dreams.

Bowen's last completed novel concerns the amazing, gawkish and overgrown figure of Eva Trout. As the novel opens, Eva is approaching her twenty-fifth birthday when she will come into a considerable fortune, inherited from her father who has committed suicide. Her mother eloped only two months after Eva's birth and was almost immediately killed in an air crash.[2] In Part I, Eva is lodging with her friend and former teacher, Iseult Arble, and Iseult's husband Eric on a fruit farm in Worcestershire. She is also friendly with a local family, the Danceys, especially with the twelve-year-old Henry. As Eva's birthday and financial independence approach, both Iseult and Eva's guardian, Constantine Ormeau (formerly the lover of Eva's father, Willy), become increasingly concerned about Eva's ability to cope with such wealth. Under the pressure of this concern, Eva disappears and rents a house in Broadstairs, Kent, which, as if to galvanize herself, she fills with electrical appliances. Her whereabouts are discovered, however, and when Eric goes to see her, she manages to make their meeting seem, at least to Iseult, adulterous. Eva then declares that she is pregnant and disappears again, this time to America. Part II is set eight years later, when Eva returns from America with a son, Jeremy: Jeremy seems to have been adopted or bought – Eva's pregnancy was apparently an uncertain mixture of fiction and fantasy – but the precise mechanism of acquisition is never made clear. Jeremy, then, is a simulacrum of a son. He is also deaf and dumb. By this time the Arbles have separated, but Eva's disruptive return brings them together again. Eva falls in love with Henry Dancey, now an undergraduate at Cambridge, and asks him to elope with her. He refuses, but agrees, under pressure, to take part in a mock departure on a train for a wedding and a honeymoon on the continent. In her final scene of departure, Bowen once again dissolves still lives on a station platform, once again stilling lives in a scene of going. As people gather at Victoria Station to say goodbye to Eva and Henry, Jeremy arrives, takes out a gun, and shoots Eva dead.

Within the unlikely convulsions of such a plot, Bowen presents what is perhaps her most grotesque, mobile and uncanny narrative of still lives.[3] As in earlier novels, stillness, catatonia, interior quietness continually punctuate characters in transit. Characterological immobilities or absences of thought run through *Eva Trout*: Eric habitually returns to rooms, for example, 'as though not conscious' of having left them (19); and Eva's effect on Professor Holman includes symptoms such as atrophy, failure or inability to think, paralysis, abeyances, lacunae (127–28). Such absences or abeyances of thought also seem to mark the body as in some sense fictional because uninhabited. On a number of occasions in *Eva Trout*, the body becomes a simulacrum of the body, empty or artificially constructed: Iseult's movements, for example, 'were those of a marionette' (23), she weeps and stays still, 'a carcase' (25); and when Eva is shaken by Eric her body moves like a rag doll (88).

In *Eva Trout*, convulsions – the uncontrolled animation of, especially, stuttering, sneezing, coughing, yawning, laughing, speaking – disrupt the immobilization of the novel by a kind of auto-convulsion therapy.[4] Stammering, for example, is presented as that moment when the body is caught up in and by its own otherness, when the body lives its own inanimation in the moment of convulsive animation, when the body is haunted by *its own body* as other.[5] Writing and therefore reading might be understood as a kind of perpetual convulsion machine alternating with the stillness, the end, the dissolution of writing and reading. The convulsions and catatonia, shivering and dream wood, the kinks and trances of reading constitute a kind of alternator, a textual generator.

In previous chapters, we have attempted to elaborate the disturbances of still lives, the ways that people are traversed by uncertain motions, emotions and mobilities. In *Eva Trout*, such disturbances take the form, above all, of convulsion. Like *The Little Girls*, Bowen's last novel is awkward, disjunctive, convulsive. This new phase of writing prompts a new critical vocabulary, a vocabulary of convulsions, mouth-events and cinematography.

MOUTH-EVENTS

It is possible to trace the extraordinary mouth-events in *Eva Trout* through particular references to the mouth – Constantine's 'deadly mouth' (104, 263), for example, or the 'French mouth exercises' (265) which Jeremy is given to make him speak. Or we might focus on references to people speaking while barely moving their lips (13), or on Jeremy's lip-reading. Or we could examine the multifarious oral convulsions of *Eva Trout* (which are significantly more prominent than in earlier novels) – Willy Trout's tic in his cheek (17); the coughing of Eva and Henry ('Both coughed: Henry with some distinction, Eva rackingly and persistently', 71); the stammering of the house-agent Mr Denge ('he stuttered, like a choked engine', 81) and Eva (84, 86); the violent yawning of Eric (97) and Eva (109, 255); Eva's effort to swallow ('as though with a throat obstruction', 135); the possibility that breathing might be dangerous ('Eva drew a dangerously deep breath', 150); Mr Dancey's perpetual sneezing (28, 156–7); and the unstable volume of his voice (29, 251).[6] There is, it would seem, a compulsive scrutiny of oral convulsions in *Eva Trout*. Crucial, in this respect, is the novel's central trope of orality – Jeremy's dumbness. Although at first sight this dumbness might suggest a blockage or stilling of the convulsive, it can also be construed as a hyperbolic stammer, one enormous convulsion, a convulsion which disrupts the very possibility of the face-event. In this way, Jeremy's dumbness is undecidably related to the fictional: while Eva, like her parents, is said to have a 'genius for unreality' (44), Jeremy, through his dumbness, is himself a kind of 'dummy' (the gun he holds is thought to be a 'stage dummy', 265–6), a fiction or 'mimicry' (222), a simulacrum of a 'real' speaker, a mutation. On the one hand, *Eva Trout* presents speaking as a kind of convulsion therapy for silence and interior quietness. On the other hand, Jeremy's silences are themselves eloquently convulsive, his unspeakingness convulses the narrative: it is he who shoots his 'mother' at the end. As we will attempt to show, these muted convulsions – both of Jeremy and of the end of the novel – are inextricably linked to other figurations of 'death', the speaking dead or deadly speech. *Eva Trout* can thus be seen as a conclusion and a convulsion of the entire Bowen *oeuvre.*

JEREMY'S PAROXYSMS

Jeremy might be thought of as a figure of reading in *Eva Trout* in his inability to hear and 'refusal' to speak. To the extent that no sound comes out of a written text, we are, like Jeremy, lip-readers – or, more generally, mouth-readers[7] – of Bowen's novel. But it is important to recognize that such a reading is far from immobile. Indeed, Jeremy's dumbness is itself configured as a complex of convulsions: 'Jeremy's silentness, usually, had manifold eloquent variations, outgoings, clamourings and insistencies, queries, ripostes. It took much to tie the tongue of his mind' (165). As Constantine points out, 'There are dumb devils – a frequent case of "possession"' (175). And Jeremy is known to have 'paroxysms which were the inverse of his angel nature' (162): he is taken over, possessed by these paroxysms, possessed by his other and by evil. But the equivocal syntax of Constantine's sentence is itself inhabited, possessed, by a constitutive uncertainty of possession: are dumb devils possessed or do they possess?

Jeremy is presented, in the first place, as a telepathic reader, an intrusive or transgressive reader not only of lips, but of minds. Miming a popular supposition, the portrayal of Jeremy shifts from a boy with a handicap to a boy able to exploit the supplementary, 'extra-sensory' perceptual apparatus of the mind:

> Jeremy's presence, since they had sat down to table, was never not to be felt. ... [A]t intervals, he turned his candid attention from face to face, from speaker to speaker. ... The effect was not so much of mere intelligence as of a somehow unearthly perspicacity. The boy, handicapped, one was at pains to remember, imposed on others a sense that *they* were, that it was *they* who were lacking in some faculty. ... What Eva's little boy knew, what he always had known, and, still more, what he was now in the course of learning, there was no knowing. There was a continuous leakage, and no stopping it. A conviction that the vicarage tea table was bugged, if on an astral plane, gained increasing hold on father and son. ... 'Eva,' asked Mr Dancey, 'are you quite sure Jeremy cannot lip-read?'
>
> 'Only mine,' she said. 'And those he need not.'
>
> Henry said: 'Extra-sensory.' (158)

Through Jeremy, reading in *Eva Trout* becomes a telepathic, extra-sensory reading of faces. There is a leakage or slippage in the space between Eva's answer to the crucial question and Henry's comment, which suggests that the reader must read the narrator's lips, which is to say the narrator's mind. Jeremy need not read Eva's lips because he can, as Henry intimates, read her differently, extra-sensorily. Jeremy not only receives but transmits extra-sensory perceptions. Similarly, *Eva Trout* might be said to be bugged by an extra-sensory reader, leading to a continuous leakage of convulsive energies out of the novel. Such a leakage, or reading, would entail the dissolution of the novel.

MAKING FACES

Jeremy's dumbness, his speaking face and his disquieting ability to read lips, faces, minds, may be elaborated through a consideration of Leopold in *The House in Paris* and the rhetorical trope of prosopopoeia or 'face making'. At a crucial moment in *The House in Paris*, Leopold, who has just been sexually conceived by Max and Karen, is textually conceived within, and figured forth by, the prosopopoeia of the second-person pronoun: 'Having done as she knew she must [Karen] did not think there would be a child: all the same, the idea of you, Leopold, began to be present with her' (*HP* 151–2).

The unprecedented and singular apostrophic pronoun 'you' to refer to Leopold performs a bizarre catachresis of prosopopoeia: the address by the narrator to a fictional character radically disrupts the distinctions between textual levels, conceiving Leopold by disturbing the very possibility of fiction. Leopold becomes the reader of his own story. Characterizing Leopold in this way also suggests the undecidable but irrevocable reality of people in Bowen. Prosopopoeia both grounds and undermines figuration itself: it is the 'presentation of absent, dead, or supernatural beings, or even of inanimate objects, with the ability to act, speak, and respond'.[8] As this formulation suggests, prosopopoeia constitutes the rhetorical basis of characterization as such: novels are networks of precisely such presentations. Novels are peopled by omniscient narrators, inanimate fictions, the speaking dead. Bowen's scandalous apostrophe in *The House in Paris* is a literalization of that disturbing figuration of presenting people which we call 'characterization'. Prosopopoeia, then, is not simply another rhetorical figure, but figuration itself, the figuration of figuration, the uncanny, hallucinatory ground of the literary.[9]

Convulsions in *Eva Trout* might be thought of as the inadvertent side-effects of an impossible face-making. The masks and masked readers of *The Little Girls* have prepared us for the personifications or characterizations of *Eva Trout*: to be a person is to be a mask. And giving a face to a name is also bound up with voice, giving a voice to a face.[10] Stammering and, in particular, Jeremy's dumbness, then, pose critical disturbances of both personification – the mask of identity – and prosopopoeia. His refusal or inability to speak participates in the text's more general questioning of what it is to be a person, to be given a face, a mask, an identity – to become 'real'.

MOVING PICTURES

Eva Trout displays a relentless fascination with the face both in convulsion and in immobility. Eva's guardian Constantine Ormeau, for example, has an immobile face and a fictitious life. His face, to Iseult Smith, seems to be made of 'alabaster or indeed plastic', the relation of its various parts to each other are 'for the greater part of the time unchanging', and he has 'the least mobile face one might ever have seen' (36). These locutions, if only by implication, engage with the necessity of motion. They engage with what, in its mobility, is the most elusive and uncertain of objects: the face.[11] That Constantine's face is immobile suggests at once a kind of deathliness and a living fiction, a still life. In her last completed novel, then, Bowen presents, as she does in her first novel, *The Hotel*, hotel lives, lives stilled by a sense of fictitious existence, still lives:

> Iseult took stock of him anew. Mere misgivings gave place to incredulity: he did not seem possible – did not seem likely, even. Nothing authenticated him as a 'living' being. A figure cut from some picture but now pasted onto a blank screen. To be with him was to be *in vacuo* also. She said to him: 'Do you know, Mr Ormeau, I have actually no idea what you do. What you actually *do*, I mean.'
> 'I import.'
> 'Oh, do you? – Or, where you live.'
> 'In an hotel, principally'. (44–5)

Constantine is not a living being, he is incredible, a figure cut out from his background, a cardboard cut-out.[12] Constantine *is* nevertheless '"living"': by placing 'living' in quotation marks, the text suggests that 'living' and therefore 'life' is itself in some sense fictitious. Constantine, we might say, is out to lunch ('Characteristically, he was out at lunch' [193]). Constantine *imports*, like other Bowen characters, a sense of being an hotel guest, living in an undecidably fictional world.

In her 'Notes on Writing a Novel' (1945), Bowen suggests that a convincingly real or 'living' character in a novel necessarily involves movement, action, play, even in pictures: 'Physical personality belongs to action. ... Pictures must be in movement. Eyes, hands, stature, etc., must appear, and only appear, *in play*.' She writes of the 'hopelessness' of 'mere' 'description' ('categoric "description"' as she puts it) – hopeless because 'static' (*MT* 38). She refers to the idea of an 'unmaterialized' character, that is, a character, in some sense, without 'movement': 'the unmaterialized character represents an enemy pocket in an area that has been otherwise cleared. This cannot go on for long. It produces a halt in the plot' (*MT* 39). The 'unmaterialized' character, the product of 'static' '"description"' is a pocket of resistance, endangering the movements of the novel. But Bowen's account in these 'Notes' must, like much of her critical writing, be read against the grain or beside itself. While it justly stresses the importance of movement in characterization, Bowen's account is also curiously at odds with itself, as well as with the complexity and force of her own novelistic practice. The irony of this account is to suggest that the creation of 'living' characters is a process of destruction or obliteration, a warlike operation of clearance and death. Correspondingly, a character may, like Constantine Ormeau, be incredible, static, 'a figure cut from some picture', but a character who is is *still* '"living"'. The intricacy, strangeness and comedy of such a characterization unsettles the very terms of Bowen's 'Notes'. As we hope the present study has made clear, there are only still lives in Bowen's novels: there are only undecidably materialized, moving, resistant characters, belonging to a novelistic world indissociable from the 'real' or the 'living'.

DEADLY SPEECH

Conventionally, there is, as with psychoanalysis, the talking cure. Thus, in *Eva Trout*, oral emissions can be construed as convulsion therapy, purporting to 'cure' effects of catatonia or interior stillness. Through the convulsion of, for example, a stammer or even a burst of 'continuous' speech, a character can be galvanized. But as by now may have become evident, such convulsions are themselves subject to a kind of infection by 'description' – by everything that links writing to monumentalization, immobility and 'death'. And characterological speech, people speaking, is always, among other things, a figuration of the talking dead. What Bowen's novels interrogate most forcefully is the extent to which people speaking are always figurations, figures, prosopopoeia, and the possibility that reading speech is itself inhabited or contaminated by 'death'. Reading speech is prosopopoeia: talk of the dead.

Eva's speech, especially, is subject to investigation in *Eva Trout*. Eva is presented as having, in the second part of the novel, a 'fundamental' 'mistrust of or objection to verbal intercourse' (188). Earlier, however, Eva 'express[es] herself like a displaced person', and by the time she is sixteen 'her outlandish, cement-like conversational style had set' (17). It is striking not only that Eva has such an outlandish conversational style, but that such an outlandish metaphor is employed – a figure which makes the abstract 'concrete', a metaphor which sets, immobilizing as concrete. Eva's mouthings – outlandish, cement-like, but also stammering – are, like Constantine's mouth, 'deadly' (104). Iseult criticizes Eva's use of 'however': 'it's pompous, it's unnatural-sounding, it's wooden, it's deadly, it's hopeless, it's shutting-off – the way *you* use it! It's misbegotten!' (65). Iseult's hyperbolic concatenation of adjectives indicates the excessive difficulties of representing Eva's speech, the necessarily misbegotten or impossible conception that there could be a pure and proper description of verbal discourse. These mouth-events, too, exceed the possibility of figuration.[13] *Eva Trout* records the dissolving fictions of speech. In this respect, we would suggest that there can be no talking cure, because there is no talk which is not inhabited, set going, possessed by prosopopoeia.

Eva is the 'monstrous heiress' who is 'unable to speak – talk, be understood, converse'. But her 'displaced' language is not isolated in its pathology. And it is not just speaking, but emissions generally – sneezing, yawning, swallowing, breathing – which are convulsive, potentially terrifying, dissolute. Mr Dancey, the vicar, constantly sneezes, a compulsive convulsion which wreaks 'havoc' (28) on his life and on the lives of those around him. His sneezing relentlessly disfigures him: by the end of the novel 'the disfiguration of Mr Dancey ... was complete, unsparing – unbearable' (247). The descriptions of his shattering sneezes are themselves shattering, already shattered. But Mr Dancey has difficulty in speaking as well: 'Occupationally, his anxiety was his voice, which had taken to varying in volume as unaccountably as though a poltergeist were fiddling with the controls, sometimes coming out with a sudden boom of a roar, sometimes fading till off the air' (28–9). The problem with this radio-set is that the controls are out of control, or out of *his* control, in the control of the spook. The vicar's voice is spooked but not, presumably, by God. This spook is a noisy ghost (*polter-geist*), like the vicar's uncontrollable sneezing. The vicar is spooked: he is possessed by and possesses a noisy ghost. Speaking the words of the Ghost – as a vicar ought – he speaks the words of the living dead. And in the convulsions of sneezing and speaking, the vicar is haunted, among other things, by the otherness of his body, possessed by the other of the body. His animation is, in this sense, inanimate, still.

VIVISECTIONS

One of the extraordinary things about convulsions in *Eva Trout* is their sheer force. Convulsive emissions can be devastating, like a yawn which rends the body, splitting or cutting it, still living, asunder:

> At that, [Eric] was rent by a cavernous, groaning yawn, which finished its way out through him in a string of shudders – fatigue, rage, frustration, nervous despair. He was left as though he had vomited. (97)

Within the yawn, the face is fissured: the hyperbolic 'cavernous' suggests not only the opening of a mouth, but the opening or splitting of the whole body. Moreover, Eric becomes his body, he is possessed, taken over, finished, by the convulsive shudder of this yawn and left 'as though he had vomited'. Later Eva herself yawns violently: 'it distended her rib-cage to cracking point, just not dislocating her jaw by the grace of heaven' (109). Again, the sheer violence of this convulsion is complemented by an alien possession of her body. The alien (and comic) power of the yawn, its insensible and unlocatable origin deep within the mysterious hollows of the body, figures a bodily force disembodied. The figure of the body is fissured by its own figuration, by its own figure, its own body: figuration is a form of vivisection, the yawning prosopopoeia of the body.

Crucial to convulsions in *Eva Trout* is the way that faces – Dancey's, Eric's – become uncannily, animatedly inanimate. Iseult, we are told, was originally drawn to Eva by a 'vivisectional interest' (33), that is to say, in 'literal' terms, an interest in cutting up a living person for physiological, psychological or other research: in vivisection, the living body becomes a simulacrum of a corpse. In *Eva Trout*, descriptions of people *are* vivisections, the cutting up of 'living' beings: life becomes a parody of death, but by the same rigorously morbid logic, death becomes a parody of life. This is exemplified by Constantine:

> His countenance needed nothing; it was at its best. It presented Eva with one of its masterpieces of non-expression – lightly sketched-in eyebrows at rest above lids at a heavy level, eyes unreflective as a waxwork's but less demarcated, hueless segments of glaze holding pinpoint pupils. And the lips, contrasting

> in their slight moistness with the matt finish of the surrounding flesh, were at rest also, lightly lying together as they might in a smile, though smile they did not. The now neutral shape of that deadly mouth was what held Eva's regard for longest. She had seen Constantine 'vanish' before now, but not 'at' her; the performance always had been for the benefit of Willy – who could act back in no way. (104)

The physiognomics of this description suggest, unrelentingly, what might conventionally be seen as an objectification, a depersonalization or dehumanization of the face. By stilling the face in description, the text stills life, stops it dead. Constantine becomes a masterpiece and 'his' face a countenance that countenances nothing. What is sketched in and what vanishes here, is a verbal *trompe l'oeil*: the description oscillates between that of a 'living' face and that of a picture or a three-dimensional artifact (a piece of porcelain or a sculpture). Constantine's face is an artistic construction, a fabrication, a creation and vanishing of art – 'lightly sketched-in eyebrows', 'eyes unreflective as a waxwork's', 'hueless segments of glaze', 'matt finish', 'lightly lying', 'neutral shape', 'deadly mouth'. The passage reveals the ways in which every description of a face is necessarily a vivisectional blazon. In order to enable the figuration and reading of a face, description unavoidably isolates and represents its features, unmakes and makes a face.

IMPERSON

The wall between the living and the dead is, we are told, 'very thin' (173). Vivisection or description marks the liminal intersections of life, death and fiction. All of this is encountered in one extraordinary passage, in which Eva – out of the blue, out of the dark, after eight years – receives a telephone call from Iseult, her old teacher. There is something unusual about the voice, 'a vivacity not there formerly' (192). Eva's reaction is to question the identity of her former teacher and friend: 'Had this *been* Miss Smith, or was she dead and somebody impersonating her?' (192). All she has to go on is Iseult's voice: although the impersonator had 'documented herself faultlessly', she betrays 'an insufficient grasp of the character' (192). The voice, characterized as palpable and almost visible, is a supplement for a face.

But 'something ... had not rung true': 'The voice's inflections, even, had been, if not quite parodied exaggerated, over-stretched, harshened; more than once a hollow ring had been given them' (193). This telephone call is another instance of a literalization of prosopopoeia: a voice from the dead rings, is heard and given a face. We are hauntingly presented with the voice of an absent speaker (Miss Smith) manifesting an unprecedented and improbable 'vivacity'. Rather than an impersonation of a dead person by a living being, however, Eva realizes that this phone call could involve an impersonation of a living being by someone already dead: it could be the dead Iseult impersonating herself. Like so many other convulsive moments in the novel, such a possibility is a little shocking: it galvanizes Eva, stimulates her to spasmodic action as if by an electric shock, conferring a false vitality upon her in turn:[14]

> She went halfway up in the lift, came down again – then, near a sand-filled column inviting rejection of cigarettes, was galvanized. A further possibility had occurred to her – the impersonator of Miss Smith had been Miss Smith, a deceased person purporting to be a living one. Not that she necessarily was in her coffin; no, she could well be walking about in Reading. ('Charles the First walked and talked half an hour after his head was cut off.' You put in a comma somewhere, then that made sense but was not so interesting.) But, she had given an impression of dissolution. (193)

Making sense of the unstable relationship between life and death, clearing up the mystery of a dead person walking and talking, is a question of punctuation, of making language make sense. But language poses constant resistances to such 'categoric' stillings. Reading – the occurrences of thought – is always more interesting, more convulsive, more *striking*. As we have suggested in our account of *The Heat of the Day*, there is no language or sense, no reading, no experience without a force of decapitation. Making sense of a dead person on the phone is in part a question of reading 'Reading'. Iseult, whom Eva imagines to be dead, may be walking about in Reading. But she may also be walking about in reading. The distinction is typographical, the difference between upper- and lower-case letters. 'Reading' – this sentence – disturbs our sense of the importance of capitalization. But the ghoulish paronomasia of this reading also calls us to make a phonemic distinction between the sound of Reading and the sound of reading. In order to understand this voice from the tomb, we must read the phone(me), perform a phonemic reading. Iseult is a character in a book, walking about and talking on the phone as if she were alive. But she is also talking in reading, raising her voice through the prosopopoeia of reading. This prosopopoeia, raising a voice from the dead, is a question of phonemic reading, of phoning. Dissolute in Reading, Iseult, the phonemic voice of reading, impresses the dissolution of the reading voice.

Perhaps before anything else, however, making sense involves the question of identity, of the self. And that's a slippery fish:

> Anyhow, what a slippery fish is identity; and what *is* it, besides a slippery fish?. ... What *is* a person? Is it true, there is not more than one of each?. ... Eva decided to see by examining many. She telephoned for the Jaguar and drove it to the National Portrait Gallery, of which she had heard. (193–4)

To recognize that identity is a slippery fish, is to catch, at least in part, a sense of the slippery, fishy identity of Eva's name (Trout), and the fishy nature of Bowen's last novel (*Eva Trout*). And it is also immediately and irrevocably to start the reader off on the slippery slope of paronomastic naming in *Eva Trout*, to start her thinking about the way that Eva's surname is woven into the text like a signature: 'the kitchen fish kettle' (29); '"Why? He can't eat you; or can he?" "Certainly *not*!" said Miss Trout. (The very idea!)' (30); '"Well," he pronounced, "here's a kettle of fish!"' (33); '"Mayn't that look rather fishy?" "This is fishy." Eva ...' (57); 'Yet there are sometimes times when I think you [Eva] would rather go on being submerged. Sometimes you cling to being in deep water' (64); 'Then, what a kettle of fish!' (105); 'Trout's not a usual name except for a fish' (138); 'she's landed herself ... in a position which could be fishy' (171); 'one character who could be more than fishy' (208); 'A nice kettle of fish you have got me into!' (218); 'would you be so kind as to fish it up?' (of the revolver which will kill Eva) (226); 'Fishing about behind him ...' (263). The sliding of the phrase 'slippery fish' into the questioning of identity activates the polysemic references to fish which slip through the text and swallow up not only our certitude of Eva's identity as 'realistic', but also, in a deep sense, the very possibility of identity. The slipperiness of Eva's name entails the slipperiness of identity and of language. Is Eva a fish? What does it mean for a person to *possess*, and to be *possessed* by, the name of a fish? Can a fish be a person? In order to suggest the lubricious and even demonic force of 'Eva Trout', we might speak rather of an imperson.

STILLS

Going to the National Portrait Gallery to examine the identities of faces suggests, once again, that people are figurations, making faces. The still lives in the National Portrait Gallery do not help Eva:

> Each was his own affair, and he let you know it. Nothing was to be learned from them (if you expected learning that nothing *was* to be learned). In so far as they had an effect on the would-be student, it was a malign one: every soul Eva knew became no longer anything but a Portrait. There was no 'real life'; no life was more real than this. (196)

The pictorial representations of faces, rather than a solution to the question of identity, present a dissolution. If these pictures are real, if these still lives are as real as any other life, then the stability of life, of identity, is convulsed. Like a fish out of water, like a body in the spasm of a sneeze.

Unlike painting, photography might seem to offer clues to identity through its ability to catch, in the stilling of an instant, the face-event. At one point, Iseult goes to the Danceys' vicarage and, seeking to know 'of just *what* junk this havering life was composed' (212), looks at the contents of a writing desk. She finds a photograph of Henry which is itself a kind of fish, 'half-submerged in one of the upper waves of the depths of clutter' (212). And in the photograph, the identity of Henry has, like a fish, largely been caught: 'He had not (evidently) posed, but been stolen up upon – he flung round upon the aggressor's camera. Instantaneousness, as so often, had done the trick: a very great amount of him had been "caught"' (212). The passage suggests that mechanical reproduction is a key to the construction of identity through the capturing of convulsions and face-events – that the incommensurability of the face-event and description may be resolved by the instantaneous exposures of a camera, by stills. At the same time, however, the marine rhetoric itself (in particular, 'caught' in quotation marks) would suggest that any commensurability here is dissolved in the slipperiness of the fish-like.[15]

Any sense that mechanical reproduction provides a redemptive metaphor is further displaced by the novel's account of the incommensurability of movies – mobility, movement – and speech. After returning to England, Eva finds that 'her mistrust of or objection to verbal intercourse – which she had understood to be fundamental – began to be undermined' (188). This mistrust is inspired, at least in part, by her deaf and dumb son. During their 'inaudible years' alone in America, she and Jeremy have lived movies: 'His and her cinematographic existence, with no sound-track, in successive American cities made still more similar by their continuous manner of being in them, had had a sufficiency which was perfect' (188). This 'sufficiency' would seem to be a product of the speechless mobilities of silent movies, and their blurring distinctions between the real and the fictional, between what is and what is not 'cinematographic'. Deaf and dumb, Jeremy is literally a silent mover, a silent movie, set undecidably flickering in the distinction between *watching* and *being* a movie:

> They came to distinguish little between what went on inside and what went on outside the diurnal movies, or what was or was not contained in the television flickering them to sleep. From large or small screens, illusion overspilled on to all beheld. Society revolved at a distance from them like a ferris wheel dangling buckets of people. They were their own. ... Only they moved. They were within a story to which they imparted the only sense. The one wonder, to them, of the exterior world was that anything should be exterior to themselves – and *could* anything be so and yet exist? (189)

The omniscient narrator – at once identifying and detached – presents a fairground dissolution of boundaries between self and other, inside and outside, illusion and the real. In this movie-world, the only thing that can shatter the sense of their story would be the event of speech. It is this event, speech, which Eva thinks would be 'traitorous' (188) to these years in which 'they had lorded it in a visual universe'(189). Just as speaking will often awaken the sleeper from a dream, to speak in movie-land would be to still, momentarily, convulsively, the apparent continuum of the world, to isolate a frame, to crack the silent visual mobility of such a life. There can be other face-events – the 'stinging of their same faces', Jeremy looking and 'scanning', the prospect of returning to England 'to face the music', Eva 'sighting premonitions' in Jeremy's 'changeable eyes' (189) – but to speak is something else. To speak is to concatenate a series of convulsive face-events – sudden electrical impulses of the nerves, constrictions of the muscles, a flexing and stretching of tissues, dissonant vibrations. To speak (in) the silent years would be to expose the instantaneous ruptures which both join and irreducibly separate the frames of a movie, exposing the fiction of a fluid mobility which silently dissolves one frame into the next.

CONCATENATIONS

A movie, then, is a concatenation of images or stills – instantaneous, convulsive exposures. And just as putting a word or sentence together involves the concatenation of phonemic (or graphemic), spatial and other convulsions, putting a novel together – writing and reading – involves intensive concatenation: concatenations of events, people, faces, words, figures, and concatenations *between* these different elements. Novels are concatenations of these multiplicitous fictions. Like movies, novels can only move by being still: both are constructed through the imperceptible interstices between frames, convulsions.

Eva Trout ends with a cinematic culmination and dispersal of concatenations: the last scene involves the coming together of people – Eva, Jeremy, Henry, Constantine, Mr Dancey, Iseult, Eric, the 'mist-like phantoms' of aunts, uncles, cousins (264), and, inexplicably, Mr Denge, Eva's house-agent – on the platform at Victoria Station to witness the fictional departure of Eva and Henry as a 'married' couple. The scene also draws together the text's theorization of fictionality, its dissolution of the novel. Not only is the departure itself a 'hymeneal' (261) fiction, but the entire scene is undecidably a *staged* event. In particular, it is Jeremy, who is to be the 'protagonist', the heroic murderer of Eva, his 'mother'. He has already been determined as a kind of fictional or surrogate son – a kind of fictional dummy who does not speak, a mute mutation –

and he is now overdetermined as a performer: 'His performance. ... the child star ... he first appeared on the stage, or platform. ... He lifted out, in a manner evidently rehearsed ... "he's only acting!" ... "a child likes to play gunman". ... "Not that that's anything but a stage dummy he's got hold of". ... A child's ballet enactment of a *crime passionnel* ... he sped like a boy on the screen' (265–8). Linked to these climactic figurations of the fictional, the staged presence of Jeremy, are questions as to his and others' identities and the question of concatenation itself.

Throughout *Eva Trout*, Eva has been characterized as unable to join things – words, thoughts, memories, actions, people – together. Except during her flowing, phantasmagoric, movie years in America, she is like a novelist or like a reader unable to make sense of events because unable to concatenate.[16] At the end of the novel, Constantine begins to make a farewell wedding speech, attempting to chain together a sense of 'life', present, past and future: 'The future, as we know, will resemble the past in being the result, largely, of a concatenation of circumstances. ... Er – life stretches ahead. May a favourable concatenation of circumstances. ... No, here I become a trifle tied up, I think' (268). Constantine is tied up in thoughts, in words, tongue-tied, trying to untie the concatenated notion of life as concatenation. He stops. And Eva's 'last words' are to ask Constantine 'what is "concatenation"?' (268), to attempt to join together, to give meaning to, to galvanize her 'many' lives. The answer to her question is not, however, verbal and comes not from Constantine but from the gun of Jeremy. The denouement to 'concatenation' is dissolution: still life.

How can we chain together these events, concatenate our reading? We might attempt to do so by splicing and cutting the reel of this chapter, working with the material of convulsions, face-events, prosopopoeia, stills, movies, description and concatenation. To the extent that these categories are unstable, blurred or shivered, we can acknowledge that concatenation, reading, is uncertainly, unceasingly interrupted by convulsions. Our reading, our compulsive concatenation of events is also, at the same time, determined by convulsions and subject to dissolution. Reading, our reading, is dissolution. Reading is fictional, a form of prosopopoeia. It gives voice – if only in a dissolute silence – to dead words: our mouths become deadly mouths, our speech deadly speech. To read a novel is not only to speak with the dead, but also to speak the dead. Reading is a raising of our own dead voices.[17] These voices, however, are unmasterable and do not belong to us. In reading, we are figured by prosopopoeia: we too make faces and our faces are made. We speak the words of 'still lives'. We confer a mask on a novel and on ourselves, we make our person and we are multiple and other. Reading is prosopopoeia, the dissolution of lives.

A DISSOLUTION

Still lives are movie-lives, going, in the instantaneous mobility of the convulsive event, of reading. A dissolution: mobile, fluid and uncontainably still, uncontainable still.

Notes

Notes to the Introduction

1. Such comforts would include assumptions about the status of characters or 'people' in novels; the nature of novel-reading as an 'experience'; the possibility of closure or novel-ending; the stability or certainty of the temporality and ontological status of narrative 'events'; the representational or referential possibilities of language; and so on. The rereadings advanced in the present study follow on from work in recent years by, in particular, Hermione Lee, Dominique Gauthier, John Hildebiddle and Phyllis Lassner. See Hermione Lee, *Elizabeth Bowen: An Estimation* (London: Vision, 1981); Dominique Gauthier, *L'Image du réel dans les romans d'Elizabeth Bowen* (Paris: Didier Erudition, 1985); John Hildebiddle, *Five Irish Writers: The Errand of Keeping Alive* (Cambridge, Mass.: Harvard University Press, 1989) Chapter 3; Phyllis Lassner, *Elizabeth Bowen* (London: Macmillan, 1990). Each of these critics has begun to develop Bowen criticism away from the often extremely reductive and normalizing accounts of earlier studies. In this sense, our book builds on their work in emphasizing the strangeness and disturbing power of Bowen's writing. Nevertheless, even these more recent studies tend to be hampered by a number of preconceptions which have characterized Bowen criticism from the start. Earlier books on Bowen include Allan E. Austin, *Elizabeth Bowen* (New York: Twayne, 1971) and Edwin J. Kenny, Jr, *Elizabeth Bowen* (Lewisburg: Bucknell University Press, 1975). For a recent collection of Bowen criticism claiming to collect 'the best criticism that is available upon the writing of Elizabeth Bowen' (vii), see Harold Bloom, ed., *Elizabeth Bowen* (New York: Chelsea House, 1987).
2. This is not to say that there are not other, more obviously 'distorted' readings of Bowen. A good recent example of this would be Maggie Humm's *Border Traffic: Strategies of Contemporary Women Writers* (Manchester University Press, 1991), which ludicrously claims that Bowen's work was concerned with 'promoting a retreat to the supposed humane values of rural life' (42) and that it exemplifies a 'turn to religion, to the past, to exotic places [and] to a private morality' (214, n. 12).
3. Cited by Bowen in her essay on Proust, 'The Art of Bergotte', in *Pictures and Conversations* (London: Allen Lane, 1975) 100.
4. See Leo Bersani, *The Culture of Redemption* (Cambridge, Mass.: Harvard University Press, 1990).
5. Elizabeth Bowen, *Afterthought: Pieces about Writing* (London: Longman, 1962) 9.
6. *The Diary of Virginia Woolf, Volume III: 1925–30*, ed. Anne Olivier Bell (Harmondsworth: Penguin, 1982) 34.

7. The pervasiveness of 'dissolution' in Bowen's novels has been perceptively noted by John Hildebiddle, in his *Five Irish Writers*. Hildebiddle helpfully suggests that 'Bowen so insists upon the word *dissolution*. ... [that] One might more accurately speak of *dissolutions*' (95). He goes on to argue that 'What dissolves is not just the world of visible signs and landmarks. ... Memory and imagination, and even language itself begin to dissolve' (95–6).

Notes to Chapter 1: Abeyances

1. Friedrich Nietzsche, *The Will to Power*, trans. Walter Kaufmann and R. J. Hollingdale (New York: Vintage, 1968) 268.
2. We shall employ the notion of 'figure' throughout this study to suggest, not least, characterization itself. A figure is at the same time a rhetorical trope and a human embodiment, and while it involves the artificial representation of the human face and body and is *bound up* in fictionality, drama and the pictorial, it also *is* those forms. Finally, figure *gives* form or shape to something, so that to describe or embody or represent a person is to give that person bodily form.
3. Our use of the word 'catatonia' should not be construed as merely or strictly clinical (whatever that might mean); but see Lawrence C. Kolb, ed., *Modern Clinical Psychiatry*, 9th edn (Philadelphia: W. B. Saunders, 1977) 406: 'In spite of the apparent ideational poverty, there seems to be every reason to believe that ideas and representations are by no means absent [in catatonia], but rather are centered on a dominant ideo-affective constellation.' The medical literature on catatonia offers few attempts to map the interior of this thought. One such account, however, is given by Oliver Sacks in *Awakenings*: a patient with catatonic symptoms suffering from encephalitis, 'Ros R.', describes such a state as one of thinking about 'nothing'. Sacks asks Ros *how* this is possible:

   > One way is to think about the same thing again and again. Like 2=2=2=2; or, I am what I am what I am what I am. ... It's the same thing with my posture. My posture continually leads to itself. Whatever I do or whatever I think leads deeper and deeper into itself. ... And then there are maps. I think of a map; then a map of that map; then a map of that map of that map, and each map perfect, though smaller and smaller. ... Worlds within worlds within worlds within worlds. Once I get going I can't possibly stop. It's like being caught between mirrors, or echoes, or something'. (*Awakenings*, rev. edn [London: Pan, 1982] 69).

4. Robert M. Goldenson, ed., *Longman Dictionary of Psychology and Psychiatry* (New York: Longman, 1984), 'cataplexy'. See Kolb 406–7:

   > Many psychiatrists look upon catatonic stupor as a profound regression, a dramatization of death. Attention is called to the similarity

> between catatonia and the instinctive immobility reaction exhibited by certain animals when confronted with a life-threatening situation. Arieti has suggested that the immobility of the catatonic has its origin in family transactions wherein criticism is directed toward action tendencies of the growing child and is accepted by the compliant child. Catalepsy then is an expression of compliance to the demands of others ... it may symbolize an ambivalent negativism and be used to discharge hostility in a passive way.

5. In this chapter we shall rely on the term 'catatonia' as a generalized condition of physical and mental immobility, including the symptoms of catalepsy and cataplexy: elsewhere in this study, such abeyances will be referred to, for example, in terms of interior quietness.
6. By contrast, moments of movement seem to offer a redemption from the catatonia of stillness: for example, 'The rush of air and the movement had made [Sydney] come alive again' (157).
7. See 62: 'you really are too clever sometimes to understand me'; see also 52 and 93, on Sydney's cleverness.
8. Compare *LS* 34, when, for Lois, 'not to be known seemed like a doom: extinction'.
9. See *TN* 132–4 and *HP* 151–5.
10. Similarly, it is a sign of Henrietta's maturation in *The House in Paris* that 'she longed to occupy people's fancies, speculations and thoughts' (*HP* 24), and 'she had never met anyone without immediately wanting to rivet their thought on herself' (32).
11. Another important question of thought in *The Hotel* is that of the ownership of thoughts – whose thoughts are 'my' thoughts? – and the question of the public/private status of thoughts – explicitly addressed, for example, in a conversation between Ronald and Eileen (129–30).
12. It is this work of deferral, this logic of the slipping away of still lives, this inscription of movement at work even in figurations of the catatonic, that we shall focus on in the next chapter, in terms of the notion of going.
13. Dolls and doll's houses are often presented as analogues of people and houses in Bowen: see, for example, *HP* 22, 26; *WL* 42, 60; *CS* 109; and an example from 'real life': in a letter from 1935, Bowen recounts to Virginia Woolf the experience of looking for a house to buy: 'It is impossible to believe that the people discovered in rooms sitting stiffly about as dolls in a dolls-house attitudes [sic] are not to be sold with the house' (*MT* 211).
14. The logic of hotels here is elaborated in Chapter 6, below, in terms of the logic of 'sheer kink'.
15. In Greek laúra signifies lane, passage, alley. Laura's name is emphasized by its homophony with Lois's brother's name, Laurence, and indeed, by Lois's name itself. See 172, where, on being kissed, Lois bends back into the laurels which make a creaking noise.
16. See 157: Lois regards another British soldier, Daventry, who seems to be undergoing some kind of breakdown, as 'hardly even a person'.

Notes to Chapter 2: Shivered

1. For moments when the novel itself refers to the notion of tragedy, see for example *TN* 185 and 235.
2. On tragedy and audience, see Howard Barker's *Arguments for a Theatre* (London: John Calder, 1989), especially Barker's stress on the sense that 'After the tragedy, you are not certain who you are' (12).
3. See Bowen's own discussion of, for example, 'immobility' and 'anti-static verbs' (*MT* 284–5) and the sense of constant movement and mobility implied in her observation that '*everything* put on record at all – an image, a word spoken, an interior movement of thought or feeling on the part of a character – is an event or happening' (*MT* 45).
4. We say 'auto-thanato-mobile' rather than 'death-drive' for a number of reasons. In particular we do not wish to propose any subordination of Bowen's text to the theoretical efficacy of a notoriously problematic psychoanalytic concept. Rather, we would argue that *To the North* furnishes a critique of the Freudian notion of the death-drive, indeed that *To the North*, in relation to psychoanalysis, *rewrites* the death-drive. Freud first theorizes the death-drive or death instincts in *Beyond the Pleasure Principle* (1920): *Pelican Freud Library*, vol. 11, trans. James Strachey, ed. Angela Richards (Harmondsworth: Penguin, 1984): 269–338. It is here that he formulates the principal thesis that '*the aim of all life is death*' (311). Freud frequently speaks of forms of behaviour, acts, desires, etc., as being 'in the service of' the death-drive or death instincts. As we will be trying to suggest in the present chapter, the logic of *going* may be recognized as in certain respects circumscribing or otherwise displacing a psychoanalytic notion. However unconsciously, Freud's own speculations, especially in *Beyond the Pleasure Principle*, cunningly manipulate the ineluctable silence and resistance to theorization imposed by the concept of the death-drive. See, in particular, Samuel Weber, *The Legend of Freud* (Minneapolis: University of Minnesota Press, 1982). *Pace* Freud, we would suggest, there is no drive to be disentangled from the disseminating force of that which would not be assimilable to any mastery or assurance, any theoretical classification or conceptualization – least of all a theory of the death-drive.
5. *The Art and Thought of Heraclitus: An Edition of the Fragments with Translation and Commentary*, by Charles H. Kahn (Cambridge University Press, 1979) 53.
6. Walter Pater, *The Renaissance*, Introduction by Arthur Symons (New York: Modern Library, 1919). Pater's references to the 'delicious recoil from the flood of water in summer heat', the 'whirlpool' of 'the inward world of thought and feeling', 'the movement of the shore-side', 'the race of the midstream', and the 'tremulous wisp constantly re-forming itself on the stream' may all suggest a sense of the 'river' in Heraclitus.
7. The standard study in this context is Morris Beja's *Epiphany in the Modern Novel* (London: Peter Owen, 1971). For a more specific account of Joyce and Pater, see, for example, F.C. McGrath, *The Sensible Spirit:*

Walter Pater and the Modernist Paradigm (Tampa: University of South Florida Press, 1986) 231–81; and for Woolf and Pater, see Perry Meisel, *The Absent Father: Virginia Woolf and Walter Pater* (New Haven: Yale University Press, 1980).

8. *The Renaissance*, 199. The phrase 'life in the moment and for the moment's sake' occurs, in the context of describing life during wartime, in *The Heat of the Day* (95).
9. See, too, the ending of *The House in Paris* which takes place at a railway station or in what the text calls 'a temple to the intention to go somewhere' (*HP* 237). We discuss these strange forms of going, arrival and departure in greater detail in the appropriate chapters below.
10. An example of 'shiver' as 'quiver' is to be found at the end of *The House in Paris* when Leopold 'shivered once' (239). The importance of convulsions in Bowen's work is the focus of our final chapter, on *Eva Trout*.
11. This phantasmagoric black hole would to some extent correspond to the shivering decribed in *A World of Love* when Antonia is at the garden fête and everything is proving manageable until she trips over a tent peg: 'Like a bullet-hit pane, the whole scene shivered, splintered outward in horror from that small black vacuum in its core' (WL 29).
12. See *MT*: 'Out of a Book' (48–53), 'Coming to London' (85–9), and 'Pictures and Conversations' (especially 295–6).
13. William Hazlitt, 'On Shakespeare and Milton', in his *Lectures on the English Poets and The Spirit of the Age* (London: Dent, 1910), 44–68. For a discussion of multiple identity in relation to Hazlitt and Shakespeare, see Nicholas Royle, *Telepathy and Literature: Essays on the Reading Mind* (Oxford: Basil Blackwell, 1991), 157–8.
14. 'Gone Away' is the title and subject of a Bowen short story, first published in 1946 (reprinted in *CS*, 758–66).
15. We discuss some of the extraordinary dimensions of the Bowenesque 'you' in greater detail in our reading of Leopold, in *The House in Paris* in Chapter 3, and in our reading of Guy's love letters, in *A World of Love* in Chapter 6.
16. John Hildebiddle is one critic who is particularly attentive to the sense that, in Bowen's fiction, 'movement is the paradigmatic condition under which people live'. See the chapter on Bowen in his *Five Irish Writers: The Errand of Keeping Alive* (Cambridge, Mass.: Harvard University Press, 1989) 115 and passim. The importance of movement is also the focus of Janice Rosen's essay on Bowen, 'Running Away from Home: Perpetual Transit in Elizabeth Bowen's Novels', in Rosemary M. Colt and Janice Rossen, eds, *Writers of the Old School: British Novelists of the 1930s* (London: Macmillan, 1992) 103–19.
17. Aldous Huxley, 'Wanted, a New Pleasure', in his *Music at Night and Other Essays* (London: Chatto & Windus, 1931) 248–57. See too Bowen's 'Pictures and Conversations' in which she writes: 'Not born ... into the age of speed, I was there while it came into being round me. ... About motor-cars ... there continued ... to be something mythical and phenomenal' (*MT* 287).
18. Browning's poem returns thirty years later, in *The Little Girls* (182). This later novel of transit is another in which car journeys figure

strongly and in which there is at least one expression of explicit uncertainty as to 'what might or might not be the connotation of the word "go"' (see *LG* 205).

Notes to Chapter 3: Fanatic Immobility

1. Elizabeth Bowen, 'Foreword' to *Afterthought: Pieces About Writing* (London: Longmans, 1962) 9.
2. J. Hillis Miller, *Versions of Pygmalion* (Cambridge, Mass.: Harvard University Press, 1990) 21.
3. Putting it in rather polemical terms, Woolf's narrative follows the convention of linear temporality while Bowen's presents a radical achronology which suggests that a single day can never be present to itself.
4. See, for example, Nicolas Abraham and Maria Torok, *The Wolf Man's Magic Word: A Cryptonymy,* trans. Nicholas Rand (Minneapolis: University of Minnesota Press, 1986), and Esther Rashkin, 'Tools for a New Psychoanalytic Literary Criticism: The Work of Abraham and Torok,' *Diacritics*, 18 (1988) 31–52.
5. See 89: a letter from Mme Fisher to Karen is, Karen says, 'in my mind': 'in', rather than 'on', suggests a telepathic inhabitation. And compare the similar gesture of telepathy performed by the shell-shocked Daventry in *The Last September*: 'Mr Daventry, looking hard at her, put the palm of his hand to his left temple with a curious, listening air, as though to see if a watch had stopped' (*LS* 156). In a corresponding gesture, in *A World of Love*, Jane 'drew her fingers slowly across her forehead, as it were as a dragnet for her thoughts' (*WL* 41). Bowen comments on telepathic reading in an essay entitled 'The Bend Back' (*MT* 56).
6. In *The House in Paris*, Leopold and Percy Bysshe Shelley are equated a number of times, not least by the Grant Moodys, who see Leopold as a kind of exotic wonder-child – see, for example 34, 204, 205, 206.
7. Compare 70, on the changelessness of Karen's 'class', and the unsuitability of such people as characters for novels.
8. See, for example, Laura Mulvey, 'Visual Pleasure and Narrative Cinema', in *Visual and Other Pleasures* (London: Macmillan, 1989) 14–26.
9. In some forms of catatonia, patients record that it is precisely the frenetic activity of the brain rather than an absence or immobility of thought processes which leads to physical immobility. Consider, in this context, Leopold's thought about Madame Fisher, that 'you make my thoughts boil' (208), just as she has made Max's thoughts boil.
10. See below, for our discussion of *HP* 151–5, where Karen's meditation on the possibility of a child after making love to Max, her conceiving of a child, is also a conception of Leopold.
11. See 103 on Mme Fisher's supernatural ability to know, 182 on the evil which pervades her house, and 155 on Mme Fisher as a kind of witch.
12. Mme Fisher's account suggests that Max's suicide was engendered by her commendation: 'It was commendation he could not bear. I was

commending him when he took his knife out' (184). It is difficult not to hear within 'commendation' the resonance of a death sentence, the commendation of 'the dying or dead to the favour and mercy of God' (*Chambers*).

13. See also comments on people as being unrooted (110, 113) or 'rooted up' (83–4), and Max and Naomi as 'two twigs' (113).
14. As Bowen comments in a letter of 1935, 'Max [*for* Leopold] is the same man as a little boy' (*MT* 199). But Leopold is also, of course, his mother Karen: Ray notices Leopold's 'Karen-like small cleft chin' (214), and 'Karen's unalarmed smile appeared in Leopold's lips' (220) (similarly, see 73, where Karen's smile is 'not her own'). Nevertheless, Ray notices something other than Karen in Leopold, which he doesn't recognize because he never met Max: 'his deliberate look was from someone else's eyes. Ray saw for the moment what he was up against: the force of a foreign cold personality' (220–1).
15. Leopold is, in fact, overdetermined as what we call a 'gash of knowledge' – in the sense that he is unknown ('no one knows I'm born', he declares [59]), that he is not allowed to know himself (to know who he is or where he comes from), that he knows more than others, more than others think he knows, more than he should know, that he must never be known (because he is the product of an illicit love) and that he is what is known (he is the product of Max and Karen's carnal 'knowledge' of each other, inevitably known to be such, and the reason that their love is known). At the same time, however, the impossibility of Leopold's 'knowledge' disrupts the very notion of knowledge. See especially pages 21, 34, 59, 68, 155, 181, 193, 200, 201, 202, 219.
16. See the 'answer' to this question: 'You do not ask yourself, what am I doing? You know. What you do ask yourself, what have I done? you will never know' (152).
17. Consider also a singular use of the present tense, 'Karen remembers her hand' (151), at this point.
18. Foreign language and the foreignness of language is a recurrent motif in *The House in Paris*: Naomi, the daughter of a French woman and an English man, speaks in a 'peculiar idiom' (19): 'Often when she spoke she seemed to be translating, and translating rustily. No phrase she used was what anyone could quite mean. ... Her state of mind seemed to be foreign also.' Consider also Max's sense that 'What I say would often be right if I meant something else' (120). This foreignness might be understood to constitute a gash across cultures: 'At his words, the English Channel rose to cut them [Max and Karen] off like a blade of steel' (109). More than this, however, Bowen's still lives suggest that all communication, all social discourse, occurs between people speaking 'foreign' languages.
19. On dread, see Maurice Blanchot, *The Writing of the Disaster*, trans. Ann Smock (Lincoln: University of Nebraska Press, 1986); and see Andrej Warminski, 'Dreadful Reading: Blanchot on Hegel', *Yale French Studies*, 69 (1985) 266–75, where Warminski quotes Blanchot on 'the dread of reading': 'The dread of reading: it is that every text, no

matter how important and how interesting it may be (and the more it gives the impression of being so), is empty – it does not exist at bottom (*il n'existe pas dans le fond*)' (266). Blanchot's essay 'Reading' also opens with a consideration of the possibility of the dread of reading, in *The Gaze of Orpheus and other Literary Essays*, trans. Lydia Davis (New York: Station Hill, 1981) 91–8.

20. 'Dread' and its cognates appear on (at least) the following pages in the Penguin edition: 19, 31, 32, 40 (twice), 41, 53, 65 (three times), 85, 86, 106, 107, 114, 116, 122 (twice), 124, 126, 141, 143, 147, 152, 153 (twice), 157, 158, 161, 174, 177, 180, 184, 188, 206, 207 (twice), 215, 217 (twice), 220.
21. See also *WL* for the notion of 'belated dread' (50, 97 and 147).

Notes to Chapter 4: Dream Wood

1. Samuel Beckett, 'what is the word', in *As the Story was Told: Uncollected and Late Prose* (London: John Calder, 1990) 131.
2. See also, in *The Tempest*, Ferdinand's 'My spirits, as in a dream, are all bound up' (I.ii.487). Consider also *Macbeth*, II.ii.34 ('Sleep that knits up the ravell'd sleave of care') and Birnam as dream wood in that play. Further interrelations with Shakespeare's work could doubtless be pursued here. Suffice to say that the question of such intertextuality forms a focal point of discussion in the next chapter.
3. This detachment is ironic if only because of the extent to which *The Death of the Heart* will suggest that Anna herself, especially in her relationship with Robert Pidgeon, is haunted, still caught up in a dream wood. See for instance p.66: 'When Anna made this fuss, [Eddie] thought her a silly woman. He did not know about Pidgeon, or how badly she had come out of all that – if, in fact, she *had* ever come out of it'.
4. See too, in this context, Kathie's laughter in *A World of Love* (discussed in Chapter 6), and Robert Kelway's laughter in *The Heat of the Day*: 'It was a laughter of the entire being, racking as it was irregular in its intakes upon his body, making his face a mask of shut eyes and twisting lips, convulsing the rest of him in a sort of harmony of despair at the situation and joy in her' (285).
5. See especially *The Death of the Heart*, Chapter 6, 'The Flesh'.
6. See also Portia's diary: 'I said I did like Clara, and [Dickie] said oh she's all right but she loses her head' (226).
7. Where does such a drawing leave us? On Portia's first night at Waikiki – we may recall – it draws her into a dream of reading, into a dream wood. Portia dreams of 'sharing a book with a little girl', of reading, or rather of being unable to read, as Anna 'kept turning pages over' (140). There is a forest in the dream ('there was a forest under the window') which is 'being varnished all over' and which leaves 'no way of escape'. Portia, even after waking (it was 'Only Daphne running her bath out'), remains 'in the haunted outer court of

the dream', affected as though by 'sounds in the forest still left from the dream' (141).

8. 'He was always a rare bird' (48), as Brutt himself remarks. Or again: Pidgeon was 'just off somewhere – "on the wing", as we always used to say' (262). Here again Bowen's text suggests a curious intimacy of the human and the animal (or avian).
9. See, for instance, 15, 216, 240.
10. In inevitably different ways, this non-coincidence of self-reflection, self-presentation and self-representation could doubtless be analysed in *The Death of the Heart* also in terms of diary-writing, in particular in relation to the abyssal logic whereby a diary is, for example, 'bound to be enormously written up' (11) and figures the impossibility of the 'I' coinciding with itself. A diary would thus be incapable of accommodating the very structures of identification which appear, abyssally, to set it in motion.
11. See, too, the description of early spring on 123–4, when city traffic 'lightens and quickens' and 'even buildings take such feeling of depth that the streets might be rides cut through a wood'; and see also the 'double tree' and 'ferny grot' on 271.
12. Illustrating a bizarre oneiric logic of narrative, this brief exchange recalls an earlier one between Brutt and Portia, and another surreal kind of dream wood. Anna has remarked that 'thorough chars don't grow on every bush'. Then 'Portia said excitedly: "How funny bushes would look!" "Ha-ha," said Major Brutt. "Did you ever hear the one about the shoe-tree?"' (46–7)
13. See also the reference to Portia's 'concavities, her unconsciousness' (294).
14. It is also appropriate that the name 'Portia' evokes the importance of questions of judgement: see Ann Ashworth's '"But Why Was She Called Portia?": Judgement and Feeling in Bowen's *The Death of the Heart*', in *Critique: Studies in Modern Fiction*, **38**(3) (1987) 159–66. Ashworth argues that '*Portia* can connote only one person: the golden-haired heiress who is both "a Daniel come to judgement" and Shakespeare's chief spokesman [*sic*] for the quality of mercy' (159).
15. For a fuller discussion of caryatids in Bowen, see Chapter 7 on *The Little Girls*.
16. This oneiric folly of what is unfinished cannot be dissociated from the ultimate dream wood, the ultimate piece of dream wood furniture or the ultimate dream wood edifice, in other words, the dream wood of a coffin or death. As Matchett (who is more than once associated with coffins: see also, e.g., 76) tells Portia, earlier on: 'Finished? You show me one thing that is ever finished, let alone everything. No, I'll stop when they've got me screwed into my coffin, but that won't be because I've got anything finished' (235). This identification with 'death' should not be taken as implying any simple, final referent for the term 'dream wood'. In this context we might suggest that there would always have to be a telephone network to link up – and disconnect – the logic of such an identification: this might be one way of starting to think about 'the upright telephone coffin' (298) from which

Brutt calls Windsor Terrace and which thus renders possible the curious closure of this Bowen narrative.

Notes to Chapter 5: Sheer Kink

1. Cited by Victoria Glendinning in *Elizabeth Bowen: A Portrait* (1977; Harmondsworth: Penguin, 1985) 152–3.
2. See Barbara Bellow Watson's 'Variations on an Enigma: Elizabeth Bowen's War Novel', in *Elizabeth Bowen*, ed. Harold Bloom (New York: Chelsea House, 1987) 81–101. Watson too explores *Hamlet* as what she calls 'the literary forebear of this novel' (82).
3. The terms 'dramaturgic telepathy' and 'textual telepathy' refer above all to the curious phenomenon whereby one character in a dramatic or other literary work utters some word, phrase or idea which has already been expressed by another character but without the former's knowledge. For a more detailed account see Nicholas Royle's essay, 'Some Thoughts on *Antony and Cleopatra* by Moonlight', in his *Telepathy and Literature: Essays on the Reading Mind* (Oxford and Cambridge, Mass.: Basil Blackwell, 1991) 142–59.
4. This doubling or kink presupposes (as elsewhere in this volume) a logic of further multiplication. Additional analogies can be made, for example, between Cousin Nettie and the Ghost in *Hamlet* or (as Barbara Bellow Watson suggests) between Cousin Nettie and Gertrude ('Variations on an Enigma', 94).
5. Phyllis Lassner indicates a corresponding kind of logic at work in *The Heat of the Day* when she observes, in her study *Elizabeth Bowen* (London: Macmillan, 1990): 'Although Kelway does collaborate with the enemy, his treachery seems authentic and real only as Stella is involved in interpreting it' (125).
6. The elaboration of a Bowenesque erotics of undecidability and a notion of 'sheer kink' in more specifically sexual and erotic terms might be made by way of a recent essay by Parveen Adams entitled 'What is a Woman? Some Psychoanalytical Dimensions', in *Women: A Cultural Review*, **1**(1) [1990], 38–41. Adams concludes her essay by proposing a simple but extraordinary reformulation of the question 'What is a woman?' as: 'What is perversion?' (41).
7. Such an immemorial demand is also figured by Cousin Nettie, for instance, when Roderick comes to visit her at Wistaria Lodge: 'She marvelled: "So you remembered me though you never met me? Are you called Victor too?"' (207)
8. See too Barbara Bellow Watson's emphasis on the hallucinatory in her observation that 'Often in *The Heat of the Day* one may see what is not there, fail to see what is, or see clearly something that is not what it seems. There is darkness or too much light' (97).
9. The significance of gloves in Bowen's writing would merit far more extended discussion than can be offered here. For where, with a Bowen text, does the significance of a glove cease? Like an umbrella in

Nietzsche or like Cinderella's slipper, it is that which is left behind and forgotten yet that which binds and generates narrative: Stella drops her glove and Louie's fascination with it is what essentially conducts the narrative from this point (see, e.g., 247, 324). The glove figures a strange reality of the hand: in Bowen, the phrase 'hand in glove' – which is the title of a story about a glove which supernaturally takes on a life of its own (see *CS*: 767–5) – becomes as curiously unstable and resistant to fixed meaning as the word 'hand' in the sense of 'handwriting' or 'author'. Bowen's work would seem to call for something like a critical theory of writing-in-gloves or gloved authorship.

10. 'Creature' can be understood in the sense of 'creation', 'dependent' or 'puppet' (*Chambers*). Thus Robert and Stella are creations or puppets of history. But their love, their relationship with one another, necessarily also belongs to that movement of going traced earlier (in our reading of *To the North*). In other words, they are also caught up in a movement, a structure and temporality of going, which can never be thought on the basis of the present or in terms of a notion of history grounded in such a present. It is in terms of this final movement – a movement which, while it can be anthropomorphized (as it is by Bowen on pp. 194–5), can only ever be phantasmagoric, can never, that is to say, be experienced or made present to perception, since every representation of it is only an appropriation which expropriates it, leaves it still moving, beyond us, unthinkably – that it would be necessary to try to grasp how Bowen's texts theorize 'history'. The possibility of history, in this respect, would appear to be identical with that of love.

11. For a fascinating account of this topic in relation to a reading of Melville's *Moby Dick*, see Leo Bersani, 'Incomparable America', in his *The Culture of Redemption* (Cambridge: Harvard University Press, 1990) 136–54. *The Culture of Redemption* as a whole is crucially concerned with attempting to work over and beyond this equation of identity and/as authority. From a slightly different perspective we may consider too Samuel Weber's remark that 'In democratic societies, one is prone to point to the people as the source of all authority; but it remains to be seen in what sense the people, as a collective subject, can claim to dictate the law to language.' (*Return to Freud: Jacques Lacan's Dislocation of Psychoanalysis* [Cambridge University Press, 1991], 175–6).

12. See, too, Bowen's Preface to her collection of wartime stories, *The Demon Lover* (*MT* 94–9), in which she describes what she finds in the stories themselves to be 'a rising tide of hallucination' (96).

13. Particularly as regards ghostliness and hallucination, Harold Pinter's screenplay of Bowen's novel provides at least one curious Hamletian addition in this context: when Roderick asks his mother whether there is a boat at Mount Morris (*HD* 53), Pinter has him say that he can see it 'in my mind's eye'.

14. The haunting presence of *Hamlet* might be pursued further by way of the very syntax of Stella's faltering, self-correcting 'Two months ago, now, nearly two months ago':

HAMLET: ... look you, how cheerfully my mother looks, and my father died within's two hours.
OPHELIA: Nay, 'tis twice two months, my lord.
HAMLET: So long?. ... Die two months ago, and not forgotten yet?
(III.ii.118–23)

15. S. L. Goldberg, 'Shakespeare's Centrality', in *The Critical Review* [Melbourne], 18 (1976) 3–22: see 5. (We are grateful to Richard Lansdown for drawing our attention to this essay.)
16. 'Shakespeare's Centrality', 6.
17. John Bayley, *The Short Story: Henry James to Elizabeth Bowen* (Brighton: Harvester, 1988) 176.
18. In this context it may seem less remarkable, then, that the central example which S. L. Goldberg gives of the 'created sense of a person' in Shakespeare's work is Gloucester's response to Buckingham in *Richard III*:

    BUCKINGHAM: Now my lord, what shall we do if we perceive
    Lord Hastings will not yield to our complots?
    GLOUCESTER: Chop off his head.
    (III.i.191–3)

    Goldberg writes: 'In the question, we are aware mainly of the rhetoric; in the reply, we are aware – very sharply [*sic*] aware – of a person' (5).
19. See *ET* 193 – also discussed in Chapter 8, 'Convulsions' – where we may find ourselves reading of a town called Reading: 'A further possibility had occurred to [Eva] – the impersonator of Miss Smith had been Miss Smith, a deceased person purporting to be a living one. Not that she necessarily was in her coffin; no, she could well be walking about in Reading. ("Charles the First walked and talked half an hour after his head was cut off." You put in a comma somewhere, then that made sense but was not so interesting.) But, she had given an impression of dissolution.' (And see also 'The Happy Autumn Fields', in *CS* 681.) No doubt we too must walk about – and carry on trying to talk about – what is so specifically 'interesting' in the context of such a reading, or in the dissolution of such a Reading. One might note a further correlation between the force of Hamlet's phrase 'My head should be struck off' (V.ii.25) – a phrase which, cut off from its 'original' syntactical context, resonates in strangely Bowenesque ways – and the word 'struck' as it appears in the passage from *The Heat of the Day* immediately succeeding the one cited in the main body of our text, above: '[Louie:] "The Yanks are struck by our character now they're here." [Connie:] "You ever seen a Yank struck?" "Well, but I saw where it said – ." "They're struck on our pubs all right: my friend and I couldn't get in anywhere edgeways the other evening."' (155). 'The main body of our text, above' – or the main body below? This footnote should perhaps more correctly be a headnote to the present essay, a headnote that would seek to detach itself from that essay specifically with a view to underscoring a certain hydra-effect or hydrafication, a

labour of ghostly decapitation and grafting that necessarily and uncannily inscribes itself in any practice or theory of cross-referencing, quotation or intertextuality. (Is this not, after all, what criticism [Gk. *krinein*] is, that is to say a question of precisely *cutting*?) Bowen's text here, sliced off from Shakespeare's, suggests in any case one possible scaffolding for a theorization of what is *striking* in the literary text, in other words for a theory of literary aesthetic decapitation.

20. So too with the kind of exemplary still life evoked in the description of Stella by herself in the lamp-lit drawing-room at Mount Morris: 'she carried the lamp to meet one of its own reflections in a mirror, and, lifting it, studied the romantic face that was still hers. She became for the moment immortal as a portrait' (173).
21. 'Decapitation' here figures an affirmative logic of dissolution, dispossession, loss of authority, identity and sense. It perhaps goes without saying that its force differs from, and in various respects could be seen to exceed, that of a psychoanalytical concept of castration. For a recent essay which is focused primarily on the significance of the guillotine in the French Revolution but which also stresses the reductiveness of equating decapitation with castration, see Regina James's 'Beheadings', in *Representations*, 35 (Summer 1991) 21–51.

Notes to Chapter 6: Obelisk

1. See, for example, Hermione Lee, *Elizabeth Bowen: An Estimation* (London: Vision, 1981) 191, 197.
2. A weak sense of 'metafiction' would involve 'simply' the idea of fiction which draws attention to itself as fiction or fiction which is *about* fiction (as in the novel about a novelist writing a novel about a novelist, etc.): it would not engage with more fundamental disturbances of the relations between what is fictional and what is not. Patricia Waugh's *Metafiction: The Theory and Practice of Self-Conscious Fiction* (London: Methuen, 1984) strives to elaborate a stronger notion of metafiction, declaring, for example, that metafiction 'self-consciously and systematically draws attention to its status as an artefact in order to pose questions about the relationship between fiction and reality. In providing a critique of their own methods of construction, such writings not only examine the fundamental structures of narrative fiction, they also explore the possible fictionality of the world outside the literary fictional text' (2). Waugh's account, however, tends to preserve or reinscribe precisely what metafiction (in a 'strong' sense) puts into question – for instance, the very notion of the 'artefact' (in the above quotation), the maintenance of an oppositional logic of 'fiction' and 'reality', and a privileging of the concept of self-consciousness (evident even in the title of her book). The 'metafictional' in the terms in which we are seeking to elaborate in the present chapter is less subject-oriented and subject-centred, and concerned rather with the citational *per se*.

3. This linking of 'heat' with 'a white-hot sword' suggests a parallel with our argument that thermo-writing, in Bowen's novel, is linked to the notion of the obelisk or obeliskine.
4. Compare in this respect Bowen's Preface (1947) to Sheridan Le Fanu's *Uncle Silas*, in which she observes of Le Fanu's characters: 'There is abnormal pressure, from every side; the psychic air is often overheated' (*MT* 105).
5. Thus, for example, Hermione Lee's suggestion that '*A World of Love* is haunted by its author's past creations' (195) takes into account neither the novel's phantasmagoric presence in earlier novels nor its haunting of Bowen's later work.
6. See the parable of the vineyard labourers in which those who began working earlier complain about the equal payment given to those who have arrived late: 'These last have wrought but one hour, and thou hast made them equal unto us, which have borne the burden and heat of the day' (Matthew 20:12). The parabolic significance of this story for Bowen's novel would no doubt include analogous senses of temporal disruptions and dissolutions.
7. More fully, the passage from Traherne reads: 'As iron at a distance is drawn by the lodestone, there being some invisible communications between them: so is there in us a world of love to somewhat, tho we know not what in the world that should be. There are invisible ways of conveyance, by which some great thing doth touch our souls, and by which we tend to it. Do you not feel yourself drawn with the expectation and desire of some great thing?' See 'Centuries of Meditations', 1:2, in Thomas Traherne, *Selected Poems and Prose*, ed. Alan Bradford (Harmondsworth: Penguin, 1991) 187. It may be noted that Bowen's 'citation' of this passage includes the (as we shall come to describe it, obeliskine) 'drawn by' instead of 'drawn with'.
8. The notion of the immemorial is most fully developed in the work of Jean-François Lyotard. See, for example, his essay on 'the jews' in *Heidegger and 'the Jews'*, trans. Andras Michel and Mark Roberts (Minneapolis: University of Minnesota Press, 1988) 1–48. For an excellent exposition and elaboration of this aspect of Lyotard's work, see Bill Readings, *Introducing Lyotard: Art and Politics* (London: Routledge, 1991). Readings defines the immemorial as 'That which can neither be remembered (represented to consciousness) nor forgotten (consigned to oblivion). It is that which returns, uncannily' (xxxii).
9. Any sense of 'firstness' concerning this love-at-first-sight is further displaced by the citational haunting here of Orlando's words to Oliver in *As You Like It*: 'Is't possible that on so little acquaintance you should like her? That but seeing, you should love her?' (V.ii.1–2).
10. Although Traherne's work was not published until 1908, this passage seems uncannily similar to Wordsworth's description of the Imagination in *The Prelude*: 'With hope it is, hope that can never die, / Effort, and expectation, and desire, / And something evermore about to be' (Book VI [1805], 540–2). Alan Bradford's Preface to *Selected Poems and Prose* provides a brief account of the fascinating history of the preservation and publication of Traherne's work, including 'the astonishing

rescue of the *Commentaries of Heaven* from a burning rubbish heap in 1967' (xi).

11. For the fate of the letters in the novel see, for example, 115, 122–4, 131 and 139.
12. This obelisk also occurs in the first edition of *A World of Love* (London: Cape, 1955).

Notes to Chapter 7: Trance

1. Maurice Blanchot, 'Reading', in *The Gaze of Orpheus and Other Literary Essays*, trans. Lydia Davis (New York: Station Hill, 1981) 95–6.
2. The key moment of trance in this respect occurs as Dinah waits to meet her schoolfriends fifty years after their last meeting: 'she ... sat tranced, becalmed in the stillness as one only otherwise is in the midst of speed' (44–5); and the novel opens with a kind of trance in a place where 'it was some other hour – peculiar, perhaps no hour at all' (10).
3. Hermione Lee, *Elizabeth Bowen: An Estimation* (London: Vision, 1981) 204. Lee does, however, go on to suggest that *The Little Girls* and *Eva Trout* are not 'merely failures of assurance' and makes the important point that these texts become 'increasingly concerned with the concept of a breakdown in language': 'That Elizabeth Bowen's highly charged, contrived and controlled style should have been reduced to the clumsy procedures of *The Little Girls* can be attributed to more than obvious reasons of old age and a dissatisfaction with out-dated formulae. The last two novels incorporate the idea of a future without any verbal "style" at all' (205–6).
4. Thus, for example, cars are dated: cars of the early sixties – Hillman, Triumph coupé, Mini-minor, Bubble car – are mentioned on numerous occasions in *The Little Girls*.
5. See 154 on Dinah, Clare and Sheila as 'revenants'.
6. See also 167 where, within a discussion of prefabricated feelings, the word 'fishy' is used (and see Chapter 8 for a discussion of this paronomastic word in *Eva Trout*).
7. As Dinah says, 'Somebody's shooting somebody else with it now, probably' (188). The gun and the child with a gun might in fact be said to 'originate' not in *The Little Girls* but in *The House in Paris* (see *HP* 220).
8. See 156, where Clare admits to having written another letter in Unknown Language, but says that it arrived too late: Major Burkin-Jones, Clare's father, asks her to write a letter to him in Unknown Language (115). Before he receives it, however, he is killed in the First World War. For more on posterity and reading, see Andrew Bennett, *Keats, Narrative and Audience: The Posthumous Life of Writing* (Cambridge University Press, 1994).
9. Frank is of a nervous disposition, it seems: Dinah secretly puts a mask on the wall of his cottage, after which, without knowing what Dinah has done, he confesses to a horror of coming home late and finding

'one of those grinning at me' (191). Frank's horror of children might be compared to his horror of masks.

10. The only exception to this unreality for Dinah is Clare – 'But *you're real*, Mumbo. ... You were there before' (163) – an exception who is, however, haunted, unstable, illusory. Clare is described as being, for example, a visitant (235), and, like her father, a revenant (85).
11. George Orwell, *Nineteen Eighty-four* (Harmondsworth: Penguin, 1954) 137.
12. For more on this passage and on the reading body in reading theory, see Andrew Bennett, 'On Not Reading', in Andrew Bennett (ed.), *Reading Reading: Essays on the Theory and Practice of Reading* (Tampere: Tampere English Studies, 1993) pp. 221–37. It should be noted that a not insignificant part of *The Little Girls* involves Dinah taking Clare to visit a mask-maker, Clare's purchase of some masks for her gift shops, and their placing of a mask on Frank's cottage wall; see especially 182–8.
13. See Dinah's comments on Clare's 'symbol shop' (180).
14. Such a list may be compared to the 'catalogue' which Dinah is making at the beginning of the novel (see 10). This opening suggests a further parallel with reading: to begin to read a novel is unavoidably to begin to compile a catalogue. (For another shopping-list and meditations on shopping, see *DH* 153–5.)
15. See Jean Baudrillard, *Simulations*, trans. Paul Foss *et al.* (New York: Semiotext(e), 1983).
16. 'What really expresses people?' asks Dinah, 'The things, I'm sure, that they have obsessions about.... You know, a person's only a *person* when they have some really raging peculiarity' (15); the object of the second collection of objects to be buried 'for posterity' is, Dinah claims, to preserve the specific identity of herself and her friends and acquaintances (14–15). The collection ironically suggests, however, that there is in fact very little to differentiate people (10). For an interesting discussion of this idea more generally, see Ian Hacking's essay, 'Making Up People', in Thomas C. Heller *et al.* (eds), *Reconstructing Individualism: Autonomy, Individualism, and the Self in Western Thought* (Stanford: University of California Press, 1986) 222–37.
17. This analogue is made explicit by Clare, speaking 'as a shopkeeper': if you got rid of the prefabrications of contemporary emotional lives, she claims, 'You'd put more than half the world out of business, including novelists' (168).
18. For a recent empirical study of the trance of reading, see Victor Nell, *Lost in a Book: The Psychology of Reading for Pleasure* (New Haven, Conn.: Yale University Press, 1988).
19. This undecidable sense-making quality of the name is what Joel Kuortti has named 'nomsensical': see his '"To be born again ...": Reading Salman Rushdie's *The Satanic Verses*', in Bennett (ed.), *Reading Reading*, pp. 69–82. Compare also the duplicities of Robert Kelway and Harrison in *The Heat of the Day*. Names and their instabilities are constantly highlighted in *The Little Girls* in other ways: they can, for example, be ghostly (119), as well as the subject of irritation (33), confusion (55), or half-veiled ridicule (Francis on Mrs Artworth: 202). In her

review of *The Little Girls*, Christine Brooke-Rose points to naming in the novel as one of Bowen's 'main affectations' and includes a substantial list of, especially, euphemistic namings in the novel ('Lady Precious Stream', *The London Magazine*, 4(2) [May, 1964] 84–5).

20. A different kind of apocalypse – the end of the world – is also figured at the moment of burial fifty years earlier: 'The outside world, when they left it, had been extinct rather than, yet, dark' (116).
21. See 51–2, where the change of name is mentioned in the context of a reference to 'that bristly goddess' (i.e., Artemis or Diana).
22. Like posterity, the *avant garde* is constituted by its reception in (an indefinitely deferred) future: once the *avant garde* art-work is 'received' and 'understood', it becomes canonical or at least part of a tradition, and no longer *avant garde*, once it is read it can no longer be read as *avant garde*. (Another *avant garde* person in *The Little Girls* is Sheila: 'Sheikie always was *avant garde*' [150].)
23. See, for example, Allan E. Austin, *Elizabeth Bowen* (New York: Twayne, 1971), Chapter 4; Hermione Lee, *Elizabeth Bowen: An Estimation* (London: Vision, 1981), Chapter 7.
24. See 235 on Clare as a 'visitant'.
25. The name 'Mumbo' is on Frank's mind, no doubt, having just been mentioned by Dinah, who does not tell him to whom or what it refers.
26. See, for example, Edwin J. Kenny, *Elizabeth Bowen* (Lewisburg: Bucknell University Press, 1975) 93.
27. In this sense, the tragedy of Shakespeare's *Romeo and Juliet* is the inability of either Romeo or Juliet to revoke their names – despite their claims in II.i.

Notes to Chapter 8: Convulsions

1. André Breton, *Mad Love* (*L'Amour Fou*), trans. Mary Ann Caws (Lincoln: University of Nebraska Press, 1987) 10. See also *Nadja*, in *Oeuvres Complètes*, I, ed. M. Bonnet *et al.* (Paris: Gallimard, 1988) 753: 'La Beauté sera CONVULSIVE ou ne sera pas.'
2. This repeats very precisely the parental deaths in *The Little Girls*: Dinah's father killed himself and her mother died of Spanish 'flu.
3. See Hermione Lee's comments on *Eva Trout*'s 'preposterously haphazard plot' (208), and *Eva Trout* as 'an unfocused and bizarre conclusion to [Bowen's] opus' in her *Elizabeth Bowen: An Estimation* (London: Vision, 1981) 206; and see John Hildebiddle's unfortunate remarks on this as 'the last (and, sadly, by far the worst) of her ten novels', in his *Five Irish Writers: The Errand of Keeping Alive* (Cambridge, Mass: Harvard University Press, 1989) 5.
4. See Benjamin B. Wolman, ed., *International Encyclopedia of Psychiatry, Psychology, Psychoanalysis, and Neurology* (New York: Aesculapius, 1977) III, 373: 'Patients with catatonic syndrome of motor inhibition, muteness, negativism, posturing, mannerisms, and stereotypy will often respond rapidly to convulsive therapy'; and compare James

B. Lohr and Alexander A. Wisniewski, *Movement Disorders: A Neuropsychiatric Approach* (Chichester: Wiley, 1987) 227: 'Severe catatonia is probably best treated with ECT.'

5. Convulsions – coughing, sneezing, even breathing – are included in Charles Darwin's consideration of 'reflex actions', in *The Expression of the Emotions in Man and Animals*, in *The Works of Charles Darwin*, ed. Paul H. Barrett and R. B. Freeman, vol. 23 (London: William Pickering, 1989) 26–31. What is interesting about Darwin's discussion of these 'actions' is his very clear uncertainty over the extent to which they are 'voluntary': coughing, sneezing, etc., constitute liminal 'actions' which can, to some extent, be controlled. And, as Darwin suggests, the voluntary or 'conscious' attempt to produce such mouth-events may actually interfere with the actions: 'The conscious wish to perform a reflex action sometimes stops or interrupts its performance, though the proper sensory nerves may be stimulated' (28) (as when we cannot swallow because we are thinking about swallowing). In his discussion of patients in the acute phase of encephalitis, Oliver Sacks relates convulsive movements to catatonia, when he notes 'a wide spectrum of tics and compulsive movements at every functional level – yawning, coughing, sniffing, gasping, panting, breathholding, staring, glancing, bellowing, yelling, cursing, etc.' (*Awakenings*, rev. edn. [London: Pan, 1982] 17).
6. *The Little Girls* is similarly convulsive: see, for example, representations of coughing (11); Dinah's writing as 'tangled convulsive sheets' (27); the idea that 'having' a memory is like having a seizure (39); references to deep intakes of breath (69, 140); Clare's 'spasms by which her face was apt to betray thoughts' (43); her 'electrical happiness' (59); and the idea that there might be, though seldom is, 'something convulsive about change' (154). Similarly, in *A World of Love*, Jane draws a breath 'big with risk and exhilaration' (69), and Fred gives a 'violent obsessive yawn' (82).
7. Reading as lip-reading: the poet David Wright, who is deaf, reminds us that lip-reading involves, also, the reading of other parts of the face – the eyes, for example – as an indication of intonation (*Deafness: A Personal Account* [London: Allen Lane, 1969] 115), and that the primary indicator is no longer sound but movement ('from the very first my eyes had unconsciously begun to translate motion into sound', 22): 'listening', for the deaf, involves looking at the moving face. To the extent that Jeremy provides a model of reading (in) *Eva Trout*, reading involves the scanning of mobile faces.
8. Pierre Fontanier, quoted by Bernard Dupriez in *A Dictionary of Literary Devices*, trans. Albert W. Halsall (Hemel Hempstead: Harvester Wheatsheaf, 1991) 357.
9. See also Paul de Man, 'Autobiography as De-Facement', in *The Rhetoric of Romanticism* (New York: Columbia University Press, 1984); and see Dupriez, *A Dictionary of Literary Devices*, 358, on the hallucinatory nature of the figure.
10. See de Man, 'Autobiography as De-facement', 75–6: prosopopoeia is 'the fiction of an apostrophe to an absent, deceased, or voiceless

entity, which posits the possibility of the latter's reply and confers upon it the power of speech. Voice assumes mouth, eye, and finally face, a chain that is manifest in the etymology of the trope's name, *prosopon poein*, to confer a mask or a face (*prosopon*)'. 'Giving a Face to a Name' is the title of Cynthia Chase's essay on prosopopoeia in the work of de Man, in her *Decomposing Figures: Rhetorical Readings in the Romantic Tradition* (Baltimore: Johns Hopkins, 1986) 82–112.

11. As Patrizia Magli, glossing Jacques Lacan, puts it, 'The roles of its individual actors, such as the nose, eyes, eyebrows, mouth, all belong to the indefinite time of their action, to a fluctuating and unstructured logic, one based on the genesis and the relationship between movement, stasis and variations in speed.' See 'The Face and the Soul', in *Fragments for a History of the Human Body*, ed. Michel Feher *et al.*, vol. 2 (New York: Zone, 1989) 87.
12. In *Eva Trout*, buildings (houses, castles, hotels) which are often so uncannily alive in previous novels, have become cardboard cut-outs, childish drawings: 'As for the castle, it looked, from here, as though cut out, flat, from a sheet of cardboard' (13); 'The house was itself ... not unlike a house in a child's drawing' (16). And from the perspective of the present chapter, it is significant that at least one facial description is figured in terms of a building: Eric 'looked like a searchlit building' (20) – an inversion of the conventional trope of a building looking like a face or facade.
13. See 194, for similar concatenations of adjectives in order to attempt to understand identity through the still lives of the National Portrait Gallery, and 256, for another collection of adjectives which attempt to define the indefinable Jeremy.
14. See 'galvanize' in *Chambers*. Eva is also galvanized earlier, in Part I, Chapter 9 (108). See also 20, where an Anglepoise lamp is directed at Eric's face: 'Electricity, making just more than lifelike the general ruddiness of the colouring'. For a description of people as electricity conductors, see *WL* 67–8.
15. See also 194, where Henry is said to resemble the still lives in the National Portrait Gallery.
16. See, for example, the beginning of Part I, Chapter 5: 'Time, inside Eva's mind, lay about like various pieces of a fragmented picture. She remembered, that is to say, disjectedly' (46); or Iseult's comment on Eva's thoughts: 'they're rather startling, but they don't connect yet' (62); or the idea that Eva 'had been left unfinished' (51), that she is characterized by 'instability' (102) and 'disorder' (103).
17. See Garrett Stewart, *Reading Voices: Literature and the Phonotext* (Berkeley: University of California Press, 1990) for an account of the importance and inevitability of a silent voicing at work in reading. At one point in his impressive and valuable book, Stewart comes close to articulating this notion of the prosopopoeia of reading: 'The self-"disfiguring" inscription analyzed in de Man's deconstructed *rhetoric* may therefore be further isolated and unstrung ... within the dyslocutionary force of phonemic reading' (156).

Index